OUR ISLAND STORY

'London itself is a central character here, as seen through the eyes of now 80-something queer quantity surveyor Charlie. We join him on the night of his twin brother's funeral and as he tries to write a eulogy (while getting increasingly sloshed), Charlie recalls the city's journey from the idealism of the actual 1930s Peckham Experiment – which encouraged working-class families to actively participate in their own well-being – to institutional corruption; the power cuts of the three-day week, the rise of Enoch Powell and, above all, the devastating collapse of the tower block that his brother built . . . there are shades of the great Gordon Burn in Ware's portrait of period, place and class.'

STEPHANIE CROSS, *Daily Mail*

'The novel begins on the eve of JJ's funeral, with Charlie struggling to write a eulogy for his 85-year-old brother. Confined to a mobility scooter ('like Dennis Hopper on Medicare') and drunk on brandy, Charlie is a seductively irreverent narrator. Witty, wise, queer and possessed of a fierce social conscience, he revisits their parallel lives in a fluid monologue that's as Beckettian as it is Steptoe and Son. Ware is refreshingly sharp on twin psychology: 'I never believed I'd bury him. I'm older. Surely it should fall to you to bury me . . . No one wants to be last. We should have gone together . . . A plane crash.''

JUDE COOK, The Spectator

"Deeply impressive . . . one of the most moving novels I have read in some time."

KEIRAN GODDARD, *The Guardian*

GUY WARE is a critically-acclaimed novelist and short story writer. His work has been listed for many awards, including the Frank O'Connor International, Edge Hill and London Short Story Prize, which he won in 2018. *Our Island Story* is his fifth novel. Guy was born in Northampton, grew up in the Fens and lives in southeast London.

ALSO BY GUY WARE

NOVELS
The Fat of Fed Beasts
Reconciliation
The Faculty of Indifference
The Peckham Experiment

SHORT STORIES
You Have 24 Hours to Love Us

GUY WARE

OUR ISLAND STORY

SALT

SHEFFIELD

PUBLISHED BY SALT PUBLISHING 2024

2 4 6 8 10 9 7 5 3 1

First published in Great Britain in 2024 by
Salt Publishing Ltd
18 Churchill Road, Sheffield, S10 1FG United Kingdom

www.saltpublishing.com

Salt Publishing Limited Reg. No. 5293401

A CIP catalogue record for this book is available from the British Library

ISBN 978 1 78463 313 4 (Paperback edition)
ISBN 978 1 78463 314 1 (Electronic edition)

Typeset in Neacademia by Salt Publishing

Printed and bound in Great Britain by Clays Ltd, Elcograf S.p.A

For Sophy, always

And for Frank and Rebecca:
may you make a better job of it

"O Father Neptune," she said, "let Albion come to my island. It is a beautiful little island. It lies like a gem in the bluest of waters. There the trees and the grass are green, the cliffs are white and the sands are golden. There the sun shines and the birds sing. It is a land of beauty . . . Let Albion come to my island."

H. E. MARSHALL, *Our Island Story*

ONE

DENIS GULPED DOWN a mixture of ozone and salt water, wrestled his diaphragm into place, and bellowed: "February's a shitty time to die."

The woman beside him shook her head carefully, eyes closed, and shouted back, "I'm ready."

They clutched tight to the rail as the boat rolled over the swell and plunged deep into the trough ahead, leaving their stomachs somewhere up above the belching funnel. Again. The ferry crawled up - again - then paused, taunting them, at the lip of the abyss. But they weren't dying. That wasn't what he meant. The roaring wind was cold as pity; the spray soaking his inadequate stolen jacket colder still; the constant, thought-devouring threat of sea-sickness - despite his having long since hurled overboard the morning's tea and bacon roll - would not let him be; but all this, this *unpleasantness*, ultimately just proved he was alive, and likely to stay that way. If heavy seas had been enough to sink this tub, they'd all have drowned three hours ago.

The deck disappeared from under his feet. Again. Closing his eyes made it worse. Keeping them open, though, made the lead-grey sky swipe viciously into lead-grey sea. A pair of empty bottles chased each other back and forth through splashes of vomit.

"I meant my father," he shouted, after a while. Dying, he meant. These were hardly ideal circumstances, but there was no harm in garnering a woman's sympathy. It was practise, if nothing else.

She said, "You're Denis Klamm?"

Her voice rose, but it wasn't really a question. Had they met before? He hoped not. People who knew him were prone to outbreaks of justifiable emotion, even violence. Right now, he wasn't strong enough for either. But before he could deny himself, she shouted, as if she were the first to ever say the words, "I'm sorry for your loss." Maybe bellowing against the wind helped. Also, she wasn't to know, but she *was* the first to say them to Denis. His mother wrote texts, when she wrote at all, as if they were telegrams, invoiced by the word. This one had read: "K's dead. Funeral Monday. Not optional." He'd been in the pub at the time – admittedly not something a bookie would have bothered giving odds against – and his mates had said things like: *Shit, that sucks*; *He had a good innings*; and *Does that mean you're rich?* Which – the rich thing – it might. He'd honestly never thought about it. He was not short of faults, and was usually skint, but nobody would ever have called him a grave robber. He bought a round on the strength of his prospects, then had to borrow the fare for the ferry. The only one with any cash to spare was the idiot who'd said *He had a good innings*. Which was surely more stupid than *sorry for your loss?* K had never played cricket. Eighty wasn't even a great score. Who'd want to get out on eighty? Plus K had been pretty much gaga the last few years, parked in a home, which – although Denis was no expert – didn't sound like much of an innings for anybody. Not life's best blessing. On the other hand: K. Leader of Leaders. Elder statesman and greasy eminence. Not bad for a chancer who washed up on the Island with nothing but a baggy tweed suit he'd won in a bet and a tall story about a job offer. Hauled up by his own bootstraps. Or the laces of his hand-made brogues. That was the story he told Denis, anyway. Like all good stories, the details varied with the telling.

Still: *sorry for your loss*.

He had to say something, so he said thank you, which she took as an introduction.

"I'm Lucy."

He said nothing. She already knew his name.

"Lucy Neave? I used to work for your mother?"

Oh, God. If those were questions, they weren't the ones they pretended to be. *Don't you remember me?* That's what they meant. And he didn't. He'd only spoken to her because she was there. A woman, half drowned in a cagoule. Early forties, at a guess. Long face all nose, like a rodent. Tiny mouth, tiny teeth. Were ferrets rodents? Ears glued on like Mrs. Potato Head. Of no real interest, was what he was saying. Not saying, obviously. But still: a woman. There. At a time of trial. And then it turns out she knows him. Fuck's sake. He hasn't been back in seven years and the one person he talks to knows him. Knows who he is, anyway. That was the trouble with the fucking Island. But no, he doesn't remember her. A lot of people had worked for his mother.

Pointing briefly past the bow, then grabbing the rail again, Lucy said: "Is that it?"

Ahead, on the plunging horizon, through the spray and the rain, he could just about make out something black against the grey. It could have been the Island. Or it could have been another boat. An oil rig. Could it? If only the horizon would sit still for a moment. Was it too big for a ship? It looked a long way ahead, but he had no real way to judge distance out here where everything was grey and black and moving up and down. He was an Islander but he'd never seen this view. He'd only ever left; he'd not come back before.

It didn't move, though. Well, it did: it swung up and down like everything else and in and out of sight, but each time they hung on the roll of a wave it was there and, each time, it got a little larger. And larger. Not just black, some white. Cliffs. Eventually, roofs, towers, above all, the Castle. The Island, then.

Home.

That evening, he told his mother he'd met a woman on the boat who used to work for her. They were eating something brown she'd given him to microwave in a spotless kitchen fitted out with enough culinary gear to run a restaurant. The whole flat was spotless, everything in it gleaming like a puppy's fur. The Election had been Thursday. She'd moved in on Friday. Today was Sunday. Three days.

3

A lot could happen in three days. Ask Jesus. When Denis was a kid and his mother, Cora Klamm, was Leader they'd always lived in the Castle. Even when she lost to Jacob King and became Leader of the Opposition, they'd still had a grace and favour apartment, even if it wasn't in the Central Block. Now she'd lost to Jacob's daughter, too, and was out on her ear. Not exactly homeless, but still. Not at home.

She ignored him. Which was about what his comment deserved. Still, they had to talk about something, didn't they? If it wasn't going to be his father?

He said, "Lucy something."

Cora stopped scrolling through her phone. "Lucy Neave?"

"That's the one."

"Hah. The part-time poet. Did she tell you I sacked her?"

"It didn't come up."

Cora laughed, but didn't sound amused. She started a long story about how, when Lucy Neave was her bag carrier, she'd gone running off to Ari Spencer about something or other that probably wasn't worth arguing about in the first place and which Denis didn't want to hear. Ari Spencer was a name he recognized, though. He'd been everywhere when Denis was growing up.

"What was she doing on the boat?"

"Same as me," Denis said. "Coming home."

"For the funeral?"

And there it was. An opening. The first time she'd mentioned the reason he was here. Now they could talk about it. His father. His father's death. The nursing home neither of them had ever visited. The fact he hadn't been home at all for seven years. Why he'd left. What he was going to do now. They could. They had all night.

"She didn't say," he said.

"What *did* you two talk about?"

"Nothing, Mum. She was just a woman on a boat."

"You mean you didn't want to fuck her."

Denis sighed. What could he say? His mother knew him better

4

than anyone, and she always said he was an idiot. She wasn't the only one.

What they'd actually talked about, he and Lucy, once the boat rounded the headland and the wind and the swell had both calmed down enough in the lee of the cliffs that they no longer had to shout, was how much smaller the Island looked than he remembered. She'd thought he was making some pissy joke about childhood memories. How chocolate bars had shrunk. But he meant it. The place *was* smaller. Where on earth was the harbour? The Hope & Anchor? The Hope & Anchor had been home when he was too young to drink anywhere else. In the Castle bars they'd known exactly how old he was. If they knew in the Hope, they didn't care. They hadn't much cared when he walked out on the harbour bar after seven or eight pints, either. Now there was no bar, and no pub.

"Full fathom five," Lucy said.

"What?"

She pointed down into the water.

"Right."

The Island was sinking. Or the sea was rising. It depended on what you believed about how it got there in the first place. Either way, it had been going on for years, bits falling into the sea, bits swallowed up. But it looked like the process had accelerated while he'd been away. The Castle still perched above everything, of course, up on the cliffs. But big chunks of the seafront – and of the City behind it – just weren't there any more.

They'd disembarked at a makeshift pontoon jetty. Lucy said she might see him tomorrow, then looked embarrassed, and quickly disappeared. Not that he tried to follow her. He'd trudged uphill to find his mother's new flat. Couldn't miss it, she'd texted. Bang opposite the Cathedral. They wouldn't have far to go in the morning.

They finished the brown thing – moussaka? Stew? It was hard to tell. Denis pushed back from the kitchen table, chair legs squeaking on the glossy tiles. He rubbed his stomach and said you couldn't beat the taste of fatted calf. Cora said he was confusing Prodigal with Idiot, and she was going to bed. Did he think he could cope with putting the plates in the dishwasher? He was surprised: not that she would treat him like a cretin – for years, he'd thought "Idiot Son" must be one word so often did he hear it uttered in a single breath – but that she might be going to bed. She'd never been the early-to-bed-early-to-rise type, even though she was up skewering worms before dawn most days: much more school of four-hours-kip-is-quite-enough. She seemed to believe sleep deprivation kept her vicious edge vicious. Could sudden electoral rejection have mellowed her? It seemed improbable. More likely, she just wanted to get away from him, her idiot son.

She said he could sleep on the sofa. The flat was immaculate, but it only had one bedroom and she wasn't going to share it. He shuddered at the thought and wished her good night.

She told him not to sleepwalk, and not to piss off the balcony if he did. Which was unfair, Denis thought. It was K who had pissed off balconies. In fact, she said, she'd better lock the sliding door. It wasn't as if he could upset the neighbours – these flats were pretty much all empty – but they were twelve floors up and he'd make a right fucking mess of the Close if he took a header from there.

"Mum."

"You say that, but you know what you're like. Or maybe you don't. Hard to say, what with Dunning-Kruger and all that. Anyway: sleep tight, don't let the bedbugs bite. If they do, bite back. Your poem is by the bed."

"Poem?"

"For tomorrow. You're reading a poem. I got it off the internet. Try not to bugger it up."

"I . . ."

But she'd gone, shutting the door behind her.

He was twenty-five years old. He had nothing but a stolen jacket, a half-completed course of antibiotics for a venereal disease he'd known longer than most of his friends, and his mother thought he was an idiot. On the other hand, the sofa was about eight feet long, had never been used, and was more comfortable than any bed he'd slept in for the last seven years. He would read the poem in the morning.

In the morning Cora microwaved porridge, which turned out to be about as disgusting as it sounds. Outside, the best you could say was that it wasn't actually raining. Or at least not raining yet. Across the Close, the Cathedral squatted, vast and sullen, like a giant toad in a party hat. School trips pointed out both the flying buttresses and thirteenth-century windows on the one hand, and the post-war glass roof and needle-thin titanium spire on the other. Most Islanders hated it, one of the few things that united them. The restoration was too half-hearted for modernists, but an abomination to traditionalists. Only conspiracy theorists had any time for it: the place was such an obvious mish-mash, it just had to be a Simulator's joke. Denis didn't much care either way. He was K and Cora's son: he'd been dragged to church time and again for one occasion or another – tie straight, collar tight – but religion had played no real part in his upbringing. K always said these days opium was the opiate of the masses, while mass was the consolation of the deluded few. Cora kissed crosses with the same dutiful revulsion she brought to kissing babies, applying her thickest, most purple lipstick whenever a campaign demanded either. It was Jacob King who got into bed with the Bishop, if Denis remembered rightly. And where had that got him?

"Wake up, stupid. Chop-chop. Time you were at the dry cleaners."

Cora was tapping the back of her wrist, where a watch might have been if she were wearing one.

"What?"

"You don't think you're going like that, do you?"

Cora pointed at the tee shirt he'd been wearing for two days. In his holdall was another just like it, except less clean. He'd been between flats when the news arrived. Most of his clothes were in a bedroom whose rightful tenant wouldn't let him in. Unless she'd already tossed them in a skip. Apart from the shirts, the sum total of his possessions was a pair of socks, a pair of boxers and the jeans he'd travelled in, plus a leather jacket belonging to the woman's previous boyfriend that had been hanging in the hallway when she'd thrown him out. They'd been much the same build, it turned out; the jacket was a decent fit, but hardly the thing for a state funeral.

"There's a suit of your father's waiting at the cleaners. I took it in for another funeral a couple of weeks ago – do you remember Donald Price? – but in the end K was too ill to go. Or too drunk," Cora said. Or off his face on the antidepressants the nursing home inmates traded like kids with marbles. In any case, the suit was just waiting there. No good letting it go to waste. He could pick it up, get a decent shirt and tie while he was at it. Denis said it wouldn't fit. Cora said they could give it a nip and tuck, but it turned out there wasn't much that could be done in the thirty minutes available. The suit hung off him like dustsheets on abandoned furniture. He topped it off with his father's black cashmere overcoat and felt like a clown. A miserable, diminutive clown. He was always so much smaller than his father. Even when his father was dead.

When he got to the Cathedral, though, he wasn't the only one in fancy dress. There must have been a thousand people, all told, not an empty pew in the house; and not one of them looked normal. The Bishop, obviously, set the pace: all outsize Elton John in oyster silk and golden thread, plus a curly Bo-peep walking stick and pointy hat twice as high as any policeman's helmet. But the police could hold their own: Commander Cole was dressed up to invade Ruritania. One of those hats that look like an upside-down boat, pointed back and front, with tassels; enough braid on his jacket to trim a cinema curtain; waistcoat, breeches, mirror-gloss top boots up to his knees; and, best of all, a *sword*. It rattled every time he had to stand, and made sitting down again something of a performance. K would have split his sides. Even Denis's mother, all four foot two of her, was shellac-ed out in something shiny black and brittle, like a giant beetle, plus a hat and a veil and an ebony-black, silver-tipped walking stick she hadn't used when he left home, and probably didn't need. She'd always been as strong as an ox, and built like one, too. Perhaps it was for beating off admirers, now she was a merry widow.

Merry?

He had to laugh. It was only watching this carnival of fellow clowns that would get him through ninety minutes of Bishop Grendel MC-ing prayers, hymns, psalms and obsequies, throwing himself into it like a TV game show host in the death spiral of a failing career. And that was before they even left for the cemetery. It was going to be a long morning.

Some triggered liturgical memory of those in peril on the sea had sent his thoughts wandering idly back to yesterday's boat crossing when Cora whispered, "You ready?"

Ready?

"You're up."

Oh, shit: the poem. He had it. He was pretty sure he had it. Yes, here it was, in his father's suit pocket. He hadn't read it, though. He'd meant to, but Mum had been nagging, and then there was the cleaner's and . . . And that could be a good thing, right? It might sound fresher – if it wasn't rehearsed?

The Bishop motioned to an ecclesiastical flunkey who ushered Denis half a dozen steps from the front pew to the pulpit steps. He'd have to climb them for himself. Up he went, half-expecting the scaffold trap to swing open beneath his feet with every step. A semi-spiral and there he was, gazing out over a tidal drift of faces that wouldn't stay still. He gripped the pulpit rail as tightly as he had that of the ferry. He said, "K was my father . . ." and read the poem, one word at a time. It made no sense, but that was poetry for you, wasn't it?

"Well," his mother said when he sat down again, "perhaps he didn't deserve any better."

A long, long morning.

But then, there was Jessica. Jessica King.

While Cora sat grumpily in the front pew resting her face on

9

her hands and her hands on her stick, the newly elected Island Leader ascended the pulpit steps in a rustle of tailored silk and self-possession.

Twenty-three.

Two years younger than Denis. Whispering, or at least not shouting, his mother reminded him they must have been at school together, before the whole "Child" thing became unbearable, and her father took her out. He couldn't say he remembered. Which didn't mean it wasn't true, Cora said, just that he was an idiot. There were impatient shuffling noises from the pew behind. The Bishop was staring at Cora. "What?" she whispered again, loud enough for the choir to hear, "I'm the fucking *widow*. I'm overwhelmed by grief."

From the pulpit, Jessica was hitting her stride. "In his time, K was a *colossal* figure in the life of every Islander," she said, with the slightly offbeat emphasis of the political speaker. "As *Leader*, he had put the *Island* on the map." Which might have been technically true, Denis thought, if you believed the rumours; but nobody he'd met on the mainland could have found the place without GPS and military air support. "He gave us pride in ourselves," Jessica said, "a belief that we can do *whatever* we set our hearts and minds to. And that's not all," she said. "As *a role model*" – the phrase caused a sharp intake of breath from Cora, as it would have from his father, Denis knew, if the old bastard hadn't been dead – "he showed how a *truly* strong, *confident* man could step back from the limelight to support his *wife*, Cora" – she beamed down at the front pew, ignoring the scowl on Cora's face – "in Leadership and opposition. And to support his *son*, Denis, through the trials and tribulations of growing up inside the Castle." Here it seemed to Denis that she was looking not at him, but over his head to the second pew, where her own father sat between Ari Spencer and the police commander. Whether in tribute to his qualities as a parent, or silent condemnation, Denis couldn't say. "He was," she said, "an *example* to us all."

She paused, looking down at the lectern, although she was speaking without notes.

"*But*," whispered Cora loudly, jabbing Denis with her elbow.

"But," said Jessica, pausing again in case anyone missed the change of gear before plunging on to remind them that a Leader's work is never done, and they would squander and betray all that K had achieved and sacrificed for them if they did not now set aside their differences and come together to save the Island they all loved from the rising sea; to eradicate the scourge of homelessness; and to bring justice to the loved ones of those who had died ten years ago in the Cathedral Close – here Denis detected nervous shuffling in the pew behind – just yards, Jessica continued, from where they were now gathered to remember and consign to peace the very best among them.

"We that are young," she wound up, clearly heading for the home straight, "might never see so much, nor live so long. But it is our duty, our privilege and our *destiny* to build the Island K would want to see."

"Election's over, bitch," hissed Cora.

And you lost, Denis thought. What did you expect?

An hour later, as a north wind threatened rain, and the New Cemetery's raw, scarred earth clung to their shoes like shit on a sheep's backside, the mourners sighed in collective relief at the proclamation that they were are all dust and to dust they would return. Not long left now, they knew.

The Bishop – divested of his robes and his preposterous hat, but nonetheless imposingly tall and surprisingly wide (as broad, his rivals sometimes sniped, as the way that leadeth to destruction) – claimed the dead were blessèd which die in the Lord, for they rested, apparently, from their labours. Whatever Jessica said, thought Denis, it had been years since K did anything you could honestly call labour. Decades. She'd been right about one thing, though. However good or bad their parents, it hadn't been easy growing up inside the Castle. They had that much in common. But it looked like Jessica had made a better job of it. Discreet, stylish black hat, black skirt suit, black stockings, black shoes, her pinned-up, tied-back black hair, all at odds with the shine in her eyes, the glow of her face, the hint of a smile, as if she knew how ridiculous all this seemed. Was he imagining it? Possibly. But there was no doubt she was upstaging his mother at her own husband's funeral. Which was fine by him. While they waited for the coffin to be carted out and bowled into the hearse, he asked Cora why, if she was so pissed off about it, she hadn't given a eulogy of her own. She'd made him read a poem, hadn't she? Cora said, "I'm over-fucking-whelmed, Idiot Boy. By grief."

Then the Bishop declared that unto the King eternal, immortal, invisible, the only wise God, be honour and glory for ever and ever. And they all said: Amen. Except K, of course.

Afterwards, they hung about in the bitter wind, trading brief lies about the deceased, mentioning to each other matters of business they'd have to talk about soon, when all this was over, and waiting for the funeral directors to three-point turn the empty hearse and draw the limousines up as close as they could to the graveside.

TWO

WAITING FOR THE cars, for each other, for the respectful time to leave - *you can't just walk out, can you? Not on K's widow; not on the new Leader* - mourners drifted in and out of small knots, couples and awkward, malformed circles. Ari Spencer was keen to exploit an opportunity. The first reviews should be trickling in right now. Busying himself with his phone, his watch, with re-reading the order of service - anything to discourage the approach of supplicants - he floated from the fringe of one conversation to another.

- *It was well cut, all right. For someone twice his size.*
- *And that poem? Hallmark by Alexa.*

Ari hovered, assimilating intelligence, half an eye out for the principals.

- *It's a long time to be married. Fifty years?*
- *Overwhelmed with gre-lief.*
- *Ha. Not impossible. But still.*

And . . . move.

- *Rain? It's February. Of course it's going to rain.*

A nod to Sally Porter and Peter Whatshisname; and - turn.

- *Could have said something, don't you think? Or better not? More dignified?*
- *Dignified? Cora Klamm?*
- *Ha, ha.*
- *Ha ha ha.*

All right, Ari thought. It wasn't even funny. Forget Cora. Cora lost. What he wanted to know was: what had they made of the speech? Jessica's speech. The one she wouldn't let him write.

- *What I want to know is: why don't we just float?*

– *Why an island doesn't float?*

– *Yeah.*

– *Well, I suppose it does. Tectonically.*

– *Tectonically, yeah, all right. Sort of. Though for your information tectonic plates don't really float. It's more, the whole lithosphere is in a sort of constant churn. But your point stands. As an analogy.*

– *An analogy?*

– *But what I want to know is: how does that help?*

– *You brought it up.*

Denis was already handing his mother into the first limousine, Cora leaning heavily on the stick she didn't need, Jessica diplomatically holding back. It had been Ari's idea to put her in with the surviving Klamms. A sign of her new status. He wondered how *that* conversation would go.

– *Because it should float, by rights, shouldn't it? If the Island's simulated? It wouldn't be part of the continental plate, and it should just float on the water?*

Ari loved this stuff. He told himself it was work, but it was more than that. It wasn't what he was looking for, specifically – wasn't about Jessica – but it was his stock in trade. The psychopathology of nonsense. He ignored Jacob's signal that the second limousine was ready. He wanted to hear where this was going.

– *So why's it sinking, then?*

– *We've sprung a leak?*

That's beautiful, Ari thought. He held a finger up to let Jacob know he'd be there in just one minute.

– *So all we've got to do . . .*

– *Is plug the hole.*

– *Genius.*

– *Genius.*

Which was about as much as Ari was going to get, because Jacob and Commander Cole were already in the second car; and Diana Ford-Marling, who should have been riding with them, hadn't even turned up. A bold move, Ari thought; he should come back to that.

He took a last look at the two men congratulating each other and thought: but what if the Island isn't a Simulation after all? What would they say then? They'd say that we're all doomed, obviously.

The wisdom of crowds was much overrated.

An empty hearse is a display case for death. The glittering space makes the absence of the dead more concrete than an actual coffin. In the first limo, just behind, the mood was lighter than Ari might have predicted.

"Dear God," said Cora the moment the men in professional black had gently closed the doors on them, "death brings out the worst in people, doesn't it? Do you know what Sally Porter said?"

"Who's Sally Porter?" Denis asked. There were two rows of passenger seats, two sets of doors. Denis was in the first row, his mother and Jessica sat next to each other behind. Somebody was having a laugh, at any rate.

"No, darling. If she'd said *that* it might at least have been original. What she said was: *he'd had a good innings*. Nobody says that, really, do they?"

Yes, thought Denis. Apparently they do.

"But who is she, Mum?"

Cora didn't answer, so Jessica explained. "She's the Authority's Finance Director."

"As if he ever played cricket," Cora said.

The car pulled away, at the pace of the walking wounded. Denis thought talking to Jessica would be more fun than indulging his mother, and turned awkwardly to speak over his shoulder. "Did she know him?"

"I doubt it," Jessica said. "She'd have been a trainee when your father was Leader. Fresh out of college."

"Just his type," Cora said. "When K was Leader, you weren't even born."

It wasn't obvious if she meant Jessica or Denis, but either way it would have been true, or thereabouts. Her story was that she'd given birth on the campaign trail for her first election. Not that you could trail far on the Island. They didn't even have a bus. So Denis had been born in hospital, like pretty much everybody else. All the same, it happened while Cora was campaigning to succeed his father. She took two days off, dumped him in K's arms with a case of formula and a mountain of disposable nappies, then went straight back on the road. Male politicians did it all the time, she said: so why not? She wasn't going to let a little thing like childbirth get in the way of becoming the Island's first woman Leader since the Romans snuffed out the underfloor heating and buggered off back to Italy. Denis suspected she'd secretly hoped to hang on till after the election. Then she'd have been not just the first female Leader of modern times, but the first to give birth in office: that would have set the bar pretty high for any would-be followers. But K wasn't up for bonding with a newborn. He dropkicked the bundle straight on to a scrum of nannies and babysitters, and swapped formula for whisky. Which might have been why Cora never got a second shot at calving on the Cabinet table.

Denis was an only child, then, abandoned – or so he had spent several years telling young women in student bars – by both parents. As a ploy, it worked. Not always, not often, even: but often enough for him to keep it up, and then finally to realize that the kind of women most susceptible to its spell were just those he had least interest in himself. Etiolated, droopy girls who decorated handwritten love notes with birds and flowers painstakingly inked in several colours and slept with cuddly toys older than their teeth. With their hideous, unnatural postures – the toys, not the girls – their patches worn to raw fabric and their missing facial features, they had begun to remind him of documentaries about the Somme, and did little to encourage his already weakening lust.

Jessica King, though?

They had so much in common, didn't they? Growing up inside

the Castle, the children of politicians, his mother lost to the demands of duty and ambition, hers to . . . whatever it was her mother died of. An accident? Cancer? It didn't matter: the point being that Jessica was motherless. She would understand.

He said, "Thank you, by the way. For what you said about my father. It was very . . . touching."

Touching was a good choice, he thought. Subtle; subliminal. Also best to steer clear of the political stuff. It would only wind his mother up.

"Thank you," Jessica said. "Your reading was very moving, too."

She was lying. But he didn't mind. She was lying to flatter him: that had to be a good thing, right?

"He sounded like a fucking robot reciting a railway timetable," Cora said.

"Thank you, Mother."

"You're welcome. You're just not cut out for stardom, little one. I remember once," she said, turning to Jessica, "at primary school, he was the Jacob in *Our Island Story*. Because of me, I dare say. But anyway, he splits his trousers and forgets his lines. Desperate to get off, he yanks a door handle so hard the whole set collapses. Best show they ever did."

"I was there," said Jessica. "I'll never forget it."

That's right, he thought. She was only a couple of years younger. Odd that he didn't remember her, in the circumstances. Given who she was. It must have been weird, though, seeing her dad and her infant self on stage. The pair of them fished out of the harbour when she was three. Everyone knowing the story, the prophecy. Learning it in school, acting it out every year. Everyone knowing she was the Child. That her dad would be Leader, and she'd grow up to be Leader and everything on the Island would be hunky-dory. Milk and honey. Meanwhile he would grow up, escape to the mainland and squander his allowance – when he had one – on beer, cigarettes and crypto-currency scams, while spending long afternoons in shabby pubs swapping conspiracy theories with equally underemployed

17

young men. But he'd played her dad, on stage, which was a bit messed up, and he probably shouldn't think about, right now.

She remembered him. What more could he ask?

He turned in the seat, avoiding his mother's eye. Jessica smiled, carefully, the way you might placate an unpredictable drunk.

Here goes, he thought. Cabin crew prepare for landing.

Conversation in the second limousine was desultory.

"We that are young, eh?" Ari offered.

After a while, Commander Cole said, "Are we?" He shifted his ridiculous cocked hat from his right knee to his left. Getting in and out of the limo with a sword had proved unnecessarily difficult. Now it lay across his lap as if he were preparing to disembowel himself. "I don't think we can honestly say that."

Ari wondered if there was anything more camp than *hara-kiri*. He said, "It's a Donald-ism."

"It's Shakespeare," Jacob said. "*King Lear*."

"I only ever heard Donald say it."

There was another pause. The rain had finally started and they watched the wet streets pass.

"Personally," said Jacob, "I know I've seen enough and lived too long."

Bob Cole said, "Oh, you can't say that." After which none of them said anything for a while.

Jacob took off his glasses and polished them on his shirt. "The worst is not so long as we can say: this is the worst."

"Where there's life there's hope, eh?" Bob Cole said. Then, remembering where they'd been, he added, "Sorry. Not quite the time."

"That's not what it means, anyway," said Jacob. "More like the opposite."

"Where there's hope there's life?"

"Where there's life things can always get worse."

"Amen," said Ari.

"Well I certainly caught the happy bus," said Commander Cole. Then he said sorry, again.

After a while, Jacob said: "What *were* you thinking?" He shook his head. Ari didn't answer.

"It was bad enough in the Election. But she's Leader now."

This isn't the time, Ari thought. You know this. He said, "It wasn't me."

"It's your job."

"She wouldn't let me write it."

Jacob shook his head again. "All she had to do was be nice about a dead man. No one had to believe it. Why didn't you stop her?"

She's your daughter, Ari thought. You should know. He had no children himself, though. Perhaps he should make allowances? Jacob had lost a leadership challenge to his grown-up daughter, even if he hadn't publicly contested it; Ari had jumped ship – again – to make it happen. Jacob must have known it was coming. It was the story, after all – the Child could not become Leader without challenging its father – and even if he never believed *Our Island Story*, he could hardly be surprised when others pretended that they did. But knowing your fate doesn't make it any easier to live with, Ari had to accept. Everybody knows they're going to die. Everybody *knows* the Island is sinking. That doesn't mean they'll do anything about it. And just because it was sinking faster than ever, Jessica's accession had been required earlier than they'd planned. Jacob knew all this. The brittle stalemate they'd so carefully constructed had been breaking down; the message cycle had to turn from cynicism to hope. Where there's hope there's life, as Commander Plod just put it, wiser than he knew. But Ari hadn't catered for a Leader who might not realize that hope was just another form of cynicism. He hadn't had to deal with a Child before. Not in office.

Jacob peered out of the rain-spattered window as if the answer might lie somewhere out there in the murk. "*Can* you eradicate homelessness? Is that even possible?"

It might be, Ari thought, if the Island's houses didn't keep falling into the sea. But that wasn't the point; Jacob knew that, too. It was just grief talking.

Commander Cole shifted his hat back from his left knee to his right. "Didn't somebody once say the poor are always with us?"

You could always trust a copper for a little homespun wisdom.

Jacob ploughed on. "What are you going to do?"

Ari bit his tongue. Was Jacob unhinged enough to bring up the justice bit of Jessica's triple pledge? One thing Ari would definitely do was make sure Bob Cole took the fall for the demo and the deaths. Early retirement, pension intact. He'd floated the idea as soon as it became obvious Jessica was serious about the inquiry. But now was not the time to bring it up. As for the homeless, what was there to say? Jacob had been Leader for a decade; Ari had to make allowances. He'd lost a daughter just as Cora had lost a husband. More so: Jacob loved his daughter.

Ari just thanked God – not that he believed, but thanked Him anyway – that Diana Ford-Marling hadn't come; she'd have been there in the car with them, which would have only made matters worse. But why hadn't she?

⁂

Lucy walked from the New Cemetery to the Castle, just as she had walked to and from the Cathedral. If Ari had known she was back on the Island, she might have had a place in a car somewhere. Somewhere at the back of the cortège, but still. It was possible. If he'd known why she was here.

She didn't mind the walk, though. Yesterday's crossing had been gruesome: a bit of fresh air wouldn't kill her, even if it came straight off what was left of the ice cap, spitting rain. The New Cemetery had been pretty bleak, too, even for a cemetery: all unfinished border walls and saplings still in plastic tubes, but she knew that there'd been little choice. It wasn't that the old one was full up – the dispossessed weren't really drowning, most of them, just inching further and further uphill – more that it had emptied, suddenly, apocalyptically, when the rising water undermined a retaining wall and a platoon of ancient skeletons, recent corpses and unattached body parts had tumbled indiscriminately out into the sea, where they'd bobbed about like plastic ducks in a fairground stall while the Authority's minions tried gamely to lasso them.

Her phone pinged. It was Diana. Where was she?

She thumbed: *On my way. There in 5.*

According to Diana, it was the cemetery more than anything – more than the loss of the Hope & Anchor, the rest of the seafront, the Oceanview retirement community or even two fifths of the Island's arable land – that had been the tipping point. Clamour for the Child had become irresistible. Jacob stood aside, no doubt at Ari Spencer's instigation; when it came to the election, Cora hadn't stood a chance. And when she finally lost last Thursday, she lost her party, too. So Diana was Leader of the Opposition, now, and in need of a spad she could trust. And here Lucy was: Ari's opposite number, again. Quite like old times.

Lucy quickened her step, dog-legging around a couple of sleeping bags laid out across the pavement, paper cups set out on either side.

Her first advice to Diana? Go to the funeral. Diana had said there'd be no mileage in it for her. Between them, the Widow and the Child would suck up all the oxygen. True enough, Lucy said, but sitting it out would only make her look petty. Just being there would show she was at the top table now; dignified silence was all that would be required. Diana preferred to think that rocking up to her new office at the Castle would show she'd hit the ground running. Lucy lost the argument. Not a great start, but not the end of the world. Then Jessica King had gone full messiah and Diana was nowhere to be seen. No doubt she'd heard already. Someone would have enjoyed letting her know, and of course, that someone really should have been Lucy. Hence the text. No, not a great start, but –

"Can you spare—"

She rummaged in her bag, pulled out her purse and picked a note out for the woman blocking her path.

"God bless," the woman said, but Lucy didn't think it likely.

 ❧

The cortège approached the Castle. To the right of the main gate, a rough camp built of broken pallets and plastic sheets clung to the perimeter wall. The security guard raised the red-and-white striped barrier and the limousines passed through without slowing their already dilatory pace. Before Denis could get his crucial words out, they had drawn up outside the Central Block.

"I just want you to know," his mother said to Jessica, "I don't blame you."

Jessica did not reply.

"No: I blame your father. I'm *so* glad you shafted him. I mean, you beat me; but you *shafted* him. Well *done*."

Jessica said thank you; which Denis thought, the way she said it, could have meant anything.

But his mother hadn't finished. "And good luck with all the pledge stuff. I mean it. You know I've moved into the Houghton Building? There's a woman living in the service basement."

"Homelessness is . . ."

"Disgusting. Yes. It shouldn't be allowed."

The undertakers opened the car's rear doors first; Jessica and his mother got out on opposite sides.

Great, thought Denis, stuck inside a moment longer. No, really, this was *great*. Now he could apologize for his mother. He could make a joke about how lucky Jessica was not to have one. Maybe not. Still, it was an opening, surely? If he could only get a word in.

But by the time he'd let himself out of the limousine, Jessica was already through the revolving glass doors and striding towards the lift.

THREE

T HE CASTLE WAS not in fact a castle, but a collection of civic
office blocks of varying height arranged in a semi-circle around
a Central Block, to which they were joined by covered walkways,
like the spokes of half a wheel. Half, because the Castle occupied the
high point of an Island that rose steadily, then steeply, from the east,
the north and the south to a semi-conical summit before dropping
away vertiginously in thousand-foot cliffs to the churning western
sea below. Eminently defensible, then – impenetrable, even – Jacob
had thought when he had first presented himself at the gates twenty
years earlier, the three year-old Jessica on his hip, although in reality
he would penetrate it easily enough. Still, it was no surprise the site
should have attracted the Islanders' Neolithic forebears: there was
evidence that the Romans had found the place both occupied and
defended. By the end of the first millennium the Danes – or Saxons,
or Angles or whoever was supposed to have claimed the Island for
their own – had repeatedly ringed the hill with ditches and pickets,
then crowned it with a keep built first of wood and subsequently
stone; succeeding generations had repaired, replaced and extended
it as the centuries rolled by until the Island's twentieth-century
planners decided enough was enough. Such was one theory, anyway.
As Jacob soon discovered, other explanations were available. The
most persistent held that the entire civic complex, along with the
medieval shambles at the foot of the hill; the two Georgian squares
of the city's south side and seafront; the Victorian suburbs laid out
like bricks of new money in a gangster's attaché case; the bungalows,
semis, lawns and verges of the pre-War suburbs surrounding them;
and even the low green hills and smudges of forest and heath that

could, on clear days, be glimpsed beyond those suburbs; that the very rocks on which they stood; indeed that everything visible from the highest window of the tallest block, everything except the sea itself and the sky above, had all been painstakingly constructed during the Great Simulation of the 1980s. All baloney, Jacob heard, but apt to pop up in the minds and conversation of the most surprising people. A bit like anti-Semitism, he was told, with which some of its strands had a distressing, if unsurprising, tendency to merge. If the Island had been artificially simulated by a secretive cabal of behavioural scientists, what might those scientists have been after? Where might they have got their funding? It wasn't hard to see how a bit of dubious pub-fantasy could slide into something altogether more poisonous. Especially now, when even to the faithful it must look as if the money had dried up and the Simulators had moved on to fabricate pastures new, leaving the Islanders to make do as best they could; or to drown, of course.

Dangerous baloney, then, Jacob thought: an ever more rancid sack of synthetic poison. He'd done some morally dubious things in his time as Leader, because – well, because he was Leader and it came with the territory. When you got right down to it, he had built his entire career on that other lie these Islanders loved to believe – the one about a future leader, and a future saviour, being rescued from drowning at sea. But that was harmless enough, wasn't it? If nothing else, it made the local fisher-folk more willing to pluck asylum seekers out of the water. And not to lynch them afterwards. But he'd drawn the line at Simulationism. It hadn't been that hard, to be fair. Even Ari, for whom morality was at best a flexible concept, had never stooped low enough to bring him any bright Simulation-based ideas.

All the same, the madness refused to die.

Why? Because these Islanders, he thought – watching Bob Cole struggling out of the limousine, dropping his hat and catching his sword on the leather upholstery; watching Denis Klamm gape, open-mouthed after Jessica as she swept into the Central Block while his mother stabbed the ground fiercely with her walking stick – these

Islanders were, well, *insular*. Not quite the sharpest pitchforks in the riot. Whisper it: in-bred. Prone to keep important things – like Leadership – in the family. Twenty years ago, when they'd fished him out of the harbour, Jacob had emerged blinking, wiping salt water from his myopic eyes, glasses sunk to the bottom of the sea. But he'd kept a second pair securely buttoned-up within an inside pocket. Two decades later, though, he might as well be one of them: his daughter certainly was.

What had he done?

Alighting at the Castle, only because that was where the cortège stopped, Jacob knew he had no business there. Oh, he had the *right*: he still lived in the apartment on the eighth floor of the Central Block. Only yesterday, Jessica had assured him, rather stiffly, that their change in role and status would make no difference to their domestic arrangements. But even using a phrase like *domestic arrangements* showed just how much difference there already was.

He could sleep in his own bedroom, but he was no longer Leader; she was.

His situation, he reflected, was not unlike K's. Not the being dead, but the years before. When Jacob first landed on the Island, Cora had already replaced K as Leader; but K had hung around the Castle, around his wife, for another fifteen years or so, until she parcelled him up and posted him off to St Julian's. Was that Jacob's own future?

He had no business here. Yet here he was.

To Ari, he said, "What have we done?"

The empty limousines pulled away slowly, leaving the mourners stranded alone, or in ill-matched groups.

Ari said, "We?"

"Come on, Ari. We had ten good years together."

"And you're going to ruin it now by turning sentimental?"

"It's a funeral. What better time for sentiment? Besides, I could say it was you who ruined it – by stabbing me in the back."

Ari turned to him. "You could."

"But you're right, I won't."

After a while, he said, quietly: "Fish gotta swim."

"What?"

"It's your nature, Ari. Swifts. You know swifts?"

"I know they're not fish."

"Swifts fly thousands of miles every year. Thousands. They spend ten months migrating. They eat and sleep on the wing. They copulate in mid-air. Their legs are too short to land on the ground."

"You know nature isn't really my thing?"

He did, of course. Ten years. Leader and spad: was there any closer relationship on earth? Closer than his marriage: longer lasting, too. But this particular spad was on to his third Leader. Which shouldn't have been possible.

"When did you last leave the Castle, Ari?"

"Thursday. There's been an election, in case you hadn't noticed."

"Okay. Before the election."

Ari hesitated. "I don't know." He looked up at the sky; the rain had stopped again, but the clouds remained solid and low, the colour of wet slate. It was only noon, but almost dark. "It was sunnier than this," he said. "June, maybe?"

Jacob shook his head in mock disbelief. "Do you ever wonder what would happen if you stopped?"

"Why would I do that?"

"Stop?"

"Wonder."

From inside Ari's black suit came the muted but unmistakable ping of a text arriving. He said, "That'll be a summons from your daughter."

"Ari . . ."

"I work for Jessica now."

"Good luck."

⚘

The mourners drifted away with a greater or lesser sense of purpose, according to the dictates of their diary or their conscience.

Commander Cole straightened his cocked hat, put his hand on the hilt of his sword to stop it clattering about, and strode towards the police station in Block 3, built over the entrance gate due east of Central Block. Sally Porter and a gaggle of other senior managers headed towards Block 5; the politicians mostly followed Jessica. Years ago – before Jacob's time – Cora had decided to keep her enemies close, clustering the party offices and committee rooms around her own suite on the upper floors of Central Block, and exiling the Authority's senior managers to Block 5, which perched precariously above the cliffs on the Castle's south-western fringe. Only the Chief Executive, Donald Price, had remained. His office, a sliver of space carved out between the Cabinet and the Opposition Rooms, lay on the seventh floor of Central Block, directly below Cora's own. That way, when Cora stamped her little foot – which might happen several times a day – and Donald wasn't there to witness her frustration at first hand, he would nonetheless experience its urgency through the ceiling. It kept him on his toes, Cora said. She was a traditionalist in many ways.

She was there now, lingering with her idiot son, both of them apparently as reluctant to leave as Jacob himself. She had been ousted, too, of course. She must have seen it coming – who on the Island was ever going to win an election against the Child, after all? And who, having lost three elections in a row could hope to retain control of her party? – but, still. It must have been brutal.

He straightened his spectacles, settling them on his nose, and approached with care. "This is what it comes to, isn't it," he said, waving vaguely towards the doors that had closed behind Jessica, "when they put us oldies out to grass?"

Cora straightened her spine and sucked in her stomach. "Ah, fuck off, King." She strode away, thrusting her stick into the concrete pavement as if she were hoping to stab moles.

"I'm sorry, Councillor . . . Mr. . . . . My mother is very upset. Probably."

In his mind Jacob saw the words Idiot Son capitalized, as if it were a formal title, hovering above the young man's head. He didn't really know the lad, had only encountered him on civic occasions, where he'd had nothing to do but look increasingly sullen the older he grew. But that was how Cora had invariably referred to him: *Idiot Son*; or, if K were present, *your Idiot Son*.

"Your mother," Jacob replied, "is a piece of virtue, as Shakespeare says somewhere." A piece of work, more like. Copper-bottomed. "We may have lost a great Leader," he added, wondering how much Denis would read into that *may*, "but she has lost, what's worse, a loving husband."

"You think?"

Hah. Of course he didn't. But what good would come of saying what he really thought? There had been no love lost between Cora and K for years. He had it on good authority – Ari's – that she never visited her husband in St Julian's. How Ari came by this information he hadn't asked. It was Ari's job to know such things; it didn't do for Jacob to get too close to the mechanics. That was just the way things worked. With the benefit of hindsight, though, might that have been a mistake? If he'd known more about Ari's methods, he might have seen the defection coming. Might still have been Leader. And Jessica might at least have been spared that for a few years yet.

Ah, what nonsense: he *had* seen it coming.

"Of course," he said now. "They were a great support to each other."

Like Mr. and Mrs. Macbeth, he added silently.

"I thought she despised him," Denis said. "Mind you, I haven't been back in seven years, so what do I know?"

Spotting an opportunity to tack into less perilous waters, Jacob seized it gratefully. "So, how are you finding the place? Much changed?"

"There seems to be less of it than I remember."

"I understand. Childhood memories often seem much smaller to our adult eyes."

Trite, he knew. But the young man looked at him with greater sharpness than he had expected.

"They don't usually fall into the sea though, do they?"

A fair point, Jacob conceded with a slight nod of the head. "So now you're here, what are you going to do?"

Now Denis paused before answering. Jacob guessed the real answer would be: get out as soon as he could. He was probably just wondering how polite he should be. There were rumours about his career on the mainland – using *career* in the loosest possible sense, Jacob thought: or, more precisely, in the sense of *charging around out of control*. If such rumours were true – and, again, Ari was his primary source – there wouldn't be much to keep the young man here. And no loss to the Island if he left.

"I thought I'd stick around a while. See how I can help."

"Help?"

"Do my bit for the Island."

"Well, that's . . . very commendable."

"Yes," Denis said. "I thought I'd offer Jessica my services."

Which really was a surprise. "Jessica?"

"The new Leader."

"I know who she is."

"Of course you do, Mr. King. Sorry."

Jacob shuddered.

Denis said, "Is that a good idea? Would you say?"

"I . . ."

"It is. Yes. Seize the day. Thank you."

With which he marched determinedly towards the revolving glass doors of the Central Block, and tried to push them the wrong way.

Jacob watched him go. Seize the day? The lad meant no harm. He *was* an idiot, obviously, but probably harmless. And not entirely wrong? After a suitable interval, Jacob thought, he might offer Jessica his services himself. He could still do his bit. As advisor, as mentor – the wisdom of the elder statesman to guide her youthful idealism – as William Cecil to the young Elizabeth, perhaps. Not that he would actually offer outright. That would sound too much like Jessica talking about their *domestic arrangements*. He should just make himself available. Just be there. On hand. He would let the dust of the election settle first: she would see he bore no grudge, that he was proud of her. And Ari could relax around him, too. Much as his defection had pained Jacob at the time, he understood it, saw the necessity for it, even appreciated the skill with which the manoeuvre had been executed, and had no intention of allowing it to stand between himself and his daughter. He would kiss her brow and shake Ari by the hand, when the time was right.

Just be there? Had K thought something similarly inane?

"Mr. King?"

What now? He was fast having to get used to being Mr. King again. Not *Leader*. Not even Councillor since Thursday.

It was a woman. Long, thin face, dressed in black. She must have come from the funeral, but hadn't been in the cortège. Pale, and hesitant, like one of those pets that never quite get over their fear of humans. It would come – the name – it would come, if she just gave him a moment. Lily? Lucy? That was it.

"Lucy," he said, just tentatively enough to change tack with a laugh if it proved necessary. "How are you?"

She nodded.

Yes!

"Fine, Mr. King. You remember me?"

"Jacob, please. Of course, of course. You worked for Cora."

She'd been Cora's spad. Ari's opposite number, except Ari didn't really recognize any opposition. She'd left a few years ago: why was that? Ari would know.

He said, "Are you just back for the funeral?"

"No. I mean, yes, obviously, the funeral. But also I'm working here again. For Diana Ford-Marling."

Well, somebody had to, he supposed. Personally he could imagine no worse fate. Diana Ford-Marling was a force of nature. Like malaria. Life on the mainland must really have been tough. Whatever it was Lucy had gone there to do surely didn't deserve this kind of penance?

She seemed to be steadying her nerve, screwing herself up to say something important. "So I suppose," she said at last, "the poetry will have to take a back seat for a while."

Poetry? Maybe she deserved Diana after all?

"Sorry. My agent says I need to tell people I'm a poet. To own it."

"Like alcoholism?"

She had the grace to laugh, he'd give her that.

"Anyway," she said, "I just wanted to say, I always thought you did a great job as Leader, even though I wasn't supposed to admit it. Enjoy your retirement, Mr. King. You've earned it."

Retirement? A great job? Jacob caught his breath. Well, the lack of tact explained why she'd had to leave, at any rate. That and poetry. But what had the actual trigger been? Something to do with the original drilling project, perhaps? He would ask Ari, he thought, before realizing he might not see Ari anytime soon. Because Ari had gone to meet his daughter. Because Jessica was Leader now, and he, Jacob, wasn't; and she no longer needed him.

He said, "Thank you." It was all he could do to stop the words catching in his throat. He pulled off his glasses and rubbed them against his black silk tie.

"Thank you."

FOUR

PAUSING OUTSIDE THE revolving doors, Ari wondered if he had time to change. Black suit, black tie wouldn't have been his choice. He looked up, measuring the gap between Block 2, on the third floor of which he had long ago made his unofficial home, and the Central Block, where, in response to the Leader's summons, he was already overdue. The walkways connected the blocks at different heights, none at ground level. They had been designed more with architectural grace than the weather of the northern seas in mind, and proved less than watertight during the heavy storms that now battered the Island with increasing ferocity. A couple of months ago, just before Christmas, the fifth-floor bridge between the Centre and Block 2 had collapsed altogether, leaving ragged, broken stumps sticking out like toothpicks from the mouths of grizzled gun-slingers preparing for a shootout. For Ari, the principal effect had been to increase considerably the time it took to reach the Leader's Office from his quarters – an inconvenience he could not lament aloud without revealing the secret of his living arrangements. Consequently, no decision had yet been reached on the bridge's replacement.

A black suit it would have to be.

On the eighth floor, Jules told him to wait while Jessica finished a call.

"How's Saturday?"

"Oh, you know . . ."

Ari didn't, and didn't much care, to be honest. Jules had been Jacob's PA for years and had so far survived the regime change. Ari took that as a good sign. He liked the man. More to the point, Jules trusted him, because Jacob had trusted him, and that mattered.

As for his improbably named French bulldog with its persistent psoriasis, Ari had no opinion beyond a fervent wish that they might never meet. It didn't hurt, however, to maintain cordial relations with a Leader's PA.

". . . Cute as ever," Jules continued, "but still, the *shedding*."

"Must be hell on the damask bedspreads."

"Like you wouldn't believe. And the *creams* we've tried."

Ari noted the 'we', wondering if it referred merely to Jules and the dog, or indicated some previously unmentioned upgrade to the former's love life, but didn't pursue the point. There were limits.

"So," he said, feigning outrage, "our new Leader summons me – toot-sweet, she says: now, pronto, chop-chop, lickety-spit – and then makes another call?"

"He called her."

"Who he?"

Obviously, by the rules, Jules should not reveal who the Leader was talking to, but—

"The bishop."

You're a good man, Ari thought. Aloud, he said. "Binkie? He only spoke to her an hour ago."

"That's my Lord the Bishop Grendel to you, sweetheart. He's got a bee in his pointy bonnet about something. An inquiry?"

Good man, indeed. He'd make sure Jules got a pay rise next time the chance arose. Also: good girl – woman. Whatever. Jessica obviously hadn't warned Jules to be on his guard now that she'd won. Meanwhile, Ari's hand had been tipped: he knew what he was dealing with.

A red light on Jules' desk phone went out.

"In you go," he said.

Jessica was standing by the window, a figure in black against a grey view, like one of Ingmar Bergman's cheerier moments. A seagull passed the window, mobbed by pigeons. Ari was pleased to see nothing in the office had changed. It had only been a couple of days but, still, he had wondered if there might be messages she wanted to send that she had not yet divulged to him. The two of them had worked closely over the last few weeks. They'd argued the finer details of the campaign back and forth, getting everything just so. She had never simply overruled or seriously disagreed with his ideas; but neither, he sometimes felt, had she whole-heartedly committed herself to his point of view. It was as if she were reserving judgment. So it came as something of a relief now to see the blown-up street map of the City still covering an entire wall, each church site ringed in red marker the night he and her father had planned the borehole strategy; also, to find that Jacob's sofas - installed after chucking out the immense, boat-shaped meeting table from which Cora had bullied opponents, colleagues and subordinates alike - were still in place. Jessica hadn't begun by throwing everything out. She was his third Leader, the only one he'd seen blowing out candles on a birthday cake. He had worried himself unnecessarily. It would be fine. Everything would be fine.

"Well," she said, "that's that done, anyway."

"Leader?"

"Burying the dinosaur."

"Indeed." What else could he say? If she didn't know that he was the only one who'd ever visited K, there was no need to tell her now. It wasn't as though the old man had done much more than drool and spit and provide him with an unresisting ear for the last couple of years. He said "We that are young, eh?"

"We? I've often wondered, Ari - just how old are you?"

"That would be telling."

Listen to yourself, he thought, disgusted.

"I used to think - years ago, I mean, when I was a kid - I used to think that you and Angela might, you know, have a thing."

There was nothing like a funeral to provoke unnecessary reminiscence. He said, "Me and Angela?"

"Before she died, of course."

"Well, obviously." He recalled the young woman he had interviewed and then taken to lunch a dozen years ago, and who had asked him so many questions. They had understood each other, he thought: at least, she had understood him. It was not an entirely comfortable sensation. She'd been beautiful – there was no way around that – and smart and not so much younger than he was. They'd met again, for coffee, for lunch, Ari reassuring himself that his Leader's daughter was in safe hands: nothing more. "I was too old, Leader. Even then."

"Always the court eunuch, eh, Ari?"

"I don't think I'd go quite that far."

She laughed. "No?"

"Well, maybe. Not that it would make much difference now."

He already had, though, hadn't he? Cora, Jacob, and now Jessica: he had lived vicariously, through them. But so what? It was a life. The life he'd chosen. All the same, this wasn't a conversation he was keen to pursue.

"You wanted a word, Leader?"

Turning back to the window and looking down at the streets below, she said, "I watched it, you know."

She meant the demonstration in Cathedral Close. Ten years ago: funeral-induced reminiscence was not over yet.

"From here. Well, next door. The flat. I stood at the window waiting for Angela to come and look at my homework, and I watched the protestors gather in the Close. The police formed up in Clarence Square. And for a while at least I didn't put two and two together. She'd made me translate Donne's Meditation XVII into Latin. *Nemo insula est.* You know?"

"I'm afraid Latin rather passed me by, Leader."

"Don't play ever-so-'umble, Ari. It doesn't suit you."

No? How much did she know about him, really? How much had her father shared? He never knew his own father. His mother was a committee clerk who went into early labour during a Cabinet meeting that should have ended at ten, but dragged on into the small hours of the morning before crashing to an abrupt halt when her waters broke. It was said that K himself had helped deliver him, after

35

declaring the meeting formally closed. In some versions he'd heard, K bit through the umbilical cord with his own teeth. Whose teeth he might have been expected to use, Ari never enquired, but that K had been present at his birth was indisputable; unless of course his mother had made the whole thing up. He asked her outright once; she referred him to the minutes of the meeting, where the reason for its sudden termination was dutifully recorded, although the precise contributions of the members present to the successful delivery of a healthy, seven-and-a-quarter pound baby unsurprisingly were not. His earliest memories were of the Castle crèche, where employees parked their progeny during working hours. He'd enjoyed playing with the toys and with his fellow inmates. And yet his clearest memory was of watching as one by one each of the other children was collected by a parent or an older sibling, while he waited, reading a book he had read a hundred times, a book in which a dog chased a ball that bounced across a little girl's bedroom, down the stairs, across the street – *Look out, Pongo!* – down the hill, across the park – *Watch out for the pond, Pongo!* – through the gates and up the gravel pathway to the Town Hall, where the Mayor was leading a procession of the biggest, wiggiest big-wigs in town – *Oh, no, Pongo!* – and by the time the girl and the girl's father finally catch up, red in the face, puffing and panting – especially the girl's father, who eats too many doughnuts and is not as fit as he might be (but who at least exists) the Mayor has slipped on the ball, the Mayor's wife has tripped over the dog, the brass band has collided with the aldermen and the whole glorious and dignified parade has been forever ruined. The Town Hall in the picture book had ornate stone columns around the doors and statues of former mayors on plinths and did not look much like the Castle, Ari thought, later, when he was half-grown. Besides, he thought, the Castle was at the top of the hill: no runaway ball could roll up here from the City below. It was a ship of state, floating serenely above the chaos and uncertainty beneath and all around.

He was eleven when his mother died. At which point, he had

slipped determinedly through the cracks into the heart of the Castle: leaving primary school amid the confusion of bereavement, he simply never turned up to secondary at all. When the Authority finally re-assigned his mother's flat, he commandeered a little-used meeting room on one of the quieter floors of Block 2, hacking into the Authority's cumbersome IT systems to remove all trace of its existence. He installed a makeshift pallet bed, along with a kettle and a sandwich toaster, both purloined from a staff kitchen in another block, and never moved out. Over the years, he had improved the decor and the furnishings, swapping filing cabinets for a wardrobe in which to store his limited supply of shirts and suits, installing a real bed and a bookcase for the indiscriminate collection he had assembled over the years from the books and magazines found lying under chairs or stuffed behind the radiators of committee rooms when the councillors and public had all gone home. What his education lacked in structure, it made up for in eclecticism. But it had never included Latin.

"No man is an island, Ari. *Nemo insula est.* Angela's idea of a joke. I watched the police form up in a phalanx, riot shields out and locked in place, like a Roman tortoise."

"A what?"

"I knew a lot about the Romans, thanks to Angela. I watched them creep towards the Close. Some of the protestors chucked stuff – cobblestones, bottles, bits of an old bicycle that had been chained to a lamppost. It all bounced off. I thought the whole thing would be over in a couple of minutes, as usual, but the protestors magicked up a shield of their own – huge great sheets of plywood reinforced with metal studs. They blocked the entrance to the Close. There were red and green smoke flares and the police started firing tear gas and the protestors grabbed the canisters and lobbed them back, and it was hard to see what was going on from up here. It wasn't quick, though. There was a lot of fighting, Ari. A lot of people being battered, anyway. And Angela didn't turn up for my lesson. The next time I saw her she had half her head shaved and a huge bandage. Fourteen stitches, which she said was nothing serious. Lots of blood, she said, but that's a head wound for you. Like she knew what she was talking about. We went through my translation and she told me to do it again, this time into Greek; then we talked about differential calculus and *Madame Bovary*."

Ari, much-practised, bit back his impatience. Where was all this going? He knew, really. But why the tour around the houses?

"Have you read it?"

"Yes, Leader. But . . ."

"I was thirteen. I told her I was probably too young. She said she thought she was, too. She said we should both read it again in ten years' time, when I'd be her age and she . . . she would have been the age Flaubert was when he started writing it."

Which put him in his early thirties. Ari found Emma Bovary unnecessarily hysterical; if he'd had to guess, he would have said the author was rather older. He also sensed that they were finally coming to the point, and said nothing.

"And do you know what she did then, Ari?"

He did. Of course he did.

"She died, Leader. Tragically."

Jessica looked at him sharply. "Tragically, yes. Her and six others. It's always a tragedy when it's over and we're not going to do anything about it, isn't it?"

Which *was* the point, of course.

The inquiry.

The inquiry they had promised in her election manifesto. The inquiry that Bishop Grendel had been calling about.

Jessica turned away from the window at last and motioned him towards the sofas. He hesitated, allowing her to sit first. The sofas were arranged in a horseshoe, and she chose the one at the head – which meant wherever he sat they would be at right angles, not face-to-face. Good. Despite the peremptory summons and her pointed, mawkish march down memory lane, she wasn't looking for confrontation. He sat to her left, giving him a view out of the window, although all he could see was heavy, granite-grey February sky broken by the occasional white flash of a passing gull.

He risked repeating himself. "You wanted a word, Leader?"

"Ari," she said, "we're on our own. Every time you call me Leader I look round for my dad. Could you bring yourself to call me Jess?"

Would she ever get to the point? Which, Ari knew, was that even though she'd already been elected, she was serious about the inquiry. He got that. What he would do about it was another matter. He said, "I could . . ."

"But you won't?"

"It seems unlikely, Leader."

She sighed.

"You have to get used to it, Leader. You can't live in your father's shadow. That's why you're Leader now."

"You're right. You're always right, aren't you, Ari?"

It would be best to show he knew that he was being teased. "I have my moments."

She paused again, as if steeling herself to step into new territory. Which was all very well, but it wasn't as if there weren't a thousand other things he could be doing. Or stopping other people do.

"And then the bishop rang?" he prompted again.

Jessica returned to earth. "That's right," she said. "Though you aren't supposed to know that."

"I can't be right all the time, can I, Leader, without knowing things I'm not supposed to know?"

"Fair enough. The call was about the same issue, anyway."

"Which was?"

As if he didn't know.

"Bob Cole spoke to me this morning, at the funeral. He asked where we are on the Cathedral Close Inquiry."

A tad insensitive in the circumstances, Ari thought, but not unhelpful. He preferred to see the other players' cards before selecting his own. He said, "I've already told him to check his savings and investments. What did you say?"

"That we were considering the best way forward, and would let him know."

Ari nodded. Non-answers had their uses, too.

"And *he* said," Jessica continued, "that I should watch my back on this one, and in particular to look out for my spad."

There is a kind of silence that isn't silent at all: it is filled with muffled screams and the sound of fists punching walls.

"What do you think he meant by that, Ari?"

He knew exactly what Bob Cole meant, the ungrateful bastard. He meant that if the inquiry were to criticize him too forcefully, then he would have no choice but to be explicit about Ari's own role in the events of that day.

He said, "I've no idea, Leader."

"Really? I thought you always knew?"

There was a sharpness to her tone he hadn't heard before, and didn't like. He said, "Bob was always very thick with Donald Price. And Donald had some strange ideas about my degree of influence." Donald, he happened to know, had somehow come by the idea that Ari had actually been involved in setting up the supposedly secret demo before quietly instructing the police Commander to employ maximum violence in its suppression.

Jessica gave no indication of whether she had swallowed his rather obvious attempt at misdirection, preferring to change tack, again; but there was none of the "call me Jess" warmth in her voice when she said:

"And then there's the bishop."

Just so. "Did you tell him we're considering it and will let him know?"

Please tell me that you did, Ari prayed.

"He wants to chair it."

"He . . . shit."

Jessica raised an eyebrow. "Did you have another candidate in mind?"

He did, as it happened. He had long since come to the conclusion that the best way to limit the damage would be to chair the inquiry himself. Sometimes, there was nothing like hiding in plain sight. What he hadn't yet worked out was how to engineer himself into the role. As an advisor, however special, it would on the face of it be totally inappropriate. And Commander Cole's less than subtle intervention could further complicate the picture. What would the old plod do now if Ari were given the task? Well, that all depended, of course, on why he wasn't satisfied with a sack of cash and a quiet exit. What more did the greedy bastard want? And what was Binkie the bishop after, come to that?

He became aware that Jessica was waiting for an answer. Thank God he'd played his cards so close to his chest. "Perhaps. Did his Lordship say why he wanted it?"

"He said he would be perfectly placed to bring peace and reconciliation to a divided community."

"Did he, by Jesus?"

"Just so."

"I assume you're aware, Leader, that one of the . . . deceased was a member of his congregation? A very prominent and wealthy and by all accounts generous member?"

"The bishop mentioned it himself."

Bugger, thought Ari. Another fox shot: talk about hiding in plain sight. "By way of declaring an interest, I suppose?"

"I suppose so."

There was another of those silences, as Ari scrambled to work out how to retrieve the situation.

"He said something else, Ari, something I'd really like to know about."

She paused, as if there were any doubt that she had his undivided attention.

"He said the deal with my father fell with my father. When I asked

41

what he meant, he said I should ask Dad. Better still, he said: ask Ari."

"Ask Ari," repeated Ari, flatly.

"So here I am, asking Ari."

All roads, it seems, lead not to Rome today, but to his door. He had no more doubt which deal Bishop Grendel had been referring to than he had about the police commander's threat. Pick a church, the bishop had said, any church, back when Jacob had somehow been hypnotized by a purple shirt into telling him about their plan to save the Island by drilling a hole big enough to drain away the rising tide. The germ of the idea had originally been Donald's; it had come to him in the bath. Like Archimedes, he'd said. Jacob's genius – in his own eyes – had been to add a touch of real ambition: he would not only save the Island, but make it rich. It would be risky, of course. But the trick would be to dig right down through the earth's crust, and then, of course, to get the timing right: as the sea level rose, it would fill the hole; as the molten magma pushed upwards it would break through the final thin layer of rock they'd leave and encounter – what, Ari? – not the Island's heroic miners and engineers, but a column of cold water twenty-five miles high! The water would cool the magma; the magma would boil the water: if they got it just right a perfect equilibrium would be maintained. And that's not all, Jacob declaimed, as if from a soapbox in the city square, although they were alone sharing post-Cabinet whiskies in his office. Steam would rise up through the water providing free, clean and ever-lasting energy to power the Castle!

"And the City," Ari replied. "What's left of it, anyway."

"It'll be like – what's that place where everyone lounges about in hot mud writing thrillers?"

"Iceland, Leader."

"Iceland, that's it. A man-made Iceland."

Ari had never been to Iceland. He'd never left the Island. "Or maybe," he said, "when the magma hits the water it'll be more like a cork leaving a vigorously shaken champagne bottle. Hot champagne, sousing everything. Boiling champagne simultaneously scalding and drowning everyone on the Island." Had he stretched the metaphor too far?

"There are worse ways to go."

"You know it wouldn't actually *be* champagne, Leader?"

From somewhere deep in Jacob's chest there came a familiar low growling sound, as of heavy chains being dragged across rocks, which Ari had learned to recognize as laughter. "No risk," Jacob said, "no fun."

He never found out if Jacob had tried that line on the bishop, but it didn't sound as though there'd been much need. The bishop wasn't looking to be persuaded. The bishop, by all accounts, had bitten his arm off, especially when Jacob referred to the idea as the Divine Light & Power project.

"*Divine Light*, Leader?"

"I didn't mean it," Jacob said, pouring himself another whisky. "But there was a man of the cloth right there in front of me, and I was riffing on heat and power and . . . I might have made a joke? With him being a bishop, and all."

"It just popped into your mind?"

"And he loved it. Do you know how many churches there are on the Island, Ari?"

It occurred to Ari now that perhaps Jessica's evident talent for the tangential had been inherited. At the time, Jacob's question seemed to be spectacularly beside the point. That said, he *did* know. The question had arisen more than once: mostly when debating where the homeless might go once all the parks were locked, the benches were designed to stop you lying down and shop doorways had water sprinklers to wash litter out into the gutters at night (the developers said, if anyone ever asked); and, anyway, he felt the urge to spoil the Leader's fun.

"Seventeen, Leader. Including the Cathedral, the Catholics, the Baptists, the Jehovah's Witnesses and the Church of God of Prophecy open brackets House of Bread close brackets."

"All right . . ."

"Twenty-four if you include the Friends' House, synagogues, mosques and the Zoroastrian Fire Temple."

". . . let's stick with the Anglicans, shall we?"

"Ten."

"Quite. And how many do you think they actually need for their current congregation?"

"A bus stop should just about do it."

Jacob left an ugly pause where Ari thought by rights a laugh had been called for.

"My Lord the Bishop doesn't see it quite like that."

"No?"

"He does, however, see the opportunity to diversify the functional operations and maximize the revenue-generating possibilities of his existing property portfolio."

"Is that what he said?"

"More or less."

"So he'll let us turn them into homeless hostels after all?"

"No. Well, one. He said we could have St Nicholas' for that."

"The one down behind the harbour?"

"Is that where it is?"

"Not for long, Leader. Not at the current rate of erosion."

"Ah, I hadn't thought of that."

Of course he hadn't. Which was exactly why, in Ari's opinion, no Leader should ever be allowed to meet anyone alone if it could possibly be avoided. Ari Spencer's First Law of Politics.

"More to the point, Ari, he said we could use one of his redundant churches as a drilling site."

Ari rarely drank much during these late night chats – just enough to keep the Leader company. Now he held his empty glass out for a refill. It wasn't like Jacob to be bamboozled by a God-botherer, but had any real harm been done? *Divine Light & Power?* Hideously divisive, of course. Donald would loath it, which could be fun. Cora would take it as more evidence that the Leader had lost the plot. But she'd been shouting *#We'reAllGoingToFuckingDrown* so loudly

44

all over the internet that she'd be hard pressed to oppose the idea without offering anything better. The Simulationists would say God was just an outdated allegory for the Great Simulation. The bishop would argue that manufacturing an artificial island was one thing; creating the earth's molten core was quite another: that took *real* power. No, the more Ari turned it over in his mind, the more he felt his initial repugnance had been over-hasty. The Leader's slip may have been a blessing in disguise. A miracle, even. And the trick, as with all miracles, would be to make sure no one ever got close enough to look behind the curtain.

"Did he say which one?"

"He was so happy he said that we could choose."

"Really?"

"So I said, how about the Cathedral? And he said maybe not."

"I bet."

"But any of the others, he said. So that's good, isn't it? One major hurdle cleared."

It was more than that: it was a Godsend. So to speak. In Ari's mind, inspiration struck. There were politicians – Cora was one – who regarded public choice as an unnecessary infringement of her right to decide. Ari knew better: there was nothing like choice to paralyze the population.

He said, "There are nine parish churches. It's too late for St Nicholas' and we can rule out St Walstan's, which leaves seven."

St Walstan's was a rural parish on the far side of the Island. Drilling in a field in the back end of beyond might make sense to a town planner, but if you're going to announce the most ambitious political project since – well, *ever*, really – there was no point doing it where no bugger would ever see, was there?

The Leader said, "So how do we choose?"

In an ideal world, Ari thought, they would have stood together at the window, picking out the steeples in the last rays of the setting sun. But it was pitch dark, and they had to make do with the street map on the office wall. He plucked a red pen from the Leader's desk and marked the seven candidates – the older, mediaeval churches clustered close to the Castle's skirts, Victorian Gothic and '70s experiments in the further flung suburbs.

"Well, we could go by historical importance, or architectural merit . . ."

"Me being an architect?"

"Quite. But the only really valid criterion is altitude."

The Leader had been nodding along; now he stopped with a jerk. "I'm sorry. What?"

"Think about it, Leader. The location of the borehole effectively determines the limit of the inundation we are, however reluctantly of course, prepared to countenance."

"Ah," said Jacob, with renewed energy. "I get you. The higher the water rises, the fewer voters there will be left; the fewer voters there are, the easier it is to win an election. Brilliant."

Ari was pleased to see the Leader thinking politically again, even if he'd grasped the wrong end of the stick.

"Brilliant, but sadly mistaken, Leader. Whatever Cora might be screaming, those voters won't actually drown. They'll just be homeless, and move to higher ground. Up the hill. Towards the Castle."

"Aaah."

"So the higher we start drilling, the larger the displaced – and, let's face it, probably quite angry – mob will be. I doubt there's enough pitchforks on the Island to arm them all, but you get the picture, Leader."

"I do. So we go for the lowest church, the one nearest sea level?"

"That would be one possible approach."

"But? There's a "but" coming, isn't there?"

"The housing behind the harbour and what's left of the fishing village and even the seafront, where all those wedding cake terraces have been subdivided into flats and bedsits? That housing is disproportionately occupied by the . . . less advantaged members of the Island community."

Again, Jacob said, "Ah." Then added, "So it might look like – what was it they said when we let Dan Houghton rebuild these shoddy flats in Clarence Square?"

"Social cleansing."

"That's the bugger."

"Exactly, Leader."

Ari waited. He was enjoying himself. He would hold his tongue until, eventually, the Leader would have to ask.

Jacob cracked. "So how do we decide?"

And this, Ari recalled afterwards, was where his real inspiration lay. He waited a moment or two longer. This was it.

"We don't," he said.

The effect was every bit as good as he had hoped. Jacob looked stricken, like a toddler whose favourite dumper truck has been confiscated. "We don't? But this is our Big Idea, Ari. *My* Big Idea."

And the last thing you wanted to do with a Big Idea, was to try and make it real.

He said, "We let the people decide."

"The *people?*"

"In a plebiscite. A referendum. Better still, a whole series of referendums, eliminating options one by one, until . . ."

"Until they all slit each others' throats. Do you have any *idea* how divisive that would be?"

"Yes, Leader."

And there it was.

Light dawned. If they asked the people to decide, it would never happen. Jacob stepped back from the wall map, returning to the bottle on his desk. He refilled their glasses.

"So Divine Light & Power is the perfect machine for manufacturing permanent hostility. Who knew?"

"Indeed," Ari said. "And what happens to those in power when their opponents are at each others' throats?"

"They stay in power, Ari."

"Exactly, Leader."

They clinked their glasses, toasting each other.

Sinking back into the sofa, though, Jacob said, "The sea will still be rising."

"Just so."

Jacob pondered that for a moment. "So, eventually, someone will have to step in and save the Island from itself?"

Ari nodded.

Again Jacob thought before he spoke.

"I'll be long gone by then?"

Ari nodded again.

Another pause.

"But *you* won't." Jacob looked thoughtfully at his whisky glass. "*Jessica* won't."

"So the story goes, Leader."

Which was exactly what Ari was now counting on. It was what brought him and Jessica together, a decade later, here in the Leader's office that was no longer Jacob's office. Because the strategy had worked. So there was no harm in telling her about it, was there? So what did Binkie-bloody-Grendel think he was up to with all his nods and winks? Okay, the fact that they never settled on a site meant he hadn't realized the asset, as he'd probably put it to himself – and never got his hands on the cash. But the furore around each vote had done wonders for their congregations; pews that hadn't seen bums in years had filled up fast. Almost as fast as the collection plates, Ari wouldn't wonder.

He turned to Jessica. "The deal, Leader, was simply that he would let us have a couple of church sites: one for a homeless hostel, another for the borehole, and the scheme would be known as Divine Light & Power. He said we could pick any of them except the Cathedral."

"I see. And now we haven't, and he hasn't got any empty churches, he wants to let us know the offer's closed?"

Which was all very well, Ari thought, but what had it got to do with the inquiry? The Cathedral Close demo had been a more or less direct result of the referendum strategy; even if the bishop's fingers weren't quite as stained as Ari's own, he should surely think twice before stirring that particular pot?

"It must be more than that, Leader. He could just let it drop, the same as us."

Jessica's mouth screwed up the way he'd seen it when she was a child asked to choose ice cream flavours by her father; Ari found himself interested to see what she'd come up with.

"What does a bishop who has turned the tide of falling congregations, and presided over a massive increase in attendance, participation and income, what does such a bishop want next?"

"Perhaps to exercise a little power in the secular world?"

"Well, yes," Jessica said, "but why? Why does he want power?"

To protect his back, Ari thought: to stay in the game.

Jessica laughed, and the sound grated like nails on slate.

"Come on, Ari. It's not that hard."

He knew he would get used to being patronized by a twenty-three year-old he'd seen grow up from a toddler. It was part of the job, of the situation he had engineered; he just hadn't expected it to start so soon, or hurt so much.

"Ari," she said, "you're a peculiar kind of saint, but I really think your innocence is getting in the way."

Innocence? What was she on about now?

"If you weren't so devoid of personal ambition yourself," she continued, "you might see what a successful bishop wants."

And then it clicked. "To be an archbishop," he said.

"Bingo."

"That old bucket of lard thought we'd all be calling him Your Grace by now?"

"Exactly. Allowing for your irreverence."

She was right, of course. It made perfect sense. Happy for once to be heard catching up aloud, Ari said: "So he wants the chairmanship to catch some attention on the mainland? Which means raking up as much dirt as possible."

"Go on."

"Which he can then piously use to call for a process of reconciliation. Apologies, rolling heads and restitution, on the Authority's side; plus photogenic tears, saintly forgiveness and open, grasping hands from the families." What Ari didn't say was that Bob Cole's retirement wouldn't be enough: one of those rolling heads would likely have to be his own.

Jessica leaned forward, stretching out a hand toward him. For an awful moment he thought she was going to pat his knee. But if the idea ever crossed her mind, she immediately thought better of it, and let her hand drop. "So what do we think? We need a chair. Why not the bishop?"

Ari considered the options. Appeasing Binkie Grendel meant having his own role in the affair exposed: having Jessica pat his knee would be infinitely preferable to the way she'd treat him if she discovered he was to blame for the death of her beloved tutor. Not appeasing him would lead – to what, exactly? Divine Light & Power had served its purpose. The bishop would huff and puff, but they didn't *need* him any more. No, the more he thought about it, the more Ari concluded his own plan was still by far the best.

He said, "We tell him to take a running jump into his own font."

"And then what?"

"And then I chair the inquiry."

There: he'd said it. He'd work around the whole spad/impropriety issue later. One step at a time.

"And then?"

"We accept mistakes were made, and lessons must be learned. Bob Cole gets to cut his golf handicap in half, and everybody's happy. Or at least quiet."

"And where do we drill the borehole?"

Well, that was a swerve.

"We don't." Before he could consider whether it was a good idea or not, he added, "We were never going to."

But Jessica was not surprised. "I know that, Ari. I'm not stupid."

Of course not.

"I know you used the rows to divide the opposition and keep my father in power. I know you set me up to be the answer to the years of your own indecision, as someone young and fresh who'd get things done again. That whatever *Our Island Story* says, I'm here – in part, at least – because you did. And I'm deeply grateful, Ari. Really."

He waited for the 'but' to roll inexorably down the hill, taking him with it, knowing he'd have to push the bloody thing all the way back up again.

"But . . . the sea's still rising. The city's still crumbling and our farmers are Googling how to fish."

Here it came.

"And in all the time you were busy manufacturing discontent, you and my father, you didn't bother to come up with any actual answers, did you?"

Ari said nothing. At least she'd included Jacob.

"So," she said, pulling herself upright on the sofa and staring him straight in the eye, "if I'm the new broom who gets things done, you're going to have to drill me a fucking hole *somewhere*, aren't you?"

"Me?"

Jessica ignored his squeal of discomfort in favour of yet another vertiginous swerve. "Tell me honestly, Ari. What did you make of Donald Price?"

Honestly? Was she doing this on purpose? Obviously, she was. But why?

Apart from knowing a little too much, Donald had been pleasant enough – fair, curly hair, a diffident manner and a swollen prostate he'd attempted to ignore. Until it finally metastasized, he had been chiefly distinguished – in Ari's mind at least – by an eccentric faith in the perfectibility of human institutions, a faith that had somehow carried him to the top of his profession. A mystery; but there he was. He didn't baulk when Ari suggested making Jacob City Architect when he first turned up – it was foretold, after all, even if Donald was surely far too intellectual to take the *Island Story* at face value; Jacob had repaid the favour later, keeping Donald on when he became Leader himself. Donald had then spent most of his time holed up in his office tinkering with what turned out to be a perpetual motion machine built of balsa wood and rubber bands. An irrational task that was ultimately doomed to fail, of course, but one which, with Donald's superhuman patience for making tiny, incremental improvements, Ari suspected was intended as a metaphor for his rational approach to public service. There'd been a touch of the Cnut about Donald.

"Mad as a box of mercury frogs," he said. "But harmless."

"You think?"

"I do."

He did. Donald had been all right, really. It wasn't obvious how, but he'd got done all the boring things that really needed doing. The place hadn't fallen apart. Other than the bits that fell into the sea, of course. When Ari needed him to stretch a point, a way could usually be found without too much pious heel dragging.

He said, "Sally should be ready to step up, though."

"About that?"

Ari's unease returned, deeper than ever.

"Yes?"

"I'm giving you the job."

One of the books he had found years ago under a pile of unread committee papers had been *Doctor Faustus*. Only now did he understand just how the misguided alchemist must have felt when Mephistopheles turned up to drag him down to hell.

"Me? What?" The involuntary squeal was back.

"Well, you can't chair a public enquiry as a spad, can you?"

Christ, she really had been listening. All those swerves had been deliberate distraction, not madness.

"Besides," she said, "I need you out in front."

"Taking the flak?"

"Leading the organization. Getting things done, Ari."

He sighed, but swallowed it. Allowance must be made for youth and inexperience. The urge to get things done would surely pass in time.

"But you need me here," he said, struggling to keep the desperation out of his voice. He didn't mean the office itself, not literally; he meant a spot at her shoulder, just behind the throne. Out of view, but in power. "I can be much more useful as an advisor, Leader. Believe me, that's how it works."

"That's how it *has* worked, Ari. You helped my father, and Cora, cope with opposition, with resistance from the machine, from Donald, even. But Donald is dead. All that energy can be put to so much better use. I shall still want your advice, Ari, but just think how much more we can achieve between us if you have the authority to get things done yourself! We have a manifesto to deliver. A triple pledge."

If she thought that was an inducement, she still had much to learn.

"Or did you think I didn't mean it?"

He was disappointed, in a way; but it was probably his own fault. When Angela died he'd let Jessica persuade her father not to replace her. Like Ari, she had largely educated herself ever since. Unlike Ari, she seemed to have picked up some peculiar ideas along the way. Of course she had a manifesto - he'd written most of it himself. Of course she had her pledges. And they had worked: she'd been elected. Delivery was for postal workers. He had no desire to fill Donald Price's comfortable shoes, no desire to trade influence for responsibility. No desire to screw up everything he'd created over twenty years and more because someone who ought to know better turned out to believe her own propaganda. But he was the court eunuch: his desires were of no consequence at all.

"Congratulations," she said. "You've got the job."

FIVE

DENIS STEPPED SLOWLY through the revolving door, impatience at odds with both an unaccustomed timidity – what, exactly, would he say to Jessica? What service could he offer? – and the painfully slow progress of the doors themselves. Who did anyone think would use them – a family of tortoises? He had ample time to wonder whether 'tortoises' was actually the plural of 'tortoise' – it didn't sound right, somehow: could it be one of those nouns where the plural and the singular are the same, like sheep, or malfeasance? – before finding himself disgorged into the vast and largely empty space of the Central Block's ground floor atrium. A security guard almost as broad as he was tall, in a navy blue polyester suit with added shiny patches, eyed him from one corner; a second, his hands lying crossed but ready on his stomach like weapons holstering each other, turned his whole upper body slowly to track Denis's progress towards the reception desk, the muscles in his short thick neck too pumped up to permit the lateral rotation of his head. Behind the desk, two women wearing one-sided headsets and badges declaring they were "Here to help", tapped keyboards and ignored him. They continued to ignore him up to the very brink of outright rudeness before one – Kathy, her badge said – raised her head, smiled, and asked how she could help.

"I'd like to speak to Jessica King."

"How do you spell that?"

"Jessica King? The Leader?" Apparently news did not spread quickly here.

Kathy tapped her keyboard again and peered doubtfully at her screen. "We've got a Jacob King?"

"Could you speak to someone in her office, please?"

"Whose office?"

"The Leader's office."

Kathy paused for a moment before asking, with what Denis had to admit was impeccable timing: "Do you have a name?" He scoured his memory. It had been years since his mother was Leader. But in the car that morning, he'd overheard Jessica making a call. He said, "I think . . . I think her PA might be called Saturday."

Kathy looked up again. "Saturday?"

"Yes."

"Is that a first name or a last name?"

The longer she waited, the less it sounded like either. "First, I think. Do you have him listed?"

Pause.

A brief rattle of the keyboard.

"No."

There was a silence interrupted only by the faint sound of the security guards' rubber soles squeaking on the tiled floor as they waddled a step closer.

It occurred to Denis that if they hadn't updated the directory, the numbers wouldn't have changed, either. He said, "Could you ring Jacob King, please?"

Kathy looked at him sceptically. "You want to speak to Jacob King?"

He didn't – he'd only just left him – but thought it better not to explain.

"Yes. Please."

She rattled the keys again. She held up one finger and rocked her head from side to side to indicate that she was getting a ringing tone in her earpiece. Finally she stopped, paused for a moment, and then said: "There's a gentleman here who says he wants to speak to Jacob King."

Another pause.

And then, to Denis: "Apparently he's left."

55

He closed his eyes and breathed deeply. Then he said, "Ask them if I can speak to his daughter."

"His daughter? Really?"

"Really."

She did so, while conveying just how irregular and implausible it seemed. After a brief pause, she said – but not to Denis – "Oh. You think they'd tell us." She put her hand over the mike. "They want to know: do you have an appointment?"

"No," said Denis.

"No," said Kathy, into her mouthpiece.

Pause.

"They say she's very busy. Could you please call and make an appointment?"

"Call who?"

"Jessica King. That's who you want to speak to, isn't it?"

"Can you give me the number?"

She rattled the keys once more.

"I'm sorry, she's not listed."

He gave up.

Barging into Jessica's no doubt busy afternoon had probably been a bad idea, anyway. He'd envisaged a sort of impulsive but confident gesture: so keen was he to help, he just had to speak to her at once, on this, the day of his father's funeral: that sort of thing. He saw now that it might have come across as more desperate than romantic. He'd have to think of a better way to get in touch. It shouldn't be too difficult. He was K's son, after all. That had to count for something.

He thanked Kathy for all her help, and turned to leave. The security guards relaxed, and stepped backwards, the one with the neck like a gun emplacement managing to tread on an elderly woman come to complain about the Authority's failure to locate the cat she had mislaid at some point during K's first administration. She rebuked the guard in terms that Denis – whose own mother frequently swore like a sailor denied shore leave – was embarrassed to overhear.

Outside, the granite air assaulted him again. He had almost forgotten how brutal a northeast wind could be. The Island was exposed out here, no doubt about it. Left to the mercy of the elements. He turned the collar of his father's coat against the wind and wondered where to go that wasn't his mother's flat. If it was her flat. She'd been a bit evasive last night when he asked how much it had cost; most likely, there were favours involved, some old developer's debts she hadn't wanted to discuss.

When Jacob asked what he was going to do now, Denis knew he'd been expecting the answer: "Leave". He'd come to see his father buried because – well, because you do. And because his mother had given him no choice. That didn't mean he had to hang around. If there was a wake, no one had invited him. So why not leave? He was too old to be cluttering up the family home, even if there'd been a family home available. If his mother hadn't been involuntarily downsized into an expensively appointed shoebox. Her sofa was comfortable enough, and he was more than used to sleeping in his clothes, but the sooner he got back on a ferry the better for both of them. With no husband and no job, his mother was sure to throw herself into some ridiculous new adventure, and he had no desire to be anywhere near the fall out when she did. On the other hand, Jessica King was very attractive; they had so much in common. And the old man *was* her father. So when he asked, Denis had said he might stick around, to help. It didn't mean he had anything in mind, beyond wanting to see the grown-up Jessica again. Denis was proud of his career on the mainland. It took guts and skill and dedication to scrape a third-class degree and then maintain a free, open-handed, properly leisurely lifestyle without the degrading inconvenience of regular work. Someone like Jacob – like Jessica? – someone fated to lead, probably wouldn't see it that way. But, fuck it, wasn't he the child of a leader, too? Of *two* leaders, come to that. *His* story might not be taught in the Island's schools or sung in folk songs round camp fires, if anyone still went in for all that crap, but Jessica had no reason to think herself any better than he was. No reason to turn him down, to laugh in his face; or, worse, to affect a serious, sorrowful voice and explain that it was very kind of him, and all that, but it was not to be. No reason at all.

Such thoughts had carried Denis a long way from the Castle. He realized he was approaching the Cathedral, and veered sharply to avoid it. Too close to home, so to speak. He spotted an upmarket fast food restaurant, tricked out like a 50s American diner. It was nearly lunchtime; perhaps he should hole up somewhere to eat while he worked out his next steps? He peered through the window. A decent burger and a beer might hit the spot; but not here, he thought. The place was too bright. Too shiny. Even the Naugahyde booths would leave him far too exposed for his current mood. Taking another couple of corners at random, he stumbled across an old-fashioned Italian trattoria that he could tell from outside would offer homemade ravioli, calves' liver, osso buco and tiramisu. If he asked for chips with lasagne they wouldn't turn a hair. There would be fake vines hanging from the ceiling and candles stuck in old, basket-clad Chianti bottles; because it was lunchtime the candles would not be lit and, as long as he avoided the table in the window, the gloom would be deep enough to make reading the menu – no doubt a huge affair bound in leather-effect plastic containing many dishes that would, upon enquiry, turn out to be off – unnecessarily difficult. It was perfect.

It was still a little early for lunch and the place was empty. The waiter tried to seat him in the window. Denis asked for a table further back. And to one side. He handed over his father's coat; the waiter cooed appreciatively at the quality of the cashmere. He sat with his back to a huge black and white print of Marcello Mastroianni wearing sunglasses, and waited for the menu. And the wine list. Forget beer and burgers. It wasn't every day you buried your father, after all.

For all his drawn-out dementia, for all the exorbitant fees somewhere like St Julian's would have extracted, K must surely have died a wealthy man. Ari Spencer had once told Denis that only a fool could stay in power as long as K – and as long as Cora after him – without ending up far richer than they had started. Whatever else his parents might have been, they were no fools.

The waiter returned, and Denis consulted the list. Was champagne inappropriate? He rather thought it might be, but ordered a bottle anyway. Plus a Barolo from way, way down the bottom of the list where the prices reached several figures and would, in normal circumstances, have made his eyes water as much as his mouth. Would the waiter please open it immediately? It would need time to breathe. The waiter would indeed. He would also bring the champagne, and an ice bucket. Denis drank a glass, and immediately refilled it, the menu still unopened. As the son of rich parents, one recently-deceased, he was what old novels might describe as a gentleman of good prospects; as so often with such gentlemen, however, he would find it hard to lay his hands on any ready cash just now. But his mother had dispatched him to collect his father's suit with his father's credit card. There was a theoretical risk she might have cancelled it since this morning, but surely she'd had other things to think about? Besides, the prospect – however remote – of being forced to do a runner as the waiter approached, credit card reader in hand and a sorrowful look on his face, would add a little extra piquancy to what, despite the quality of the wine, would likely be a mediocre meal. He ordered the ravioli followed by – yes! – osso buco, and sat back complacently with a third glass of champagne.

Looking around, he realized that he was still alone. He had wanted to be unobserved, but a solitary meal without the muted chatter of other diners, or the private pleasure of speculating about their crimes and peccadilloes, would make him more self-conscious than eating in a spotlight. Company – especially company he didn't have to talk to – was good for the digestion. So he was relieved when two women of about his mother's age arrived and took a table opposite his, followed by three men of varying age but almost identical dress – pin-striped business suits and loud ties – who commandeered the table in the window. He remembered what he must look like himself, took off his father's outsized jacket and hung it on the back of his chair. He loosened the black tie. He undid the cufflinks and rolled up his shirtsleeves. He was ready to eat.

Unfortunately, the kitchen wasn't. Half a dozen breadsticks, a bowl of olives and the rest of the champagne successfully eradicated all trace of that morning's porridge before the ravioli finally arrived. By which time he was in the state of mild intoxication in which mapping his thoughts on the restaurant's napkins seemed appropriate. It would be as well, he thought, before moving on to the Barolo, to remind himself why he was here. The trattoria was old school, its napkins linen, not paper, but nonetheless amenable to ballpoint pen, he discovered, sketching a rather wobbly-sided coffin, along the side of which he printed: RIP. After a moment's thought and a first mouthful of red wine he sharpened the shorter end of the lozenge to a point, added a couple of funnels trailing smoke, a wavy line beneath and – hey presto! – a boat, an ocean liner, steaming across his napkin. Another swig: this stuff was really very, very good. To the left, just in front of the ship, he drew an iceberg – or was it a cliff? In the bow, facing the obvious danger, he placed two tiny stick figures, one in a rudimentary dress. Above them, a heart, larger than them both, larger than the iceberg/cliff, pierced with an arrow as long as the ship. On the cliff, or iceberg, he wrote: SOS. Above it he spelled out: Ship Of State; beneath, carefully, one letter at a time: Save Our Souls.

He sat back, contemplating his handiwork. It was not exactly the mind mapping technique he'd once been taught at college, but its message was clear enough: Save Our Souls.

Not that he believed in souls. Soul food, yes; soul music, certainly, but there wasn't – was there? – a spiritual bone in his body. Was that a contradiction in terms? Probably. Not a spiritual synapse in his – if he said so himself – highly-evolved idiot brain.

This wine was really very good. Another bottle? A half bottle, perhaps? He wasn't sure it came in halves and, anyway, there was no point spoiling the ship for a ha'p'orth of tar, was there?

Ship of State.

Good.

Ship of Fools.

No. Where had that come from?

Save Our Souls.

Arseholes.

His soul; her soul.

Better. Good.

The ravioli arrived, and he saw that it too was good. Not as good as the Barolo, of course, but you couldn't have everything in this life, could you?

With a little food, his head cleared momentarily, and he caught himself, as if glimpsing rocks through fog. It wasn't true. He was Denis Klamm. He could have anything.

He could have Jessica.

He would. If he were just bold enough. If he just showed how much he cared.

All he had to do was save the Island.

And he would. He really would.

After lunch.

SIX

JACOB ALSO FELT it better to leave Jessica to her own devices for a while. Not that he had any choice. He would take a stroll down to the shore, his first steps into retirement. Normally, he didn't get out of the Castle much. There'd been little time and no real need. Now he thought he'd take a look around. He would have liked to revisit the Hope & Anchor: it was where he'd stayed when he and Jessica were first fished out of the harbor, and he'd had a soft spot for the place until it collapsed into the sea, along with the rest of the harbour. That would have been about the time that Cora discovered hashtags, and #We'reAllGoingToFuckingDrown had briefly polluted everybody's social media. More likely, he thought, it was Lucy Neave who'd found out what a hashtag was, technology not being exactly Cora's thing. The obscenity would have been all hers, though. Pure Cora. As pure as Cora ever got.

What did it matter, now?

He was no longer Leader, Cora no longer even leader of the opposition. He'd extended the olive branch, one old politician to another, and been told to eff off for his pains. No matter.

The smooth broad road curved clockwise down from the Castle, hugging the contours of the hill until it reached the cliffs, then hairpinned back upon itself to descend into the cramped and muddled shambles of the city proper. Here there were still mediaeval buildings whose upper storeys reached out towards each other across the narrow streets, propped up on oak beams riven by cracks wide enough to slip your hand into. The overhung pavements harboured a shifting shantytown of cardboard sheets, abandoned mattresses and greasy sleeping bags; each contained the impress of a human form, if not the thing itself. He dropped a coin into a paper coffee cup, then added the rest of his change. It was the least he could do. Since last week, it was the most he could do. Ari had always warned him not to give to beggars: it sent the wrong signal, he said. Refer them to our homeless support service, he said. That's what it was for. To make the respectable feel better, Jacob thought now. To save passers-by a few coins and a troubled conscience.

He pressed on into Houghton Square, which, like most Islanders – even if he wasn't really one – he still thought of as Clarence Square. Here the shops and offices were all brightly lit at midday, each doorway boasting a security guard and no homeless people. In the centre of the square stood the single, ancient tree – or the simulacrum of an ancient tree, if that's what you chose to believe – left intact when Houghtons bulldozed the rest of the graceful eighteenth-century-slash-1980s garden square. A ring of benches surrounded the tree, a licensed refuge amongst the granite water features and low walls topped with serrated stainless steel to prevent casual relaxation. A single arm bisected each bench, however: no one could lie down here; those who sat found themselves facing outward, gazing not upon their fellow weary citizens, but at the shops or the office they had just left. There would be no respite from the duty to produce and to consume. Jacob knew the arguments – he'd *had* the arguments, endlessly – but the taxes paid by the businesses around the square would fund the city's swimming pool and library.

He cut back up through the narrow passageway that led into Cathedral Close. That morning, chauffeured in and out of the funeral service, he'd had little time to look around or take stock. Now he stood on the cobbles, his back to the great oak doors, gazing across at a brand new tower of "luxury 1, 2 and 3-bed apartments" that occupied the site of the Old Inn – which until recently had claimed to be the first pub on the Island, and which had succumbed to a tide every bit as inexorable as that which had swallowed the Hope & Anchor. Its demolition had been part of Dan Houghton's price for agreeing to fund half a dozen "affordable" flats alongside the luxury apartments of Houghton Tower. Not literally alongside, of course, but on a separate site, somewhere further down the hill, nearer to what was left of the seafront. Jacob had signed the deal: he ought to know where they were. But that had been years ago, and besides, what did it matter? The point was that they were built at all. Now he decided to follow the river down, to see if he could find them.

He couldn't.

So much had changed, or simply disappeared. These days the river disgorged itself into the sea just beyond a slim iron footbridge K had built – when it would have been nowhere near the shore – as part of a futile scheme to regenerate the right bank. Now Riverside Walk ended in cracked concrete where you had to watch your step for seagull shit. The rusted railings and steel mesh along both sides of the footbridge were festooned with padlocks, thickly accreted like ropes of mussels, each inscribed with names or initials, some with hearts and arrows: *M & E*; *Stephen ♥ Angela*; *Eva4J4eva*. Jessica had told him about the craze. Ari said they'd get a gang of men with bolt cutters to snip the locks away so that the bridge could be re-painted. They'd dredge the riverbed to clear out all the keys rusting away down there – or glinting, stainless, like artificial fish. Jessica was upset, but in the end it was just another thing that never happened.

Jacob stood on the footbridge and looked out across the bay, trying to work out where he'd scuppered the rowing boat, and from where he had been rescued about ten minutes later. He knew it would be farther out now than it had been twenty years ago, but nothing more. All water looked alike. The tale had grown in the telling, though; that much he knew. The fishermen who hauled him out had told the landlord of the Hope & Anchor – hoping he might stand them all a round of drinks on the strength of it, which he didn't – and went on to repeat the tale to each new customer over the course of that night and the next. By the time it reached the Castle, Jacob had supposedly been treading water for three days, holding Jessica above his head, insisting they save her first. He'd saved her life. Much later, Ari told him that when he briefed Cora she'd said: "He's her dad. What does he want, a fucking medal?" Ari told her he wanted a job, and she said: "As a lifeguard?" He said as an architect, to which she had replied: "Well that's a fucking odd way to go about applying." She'd had a point, Jacob conceded. But it had worked. And the rest, as they say, was history. Or myth.

It worked, Jacob knew, because he'd been going with the grain of what people wanted to believe – the heart of any good lie, the first rule any conman learns. He wasn't an Islander. He'd never read *Our Island Story*; but Ella was, and she'd grown up with it. She was the kind of Islander who made it to the mainland at seventeen and wasn't going back. The kind who cracked inbreeding jokes before anyone else got the chance. He first met her at a poker game, where she'd stared down a once in a lifetime pot with a handful of nothing, then again at an exhibition about brutalism; after that he knew it would have to be love or misery, and of course it was both. Jessica was born the following year and it was the three of them against the world. For a while it had looked as if they might even win. At night, when Jessica was asleep, or in the afternoons, in bed after a couple of drinks and sex and cigarettes, Ella would tell him about the Island, about the Child and the Great Simulation. He'd say it sounded perfect: they should go. She'd laugh and then stop laughing and say: over her dead body.

He turned back from the sea to retrace his steps up through the City. It would be easy enough, he knew then. Say as little as he could – Jacob King's second law of lying – and people would fill the gaps in for themselves. They'd want him, or someone like him; and they'd want Jessica even more. They'd want it to be true, but there was only one parent in the Island story. So, when the time came that there was only one parent, he thought it might be worth a shot. And it had worked, hadn't it? Was still working. Jessica was Leader. He'd done his bit. He could relax.

Back in Houghton Square, he took a seat between two office-workers curled up in winter coats like moths in their cocoons. They ate sandwiches and blew on hot drinks, defying the February weather. Through his own coat he could feel the cold steel bench against his thighs. A priest in a full-length cassock kicked his way through a gang of pigeons, his hands tucked inside his sleeves. The displaced birds re-grouped around the benches demanding scraps with menaces. But when the woman to his left held up a crust, a seagull swooped and grabbed it from her hand. She screamed and ducked, then said, to no one in particular, "Would you fucking believe it?" The man to Jacob's right shook his head at the injustice of it all, and returned to his own sandwich. Neither recognized him.

He sat there, chin tucked into his chest, the lapels of his overcoat up around his mouth, until his glasses steamed up. He wiped them on his tie. When he could see again, Cora Klamm was emerging from the passageway that linked the square to the Cathedral Close, working the stick she had affected for the funeral. He made no effort to attract her attention, but she spotted him anyway. To his surprise, she crossed the square, the stick lending her a rocking gait like a pirate captain in a storm.

"I see you've joined the down-and-outs," she said, as soon as she came within firing range.

"It's only fair," he said. "We're both out now."

"Bollocks to that. I'll buy you lunch."

His surprise doubled. In twenty years, discounting official functions, they'd had lunch precisely twice – both occasions years before when he was City Architect and she was Leader. Something had changed not just her mood, but the habits of a lifetime. Defeat? Widowhood?

"Thank you, kind lady," he said, touching the brim of an imaginary hat.

"Don't push it, King."

She led him to an Italian place she knew, but there were three men in striped suits and loud ties gesticulating in the window table. She said they should go somewhere quieter. They ended up in the sort of café that served Lapsang Souchong in mismatched china cups and everything to eat from a ginger nut to boeuf bourguignon, via fruitcake, Welsh rarebit and veg or non-veg shepherd's pie. Jacob opted for soup and a roll – "I'm a pensioner now" – while Cora chose the pie – "With actual dead shepherd, if you have it" – but agreed to settle for lamb. And a bottle of stout. She propped her stick against the wall, took her mobile from her bag and placed it face down on the table, as if signalling a truce. Jacob left his own phone in his pocket. It was switched off anyway.

"To K," he said, raising his empty teacup.

Cora nodded but did not respond to the toast.

"You'll miss him, I dare say."

Inane, but what else could he say? He didn't really know Cora. They had been rivals – still were, he would guess, in Cora's mind – but without any of that easy camaraderie long-standing political opponents so often develop, born of the insiders' sense of having more in common with each other than either has with their electorate, or even their own party. Jacob had been too much of an outsider himself, and Cora too crude a politician, for such cynical friendship to flourish. He was not at all prepared for her reply.

"Do you ever talk to your dead wife?"

Not by choice. It had been twenty-one years.

Cautiously, he said, "What makes you think Ella's dead?"

"Isn't that the story?"

"My story?"

"*Our Island Story*, Jacob. Grieving single parent sets off with child to find new life. Shipwreck; rescue; rise to fame; all that."

"I've never read it."

He had, of course: once it mattered. Rule three – do your homework.

Cora laughed. "Right. And Jessica replacing you is just coincidence?"

"She always was a clever girl."

"Who's going to save us all?"

To Jacob's relief, a waitress arrived with his soup. The shepherd's pie would be ready soon, she said. When she'd gone Cora said, "So you never told her?"

"Told her what?"

Cora smiled – smirked might have been a better word. "That you're a fraud."

"Aren't we all?" he said. "Parents, I mean – frauds to our children?"

Now Cora laughed for real. "I don't think Idiot Son would know the meaning of the word."

Jacob was pretty sure he would. Along with 'embezzlement', and 'pyramid scheme'. He said, "I spoke to Denis this morning."

"Yeah? Enlightening, was it?"

"He says he wants to help."

"Then we're doomed."

The shepherd's pie arrived. Cora ordered another beer, looked at Jacob. "Are you sure you won't?"

Why not? They could get drunk together. It wasn't everyday you watched your daughter headline a state funeral. Or buried your husband. Still, he was sure. Hoping to change the conversation he told her about the pigeons in the Close just before she'd arrived, and the seagull.

"So which are you?" she asked, as if that were normal.

"I'm sorry?"

"I'm a seagull," she said. "A fucking seagull."

There wasn't much he could say to that. Was he a pigeon? He didn't think so; in any case, what would it mean? Perhaps he was the priest? He wouldn't say that, either: not aloud. He scraped up the last spoonful of soup and wiped the bowl with a crust of bread. Better get back to banalities. He said, "So what are you going to do now?"

"I'm going to crap on your daughter from a very great height."

Now Jacob laughed, despite himself. "Isn't that Diana Ford-Marling's job these days?"

Cora would have made a terrible poker player. The hatred flashing across her face was unmistakable. She said, "For now."

She was persistent; he'd give her that. Resilient. Dogged. Obses-sive, perhaps. Deranged. She had lost three elections in a row. The only surprise was that she'd managed to cling on to her party lead-ership for so long. Grace in adversity would be too much to ask, but surely it was time to let go? If only out of self-respect? Ari used to say the ability to bear a grudge was what defined a politician. However badly Jacob took retirement, he knew he'd look like a philosopher next to Cora.

He said, "You have a plan?"

"That depends on Diana. Which depends on Jessica."

Jacob thought a plan that uncertain probably wasn't a plan at all. He asked what she would do, in Diana's shoes. He had nothing better to do with his afternoon.

Before Cora could answer, her phone buzzed briefly on the table beside her. She ignored it, squashed a forkful of mash into her peas, inserted it into her mouth and spoke through the food: "I'd give Jessica a bit of space. There's no mileage in pissing on the new girl while she's still new. The *Island Times* wouldn't like it. There's nothing they love more than a photogenic underdog, even if the underdog is actually Leader. And your daughter's nothing if not photogenic."

"Thank you. I think." Could he take credit for that?

"So, me, I'd give her some space. Time to make a few mistakes, let the shine come off her election promises. *Eradicating homelessness.* I mean, is that even possible?"

Jacob was uncomfortably aware he'd asked the same question just a couple of hours ago. Luckily, Cora no longer seemed to need a response. She was merely thinking aloud. Talking to her dead husband, perhaps? He doubted K would listen.

"Even Jessica must know that's not going to happen. So the question for a halfway decent opposition leader is: how will she wriggle out of it? Which means a *clever* opposition leader doesn't attack the idea, she *supports* it, all the better to mourn the awful fucking tragedy when the Leader fails to deliver, no?"

Jacob nodded, although it really wasn't necessary. So far, so straightforward.

"So that's what I'd do," Cora continued. "But Diana? She's a new girl, too. The damp behind her ears isn't just hairspray. That combination of entitlement and rich-girl neediness might make her think she has to make a mark. That the opposition's job is to *oppose*. We'll see. What else?" By now, Cora had put down her knife and fork and was ticking off items on her fingers. "Simulationism? Usually good for stirring up a fight, but I've kind of lost track of where we are on that? Diana's said some pretty full-on tinfoil-hat stuff in the past, but what's my angle? The voice of reason? The party's split down the middle, and if I make a fight of it, I can't be sure it won't be me going down in flames. Oh, I know how you – or Ari, I suppose – stirred it up every time you had a vote on that bloody stupid borehole project that never got off the ground. Or *into* the ground: ha-bleeding-ha. But you could afford it, at least until Ari upped and knocked you off your perch. You've got to hand it to that man."

Just when Jacob thought he really might have to respond, if only to protest that his leadership hadn't *all* been Ari's work, the waitress reappeared to clear away their plates. She asked if she should bring the bill, but Cora wanted the dessert menu. "I'm just getting started," she said. Jacob could believe it. She ordered brownies with ice cream *and* custard; Jacob ordered coffee. Before the waitress had even left, Cora was saying, "There's always the rising sea itself, I suppose."

"Hashtag we're all going to eff-ing drown?"

"Exactly. And where did that get me? Fucking nowhere, that's where. You know that old saying about the value of seafront property? The Good Lord's not making any more? Well, now He's into the demolition business, prices have literally fallen off a fucking cliff. Ho-bleedin'-ho. You can't give it away. I should know: most of it was K's. Which means mine, now. And the Idiot's, I suppose. But do the voters *care*? In a pig's arse they do."

While Jacob wondered why, unless there was some massive

scandal, the average voter was supposed to worry about a politician's family finances, Cora bludgeoned her way on. "Oh, they *say* they do. And maybe, just maybe, somewhere deep down in their better selves, they do. But you and I both know – don't we, Jacob? – that voters never take those better selves into the polling booth."

"So Ari always told me."

"Me, too. And I dare say he's telling Jessica right now."

Jacob tried to imagine it. Winning an election was one thing; governing until the next one quite another. Ari knew that better than any of them. He said, "She may not listen."

"Of course she won't listen! She's the fucking Child. The chosen one. But what's she actually going to *do?*"

Her phone buzzed again, and again. She ignored it.

"And, more to the point – for me," Cora continued, "what is Diana going to do in response to whatever Jessica does?"

Jacob couldn't help laughing. "I really can't help you there."

"I don't even know where she's getting her advice."

"Ah, now there I *can* help. I met Lucy Neave this morning."

"I heard she was back for the funeral. Denis met her on the boat."

"Not just the funeral."

"You mean she's on Diana's payroll? She must be fucking desperate."

Jacob wasn't sure if she meant Diana or Lucy. He said, "Also, she says she's a poet now."

"Yeah, that too." Cora shook her head. She clearly thought the world was heading downhill faster than even she had given it credit for. "You know I sacked her because she went running to Ari with some crap about me cracking up?"

The story he couldn't quite remember that morning was coming back now. He said, "I heard she resigned."

"Well, you would, wouldn't you?"

Meaning: because he'd have heard it from Ari. In fact, what he'd heard was that when Donald Price felt obliged, on the basis of some sort of bullshit political neutrality principle, to tell her about the borehole project before they'd announced it publicly, Cora hadn't been able to stop laughing for a week. Clearly, she'd thought it was Jacob who had gone insane. But he'd won the next election and Jessica had won the election after that and who was laughing now?

Jacob's coffee arrived, and Cora's pudding. She ate about half of it before saying, "The trouble is, the real answer – all that carbon-reduction-this and working-with-our-international-partners-that bollocks – is just so monumentally fucking boring nobody's ever going to do it, let alone vote for it."

But they had voted for it, Jacob thought. It had been in Jessica's manifesto. Time was, he might have enjoyed rubbing Cora's nose in defeat, but there was no need for that now. Elder statesmen could afford to be magnanimous. "Well, Jessica believes it."

Cora's phone buzzed again. Cora herself inhaled a spoonful of pudding and made a noise like a car backfiring, propelling dense chocolate grapeshot across the table, and spitting out words between choking coughs. "No. She. Don't. Doesn't. Can't."

Jacob was bemused. If there was one thing everybody knew about Jessica it was that she was going to save the Island. Cora was turning purple. Gasping for breath, she finished off her beer and even drank a little of the water that he poured her. Recovering, she said, "I don't mean she isn't genuine. Or committed. Quite the opposite."

"Quite."

"I mean: she's young. An idealist. She can't really believe in international diplomacy and patient negotiation and years and years and bloody years of boring, thankless graft? You must know better than anyone, Jacob, she's going to want to *do* something? Something spectacular? She's here to *save* the Island, not to patch it up. That's the point of Messiahs, isn't it?"

Why must he know? Because he was her father? The truth was, he had no more idea than Cora, or anybody else, what Jessica would do. The difference was, he didn't care. He was trying not to, anyway. Not that it wasn't important; he hoped she would succeed. But the details didn't matter to him now. He had retired. He hadn't chosen the moment, but there you go. It was up to Jessica now.

But Cora wasn't looking for his opinion. She polished off the brownie, set down her spoon and wiped her mouth with her napkin. "I just can't for the love of fucking God and whisky see what the something's going to be. So I can't guess how Diana will react. So I don't know how I'm going to shaft her."

"I suppose you'll just have to wait and see."

"*Exactly*, Jacob. And it's doing my fucking head in."

Fair enough. Equanimity had never been Cora's natural style, to put it mildly. And mild was the effect he was aiming at, from here on in.

This time Cora's phone not only buzzed but also emitted a squeal like a stuck pig. Or perhaps a seagull. She picked it up, swiped a code with practised impatience, read a message, flicked the screen again. Jacob could hear indistinct crowd noise, nothing more.

"Oh, for fuck sake," she said.

SEVEN

CONGRATULATIONS, SHE'D SAID. He'd left the Leader's office in a daze.

"Congratulations," said Jules.

"So she said."

He took the lift down one flight.

Marion, Donald's PA – now his PA – said, "Congratulations, Chief."

Why did it sound so much like a death knell?

He went through to Donald's office – his office – and shut the door behind him. For years he'd teased Marion and she'd told him to bugger off whenever she felt the need. It made both their jobs easier. *Chief*, she'd just called him. It's what he'd called Donald, to wind him up. He'd have to work out what to do about that later.

The Chief Exec's office was long and narrow, little better than a tunnel: a coffin, Ari thought now, albeit one with a little light at the far end. The window would have offered a decent view of the city and the remnants of the seafront, if he'd been at all interested, and if it had been possible to get past the intricate contraption of flywheels, ratchets, pulleys, pendulums and ball-bearing runs that constituted Donald's folly. The machine occupied fully two-thirds of the already limited space, leaving just enough for a desk with a chair either side. The desk was empty; Ari sat behind it. He pulled open the drawers, and pushed them shut. The last time he'd spoken to Donald here, in his office, the machine had been running, uninterrupted, for fourteen weeks; that had been a month ago, and it was running still. He watched the flywheels spin, the ratchets slowly tick, the springs coil and uncoil. It looked perfect, but couldn't be, by definition. If he listened hard enough, he could just detect the faintest click of part on part, the slightest pulse of displaced air.

The desk phone – his phone – buzzed. Marion had Diana Ford-Marling on line 1.

"For Donald?"

"For you, Chief."

"But . . ."

"The Leader must have told her."

Ari sighed.

"Uneasy lies the head, boss?"

Boss?

"Did she say what it was about?"

"She said you'd know."

That didn't much narrow things down. The woman was a force of nature. There had been Ffordes and Marlyng/Marlynge/Marlinges on the Island for longer than most species of mammals had existed. The two great families united about the time Shakespeare was learning how to spell. The Ford-Marlings had known which side of the Civil War was right, and that it wouldn't win. It was true that a younger son of a junior branch had, as a young man under the spell of Ruskin, taken up painting and attempted to restore the double ff, but the intervention of a senior aunt had steered him back on course and marriage to Diana's great-great-great-grandmother. When Cora Klamm was looking for a spad after Ari's defection to Jacob King, she decided she could do worse than appoint Diana, who was both willing and able to work for free. Besides, it never hurt to keep in with the nobs, and she was sure she could knock the smooth edges off her young acolyte. In the event, though, Cora discovered that while it may be technically possible to roughen a polished diamond, it is hard and specialist work. Where Cora slammed her feet up on any desk to hand and had a mouth that half a dozen carbolic-wielding mothers couldn't possibly scrub clean,

Diana affected twinsets, patent leather court shoes and a stare that could drop a buffalo at fifty paces, if the Island's wildlife had only run to buffalo. In a street fight, Cora would favour good old-fashioned brass knuckles; Diana, a stiletto – or perhaps a hatpin, if such things still existed – with a point so sharp you wouldn't feel it going in, and wouldn't know you were dead until the family gathered round with a tear in their collective eye. Following Thursday's count, Cora Klamm was out on her ear and Diana Ford-Marling installed as Leader of the Opposition before the spoiled votes were even tallied. Her absence from K's funeral that morning must, Ari knew, have been a calculated snub, a statement of intent. But why was her next move to call *him*? Having to take the call was just the sort of undesirable side effect of his own promotion that he'd been trying to avoid.

"Thank you, Marion." He pressed the button for Line 1 and felt his ear sandblasted by centuries of patrician in-breeding.

"Ah, there you are!"

The volume suggested she might not trust the miracle of telephony to transmit her voice unaided.

"Good morning, Councillor Ford-Marling."

"Good afternoon!"

He checked his watch: it was well past midday. He'd had no lunch, however.

"Congratulations, Ari."

"Thank you, Councillor."

Pleasantries complete, Diana evidently considered it time for brass tacks. "What exactly does she mean by it?"

"By what in particular, Councillor?"

"All that ballyhoo about homelessness and waging war on rogue landlords. She's not going through with it, is she? Now she's . . . won?"

The word evidently stuck in her throat, even if it wasn't Diana herself who'd lost.

He said, "It was a manifesto commitment, Councillor."

"Of course it was. That's not what I asked."

76

"And I expect to produce draft policy papers in respect of all the Leader's manifesto commitments."

"Really? What on earth *for?*"

"To allow Cabinet and then Council to debate their merits and propose amendments before we go out for public consultation, Councillor."

That's what Jessica had said, anyway: right after she'd said "congratulations". There was a momentary silence on the line – as there had been in the Leader's office – while Diana digested the import of his words. "Bloody hell," she said.

Bloody hell, indeed, thought Ari, idly poking a forefinger between the spokes of a slowly oscillating flywheel, and then quickly withdrawing it. It would be unfair not to let the experiment run.

"I won't say I'm not surprised," Diana said. "Not so much at Jessica. But you've been around a long time, Ari. I'm surprised at you."

He *had* been around a long time: much longer than Diana Ford-Marling, who might have countless ancestors, but was herself not yet thirty. It would be a while before she earned the right to affect such clubbability.

He said, "I live to serve, Councillor."

"Come off it, Ari. You can't think all this is a good idea?"

It was not entirely clear whether she meant the eradication of homelessness itself or Jessica's unconventional way of going about it. He suspected both, but preferred not to debate the merits of either, at least not with Diana Ford-Marling.

"My role is merely to advise, Councillor, and to implement. It is the role of politicians to persuade and to decide."

One thing about being Chief Executive: it permitted a level of pomposity he could never have got away with in the past. Curiously, as an advisor, he hadn't needed to maintain the fiction that he merely advised; indeed, his effectiveness depended on it being known that he wielded real power in the Leader's name. Now, as "head of the paid service" he could maintain strict impartiality when it suited him. Deniability. Perhaps it wasn't all bad? Perhaps Jessica wasn't quite as green as she was cabbage-looking? But then she didn't have to actually *do* the bloody job.

Diana was speaking again: "So when should we expect these policy papers of yours?"

"In due course, Councillor."

She laughed; which, again, he thought was taking things too far. "That's more like it, Ari! *In due course.* Meaning: this year, next year, sometime, never, I suppose?"

"Meaning in due course, Councillor. Is there anything else I can help you with?"

Apparently there wasn't, not right now.

He hung up, relieved the conversation was over, but uncertain how it had turned out. True, she had started off barking and ended up chuckling, which was all to the good, if a little grating. If, on the other hand, her restored good humour reflected a conviction that he and Jessica intended to park the more difficult election pledges – which, to be fair, he would have been perfectly happy to do, but Jessica would *not* – then it was entirely possible, not to say probable, that Diana would shortly begin to demand sight of the proposals, then loudly condemn any delay in their production; not because she welcomed the opportunity for debate but because, secure in the expectation that no such policy papers would ever emerge, she would see nothing but political advantage in embarrassing the Leader personally, and the Authority more broadly. It was what he would have done, in her place.

So the question was: how would Jessica respond?

And he rather thought she would respond by redoubling her resolve. Which would not help.

It was ridiculous, he thought, to let Diana Ford-Marling get under his skin. He really had been around this game a lot longer than she had. A lot longer than Jessica King, come to that. And yet . . .

In the silence that followed, Ari could hear again the swish of the pendulum and the faintest tick of the ratchet, as if the proverbial fly on the wall were rubbing its legs together on the far side of a large room.

Normally, in this sort of mood, he would have gone to visit K. But K was dead and buried.

EIGHT

Denis followed the Barolo with a dessert wine to accompany his tiramisu and a grappa to accompany his coffee. This place really wasn't bad. Not as bad as it looked, anyway. He had arrived before anyone else and would be leaving long after they had returned to their offices, their shopping, their hairdressers' appointments or whatever it was that filled their Monday afternoons. He had drunk more than any of them, more than all of them put together, and not one of them, not one of them, was on their way towards a heartfelt, life-changing gesture of undying love. Not one. Catching the waiter's eye, he tried to scribble with the fingers of one hand against the palm of the other, and missed. When the bill came, he squinted at the numbers. They were fuzzy around the edges and wouldn't stay still. Just as well – he was better off not knowing. He added what must surely have been a substantial tip and keyed in the PIN for his father's card. The pause that followed might have been more nerve-racking had he not been too absorbed in future bliss to recall the possibility of his mother having cancelled it.

He stood slowly, unsteadily, allowing the waiter to hold out his father's overcoat, then wrestled himself backwards into its arms. He smiled benignly as the waiter brushed imaginary dust from the shoulders and effused *grazie, grazie signore, arrivederci*, his accent more Bucharest than the Eternal City. Perfect, Denis thought. It would have been a travesty to ruin so utterly ersatz a Roman trattoria by hiring actual Italians to work in it. Spoiling the trireme for a whatsit of . . . whatever? Fuck it. He was doing pretty well to get "trireme".

Outside, the cold did not so much sober him up as distil all mental effort onto the task ahead. One step at a time, dear Jesus. He stumbled back towards Houghton Square in a series of looping swerves, like a novice skater deliberately crashing into the barriers to avoid falling on his face. Once there, however, the shops – jewellers, clothes shops, a specialist tobacconist – were not what he was looking for. Hardware. That was the word. What he needed was one of those shops that sells plastic buckets and mops and laundry starch and cheap hairdryers and Christmas decorations in June, or – better still – one of those gigantic sheds on a ring road opposite a computer shed, a car parts shed and a drive through burger shed, none of which he'd ever find round here. He took out his phone and tried, with fingers thickened by cold and alcohol, to Google 'nearest DIY'. After several distracting failures, the answer appeared to be: Barney's, 2.6 miles away. Was it even possible to go 2.6 miles on this piss-pot rock without falling off the edge? After Barney's, the second nearest was 346 miles, which sounded about right. But he'd need a boat. Or a helicopter. Barney's it had better be, then, but there was no way he could walk it. Not in this weather; not after the lunch he'd had. He stepped in front of an empty cab, showed the driver his phone, checked he'd take a credit card, and settled himself in the back. The cab smelled of disinfectant, sweat and pear drops all at once. The radio was tuned to a classical music station where two presenters swapped infinitesimal differences between umpteen recordings of some screechy-scratchy crap that people had apparently been listening to since 1935. Ten minutes was quite enough before Denis broke the first rule of taxi travel.

"You like this stuff, then?"

"Is beautiful," the driver said to the rear view mirror while gliding, oblivious, across a busy junction.

"Really? Why?"

"Is soul of my country." He closed his eyes on the word "soul" in a dreamy and, to Denis, frankly alarming way. Save Our Souls.

"Where's that, then? Your country?"

"Ah . . ."

Silence. If you could call the radio's cat-stomping squeal and the muffled screams of a toddler's mother as the cab mounted the kerb at a pedestrian crossing, silence.

"Your country," Denis prompted.

"Is no more."

Iznomor? Iznomoria? Iznomoristan? Was that some shitty corner of Central Asia that might or might not actually be Russia? Or the Horn of Africa, maybe?

"My country . . . not exist."

Ah, *no more*. Of course. Wait – how did that work?

"What happened?"

"Is too long." The cab stopped suddenly, sending Denis, who never bothered with seat belts, hurtling face first into the headrest of the passenger seat in front.

"Is here."

What – in his heart? His soul? Was this guy one of those refugee philosophy professors, driving a cab to survive? Or, worse still: a poet? "Your country is here?"

"DIY is here," the driver said, pointing through the windscreen.

Two-point-six miles, it turned out, got you from Houghton Square to just the sort of home improvement universe Denis had imagined. Across a car park you could land an Airbus on if it were seriously lost, he could just make out a supermarket mothership, a computer-slash-home appliance store, a sporting goods store and there, in the far, far distance, a Barney's Homestore that he'd probably need GPS to find his way around. He suggested they park a little closer, but the driver pointed at a sign too small and much too far away for Denis, in his present state, to read.

"Loading-unloading only. I drop you here."

Denis sighed and climbed out of the car. His legs seemed to have regained some semblance of rigidity; out here the steady roar of the dual carriageway at least drowned out the hideous music. He told the driver to wait while he went inside. He would keep the meter running. He was about to make the most perilous romantic gesture of his life; there was no point getting stuck out in the arse-end of nowhere. The path of true love ne'er did run smooth. Poets knew that much. But you might as well have transport.

The driver asked how he could be sure that Denis would come back.

"You think I want to stay out here? Are you mad?"

The driver shrugged. "Leave credit card. So I know."

"And how do I know you won't drive off with it?"

The driver shrugged again. "Is impasse? You want I wait, leave card."

"Okay."

It wasn't worth an argument. He handed the driver his own card, long since blocked by the bank. If the bastard drove off and tried to use it, there was a decent chance he'd go to jail.

Inside the store Denis was confronted by the massed ranks of countless aisles, all stacked two or three times higher than his head. Superglue was easy enough; padlocks he eventually tracked down in Gardening, adjacent to flat pack sheds; chains, however, proved a different matter. The Gardening section had small white links for ornamental fence posts, but that really wasn't the image he was after: more stiff upper lip than barely-contained brute passion.

"Excuse me? Where can I find chains?"

The boy – not man, Denis thought, whatever his actual age – looked as if he'd never seen daylight. His skin was pallid and pitted with acne; there was a flayed red sore around his mouth; his hand, when he raised it wordlessly to point towards Plumbing & Bathroom, was bony with protuberant knuckles, the colour of milk that had turned and separated. Thankfully, a bright yellow Barney's jacket, manufactured with a much larger person in mind, obscured everything between his engorged Adam's apple and his emaciated wrist.

"Bathrooms?" Denis asked. "Are you sure?"

"Old-fashioned toilet chains," the boy said. "That what you're after?"

It wasn't. Nice try, though, Denis thought. "I need something a bit more . . . heavy duty."

"What's it for, then?"

Denis wasn't going into that. Nothing would ruin a romantic gesture like discussing it with . . . *Graham*, he read, stitched in brown above the boy's custard yellow breast pocket. (Unless 'Graham' was the larger man to whom the jacket rightfully belonged?) "Let's just say . . . restraint. I need to secure a large, powerful . . . object."

"Restraint, eh?" Graham smiled, revealing teeth a tad less awful than Denis would have wagered. "Have you considered handcuffs?"

He hadn't. Not quite the image he'd had in mind, either, but it could work. "Do you stock them?"

Graham laughed. "No chance, mate." Then he dropped his voice to a harsh but confidential whisper: "Only two ways to get hold of decent cuffs." Despite himself, Denis stepped closer, leaning in to catch the words. "One," Graham continued, "nick 'em off a copper. Which I personally wouldn't recommend. Or, two," - a crooked finger somehow drew Denis closer still - "twenty-five a pair at Annie's Sex Boutique. So long as you don't mind a pink fur trim."

Denis jumped back as if he had been scalded. No one would call him prudish, but sex toy was exactly the wrong impression for what he had in mind. Worse even than toilets or garden fences.

"It has to be chains," he said, "heavy chains."

"Right," said Graham, straightening up. "Then you'd better try the motorbike shop next door, hadn't you?"

Of course. He should have thought of that himself. Chains weren't Home Improvement, unless your home had a dungeon. But he'd seen plenty of expensive motorbikes chained up with just the sort of chunky, oily, indisputably masculine hardened steel links he wanted. He could do without the oil, though. No point ruining a decent suit, even if it was K's. It's not like K would want it any more.

"Of course," he said lightly. "I just thought, as I was here . . ." He gestured with the glue and padlocks to illustrate his point.

Graham looked thoughtful. "I'd get the locks at the bike shop, too, if I were you. You'd be through those in a couple of seconds with a bolt-cutter. Or a butter knife."

Denis looked at the locks, then dropped them into Graham's outstretched hand. Then he looked at the floor.

"Thanks," he said.

He paid for the glue and left.

Out in the car park he could see the minicab, way off to his right. He could just make out the driver, leaning forward against the steering wheel, pen poised over a folded newspaper. Denis waved the glue and pointed at the bike shop half a mile away, but the driver was too absorbed in his crossword to notice.

⁂

A small crowd gathered to observe the squat blond man in an ill-fitting black suit and a long overcoat who appeared to have chained himself, arms wide, to the downstream railings of the footbridge that had once been a favoured spot for trysting lovers and still bore the evidence in the form of countless engraved padlocks, most of which were, to be honest, shoddy pieces of kit that wouldn't have detained the idlest thief for more than a moment, reflecting with unconscious accuracy the constancy of love affairs so immature they were unlikely to outlive the flimsiest hardware. With the passage of time, and the rise of salt water, many had succumbed to rust, fusing together into rough, amorphous clumps, like the barnacles upon the bigger barnacles upon the scarred belly of a whale, complicating their symbolism in ways that Denis Klamm - diminutive, blond-haired possessor of the ill-fitting suit and long black overcoat, and centre of the small crowd's attention - was still too drunk to pursue.

Drunk or sober, however, the impression that he alone had chained himself to anything was entirely misplaced. Behind every great man there stands a former Soviet taxi driver and a pipeline of dead parental cash. True, if Denis had been sober, the physical demands might have been easier to manage; but if he had not been drunk, he never would have tried at all.

For a start, *his* padlocks were forged of stainless steel and boron; they had thick, stubby shackles designed to thwart the toughest bolt-cutters and the only name they bore was that of their manufacturer. They fastened two security chains – each comprising sixteen 22-millimetre diameter square links that weighed a kilogram apiece – sheathed in tough, rip-resistant nylon. Altogether, the kit weighed thirty-six kilos and cost the sort of sum that would have made his bank manager wince, if bank managers still attended to the affairs of individual clients, and – more to the point – if he had paid for them himself. Leaving the bike shop with his unwieldy packages, he remembered too late that the waiting cab was far away across the other side of the car park, which now stretched before him like the Mongolian steppe. He waved and waved, but to no effect: the driver, having apparently completed his crossword, was absorbed in an editorial on the inadequacy of international efforts to tackle the climate emergency. Denis reassured himself that a journey of a thousand miles began with but a single step, but – after very few – reflected that Chairman Mao hadn't been carrying ridiculously heavy chains that wouldn't settle in just one uncomfortable position, but slid and slipped around with each and every step, forcing him to drop his burden – only to have to pick it up again, and repeat the whole rigmarole a few yards further on. Or perhaps he had. Perhaps Chinese Communists were just made of sterner stuff. After two or three goes round the cycle – lift, stagger, drop – Denis was prepared to accept that might have been the case. He had been born to the luxury of the Castle, such as it was; if his life on the mainland had not been exactly featherbedded, neither had it been likely to promote physical fitness or muscular strength. In the last seven years he had exercised precisely once, and then only because a friend dangled the promise of a female gym employee he simply *had* to see. Well, he'd seen; but the bargain wasn't worth it. After three days of pain in muscles he hadn't known that he possessed, he couldn't recall a single thing about her. Now, when he finally reached the cab, dropped his parcels and knocked on the window, he was happy to accept the driver's offer to put them in the boot, only to be disappointed when the packages were picked up and stowed away as if they had been bags of groceries. He thought he'd better have a cigarette. He offered the driver one, but was refused: "Is not good for lungs, I think?" No, Denis thought, not good for lungs or heart or anything else, but if I don't have a fag right now I'm going to fucking die. He leaned against the cab, lit up, inhaled deeply, coughed as if he were forty-eight hours off death from emphysema, inhaled again, exhaled smoothly and asked the driver if he knew the footbridge, the one with all the padlocks? "Is pedestrian, yes?" It was a footbridge, yes. The driver pointed to his cab: "No cars?" Ah. Denis explained that he wanted to be taken as close to the bridge as possible, and would then greatly welcome the driver's help in carrying his packages onto the bridge itself. After navigating an intricate route to avoid the worst of the afternoon traffic, and parking at the end of a road that terminated raggedly in a sudden cliff above the sea, the driver carried both chains to the centre of the bridge without breaking stride; Denis followed with the padlocks and the glue. When Denis asked for help in chaining himself to the bridge, however, the driver finally hesitated.

"Why?"

"Because I can't do it on my own," said Denis, who was now beyond shame.

"But why do it?"

"For love."

The driver looked sceptical. "Is true?"

"Yes," said Denis, surprising himself. "It is true."

"Then I help."

Denis climbed over the rail and perched, buttocks on a narrow ledge, face to the sea. The driver looped the first chain over the rail by his left shoulder, round and up under his right armpit, securing it with one of the padlocks. He repeated this with the second chain, looping over Denis' right shoulder and under his left armpit, securing it with the second lock. "Like bandoleers?" he said. "Like bandoleers," Denis agreed, delighted. He held his hand out for the keys, and flung them as far as he could out to sea.

"For love?" the driver asked.

"For love," said Denis.

He felt his head clasped in a strong grip and a kiss planted on his scalp, right where the hair swirled out from the crown.

He asked the driver to pour glue into the padlocks, which he did, repeating, gleefully, "For love."

"Thanks, man," Denis said over his shoulder. He faced the sea, inhaled ozone-rich air and beat his chest with his fists. "Yes!"

But the driver was unhappy. "Is not good."

"What?"

"For love. Tarzan is not good image."

He had a point. Jessica was no quivering Jane. "The guy in the shop suggested handcuffs."

"Yes? Is good idea."

"Really?"

"This you should do." The driver spread his arms wide to show what he meant, even though Denis couldn't see. "Like Jesus," he said.

"I don't think Jesus wore handcuffs."

"But arms spread. Yes? Open to world. Defenceless."

Like Christ? Denis thought. "I like it," he said.

"Don't go away."

Was that a joke? Denis felt the weight of the chains across his chest. He was going nowhere. A moment later he heard footsteps, then a fistful of black plastic strips was thrust in front of his face.

"Zip-ties, yes?"

Denis flung his arms wide, banging his knuckles against the iron railings. "Yes!"

Within seconds his wrists were securely attached. If this doesn't show I'm serious, Denis thought, nothing will. What more could a woman ask?

"Thanks, man," he said again. Then, feeling it inadequate, asked the driver's name.

"Pavel."

"Thank you, Pavel. How much do I owe you?"

Denis heard the catch in Pavel's voice as he said, "Neeshgo. Nada. Nothing. For love."

"Bullshit, Pavel. I can't do that to you. How much?"

"In my country, I am poet."

"Which is why you're not in your country any more. Here you're a cab driver: no one drives cabs for free. How much?"

Eventually, Pavel went to check the meter. Denis, buoyed by the nobility of his own gesture, tried not to hope he'd just get in the cab and drive away. Instead, Pavel returned with a portable reader and the credit card Denis had left with him earlier. Denis' own card. He named a sum that made Denis swallow hard and held the card against the reader. It could not possibly work. The signal was poor down here by the shore, and the transaction was slow to process. He was just about to tell Pavel to take the wallet out of his jacket pocket, to find his father's card, when a faint ping told him the transaction was complete and he had absolutely no idea how. It was a miracle.

"For love," said Pavel once more. "Good luck."

For love, Denis thought. By now, the first of the onlookers had started to notice the blond man in black dangling over the river mouth; after everything he'd been through, Denis had no desire to squander the mystery too soon.

"Bye, Pavel. Thanks again. And best of luck."

Pavel disappeared into the gathering crowd.

It was only then that Denis realized he hadn't returned the miraculous credit card. Ah well, he thought. That's what you get for being drunk.

&

An hour later, he had watched a boat sail across the bay from right to left, another from left to right. East to west. Probably. He had watched the river meet the sea beneath his pendent feet, watched the clear water swell gently and recede, making the rocks beneath appear to heave and wobble like a fat man's stomach. He had counted seventeen shades of grey in an ugly grey sky and had read the inscriptions on every padlock he could see by twisting his neck to one side or the other. *Sandi ♥ James. Mick & Susie; Eva4J4eva.* Eva/ever – that was cleva, if you were drunk enough, and bored enough.

He was.

He didn't know any Evas, though.

J ♥ D.

D could be Denis, couldn't it? Of course it could. Or Dwayne, or Dora or Dickhead, Dickhead.

The knot of onlookers thickened and the water soaked his shoes. He discovered just how long it is possible to hold your legs out horizontally in front of you, unsupported. (Not long.) Within a couple of hours the tide would rise to his knees, at least. In time, of course, it would rise to his waist, his chest, his neck, and would eventually overtop his head.

For now, however, Denis dutifully waved as best he could with his arms pinned out to either side, and the small crowd became a larger crowd as people joined to see what was going on. Gradually, those who had arrived first stopped watching and began describing what they'd seen. Neighbour spoke to neighbour and the story slowly spread upstream, inland, replicating and mutating like a contagious virus. Debate spread, too, around the online world: grainy phone-shot footage prompted jokes, abuse and conspiracy-based speculation in roughly equal measure. He was a suicide; a performance artist; a publicity seeking magician-cum-escapologist; a protestor. What was he protesting about? No one knew; he had no placard, no banner – which only reinforced the view of those convinced this was a stunt. *Publicising what?* demanded those more taken with the idea of performance art. Just you wait and see, retorted the publicity theorists. It'll be a marketing campaign for soft drinks, or laser surgery, or tax-efficient savings plans. Nonsense, scoffed those wanting to believe that activism could still elude the deadly grip of global capitalism – he's a hero, sacrificing himself to force the Authority to finally *do* something to save the Island. His protest, they said, put a time limit on prevarication: if something were not done before the waters rose above his neck, he would undergo a very public death. It was just a matter of time. How much time? Some said weeks, others months, but they were probably all wrong. Once the story reached the mainland a climatologist would calculate that, on the basis of current trends, it would be twenty-seven years before Denis actually drowned; but of course, he warned, no one really knew whether the future could be reliably extrapolated from the past: feedback loops within the earth's overall ecosystem were accelerating, becoming harder and harder to predict.

One young woman, whose own love life had been in abeyance for several years at this point, advanced the suggestion that the short but nonetheless handsome blond man in the ill-fitting suit and heavy chains was making a beautiful romantic gesture; that his action, far from being a protest or a sordid commercial stunt, was designed solely to capture the heart of some object of affection who, most likely, was until now entirely unaware of the overwhelming passion he or she had inspired. The woman was alone in this belief, however, and was not so much drowned out as silently ignored: those to whom she advanced her theory simply shrugged and returned to battle for the claims of politics or art or advertising.

She was, however, right.

Or near enough.

While debate raged, Denis kept his own counsel. In response to those who forced their way through the crowd up on to the bridge and whispered questions in his ear, as to those who shouted from the river banks for all to hear, he merely smiled – which most of them could not see – and nodded, and commented that the weather *was* foul, wasn't it? Viciously cold and, if it were not actually raining, the wind was whipping up an icy spray that would drench him soon enough – which comments most of them could not hear, over the roar of the wind and their own raised voices.

He could do with a drink, he thought, to keep out the damp.

NINE

"FOR FUCK SAKE, " she said again.

Whatever it was, it had put her off her pudding. She held the phone out across the table, but Jacob couldn't make out what he was looking at.

"A problem?"

"All he had to do was come home, look solemn and piss off again. How hard could it be? But: no. The little prick's only been here twenty-four hours, and he's already making a public tit of himself."

"Denis?"

"Who else?"

Jacob wondered if this could be Cora's twisted way of expressing pride in her son. Then stopped wondering, because that was ridiculous.

"What's he up to?"

"Look!" She handed him the phone, swiping the screen to replay a video. It was less than two minutes long and panned wildly, as if trying to induce nausea in the viewer; it zoomed in and out inexpertly, but gradually focused, when the crush of bodies allowed, on a small blond black-clad figure perched uncomfortably on the outside of the footbridge, facing out to sea.

❧

No two points on the Island could be very far apart as the seagull flies but inequality isn't really a matter of geography at all. In the food bank where she had spent the morning divvying up root vegetables and plastic bottles of peach-flavoured fermented milk about to pass its sell-by date, less than half a mile from where Cora Klamm sat waiting for Jacob to hand back her phone, Eva Maria's lunch was similarly interrupted, if less substantial. When her phone buzzed repeatedly, the video she found herself watching was a cousin to that at which Jacob King simultaneously peered. Eva's view had been shot from the opposite bank, the other end of the bridge, and rather earlier in the day, with far fewer onlookers crowding the scene. As a result, she recognized not one but two of the participants. Denis Klamm, of course, whose face she had not seen for years but whom, even in blurred profile, she had no trouble picking out of a crowd; also, in the first few seconds, slipping quietly out of shot, Pavel.

She made a call of her own.

Further away, but still no more than a short hop for a determined seagull, Commander Cole looked down on the City from his office above the Castle's security gate and dismissed the inspector who had stopped by to brief him on the developing situation down in what was left of Riverside Walk. He had changed, reluctantly, out of his dress uniform. After a few experimental thrusts and parries – just to experience the feel of the thing – he had hung his ceremonial sword and cocked hat back in the display cabinet immediately above the shelf on which two framed photographs – PC Cole graduating from the police academy; Commander Cole shaking hands with Cllr King – sat either side of the polished wooden truncheon he had swung performatively by its leather strap during his first, brief days on the beat.

Why did people do these things?

He meant stupid things. Not necessarily criminal things, which he found easier to understand, but things like gluing themselves to the road, living for months in squalid muddy tunnels, lobbing bricks at his officers, sleeping in doorways or, as in the present case, chaining themselves to a bridge? He wasn't stupid. He knew what they *said* – although young Klamm was apparently keeping schtum, at least for now – but why did they do it, *really*?

Do-gooders. That was the word. It didn't mean they did any good. Once, during one of their regular lunches – falafel burgers and beer in that fake diner place – he'd told Donald Price that civilians were simple. Basically, you had your do-gooders and your wrong'uns, and he'd take a wrong'un any day. At least you knew where you stood. Donald suggested it might be a bit more complicated than that, but he would, wouldn't he? Complication had been Donald's thing.

Bob remembered the conversation, and the lunch, even if it had been ten years ago, because that was the day he'd managed to show Donald a thing or two about complexity himself. Donald thought he was a plod, even if he was a graduate copper, and he had played along. "Beer or beer?" he'd said, flapping a laminated menu as the Chief Executive shuffled sideways into the vinyl booth at *Route 66*. They met up for lunch every few months. Donald obviously liked to think he was guiding the new man through the idiosyncrasies of Island life. Bob mostly let him: it did no harm. It was just coincidence this lunch had fallen a couple of days after the events in the Cathedral Close.

"Mineral water, please."

That was Donald for you, too. Bob turned to the waiter, who flicked his carbon-copy notepad open and licked a pencil in anticipation. "That's two beers, love."

"Really," Donald said. "I'm working."

"That's two *large* beers. And a bottle of pop for Daisy, here."

The waiter scribbled, tore off the top sheet, slapped it on the table and headed towards the counter, buttocks twitching. Bob had turned to watch them go. "You've got to give 'em credit."

"Who?"

"The Simulators. Phenomenal attention to detail, there."

"I . . . ah . . ."

"I mean, they could so easily have given him one of those electronic doo-dads to take the order on. But: no. This is a diner, so the waiter gets a proper pad and a 2B pencil to lick."

He watched Donald squirm, reluctant to get dragged into a conversation about Simulation.

"Mind you," he said, "I'm surprised they could find one that pretty who can actually write."

Donald couldn't resist. "Do you not think, Bob, that Simulators could have made him specially to order?"

"Christ sake, Daisy. I'm not a bloody fundamentalist."

Donald looked flustered. He was so easy to tease.

"Of course not. I was just . . ."

"Ah, forget it." Bob waved a hand between them, as if literally clearing the air. "What're you eating?"

There wasn't really any choice. The place did burgers. Burgers and fries. Some of the fries weren't made of potato, but what was the point of that? If you were going to eat something, Bob thought, you might as well eat it. Not try and pretend otherwise. You could say the same about the burgers, he supposed, but what could he do? He was a vegetarian.

The waiter was back. He placed a beer in front of Bob. He placed the second, a bottle of mineral water and a glass full of ice in the middle of the table. Didn't want to get involved, Bob thought. Very wise.

The waiter tucked his tray under one arm and pulled his notepad out of a rear trouser pocket. "Are you guys ready to order? Or do you need a moment?"

"Two falafel burgers please, love," said Bob. "And chips."

"Two falafel," the waiter repeated as he wrote. "Two fries."

"Chips."

"We don't do chips."

Bob looked up from the menu. He winked at Donald before facing the waiter. "Do you by any chance chop potatoes into sticks and fry them in oil?"

"We do. That's why we call them fries."

"Fair enough."

He held up both menus for the waiter to take while watching Donald, who looked unsure whether to be relieved or disappointed at his surrender; good, Bob thought. Confusion would do nicely.

The waiter took the menus; Bob watched him shimmy to the counter, while Donald watched Bob.

"So," Donald said.

"So," the police commander replied.

The etiquette of all working lunches is that no business be discussed until the meal has been ordered; once the food arrives, conversation again becomes general, beginning, perhaps, with remarks pertaining to the food itself, before enlarging upon current affairs not directly related to the responsibilities of those present. The window of opportunity lies therefore between the order and the eating: at *Route 66* that window was bracingly narrow, and did not accommodate Donald's natural instinct to beat around the bush. Which, as much as the quality of the burgers or the attractions of the staff, was why the place appealed to Commander Cole.

"Tuesday," said Donald.

"Cathedral Close?"

"Unless your mob ran amok somewhere else I haven't heard about?"

"My officers do not *run amok*." He prodded the words the way another man might approach a stranded jellyfish with a stick.

"So what happened?"

"Bunch of do-gooders got mixed up with some wrong'uns and started a riot. My lads and ladesses restored order."

"With extreme prejudice?"

"With the minimum possible threat to public safety. End of."

"That's not quite the way it looked from the Castle."

"It was the Castle as wanted it."

That took Donald by surprise, but Bob was just setting up the follow-through.

"Orders is orders. Straight from the horse's mouth."

"The Leader?"

Could Donald really be as surprised as he sounded?

"Well, not the Leader himself," Bob admitted, while pretending to forget a name. "His sidekick. Tiny feller. Black hair, cheekbones you could use to shave a coconut."

"Ari Spencer?"

"That's the lad. Slippery as a porn star's prick. But sound on this one. I'll give him that."

"Ari Spencer told you to assault peaceful, unarmed protestors?"

"He said – and I remember his exact words, clear as day – you can't make an omelette without cracking a few heads, Bob."

"And you thought he meant . . .?"

"I knew *exactly* what he meant."

There was a brief silence during which Donald drummed his fingers ever so lightly on the tabletop.

"And when did this conversation take place?"

"A week ago."

Which was Bob's real revelation. The official line, from both the Authority's press office and the demonstrators themselves, was that the whole thing had been a spontaneous affair, to which the police had rapidly improvised a response. By "spontaneous" the demonstrators meant "organized", but secretly. Their own supporters wouldn't have known what was happening until securely encrypted messages went out on the morning of the event. So what was Ari Spencer doing talking about it three or four days in advance? And not just giving a heads-up, but encouraging the sort of "improvised" response that left seven people dead and countless others injured?

That was the question he'd wanted to plant in Donald's mind, all those years ago. Not that he'd been looking for answers. The answers were obvious, and he was delighted with his timing when the waiter brought their burgers to the table, and the conversation to a close. Less a search for knowledge, more of an insurance policy. Who could have guessed that Donald would be dead before the Authority finally got round to holding an inquiry?

Now, though, that inquiry was finally on the way, and Ari

Spencer was sniffing round again. Asking pointed questions about his retirement plans. Do-gooder or wrong'un? Normal categories did not apply. Ari wasn't a civilian. More of an operator. Still, he could handle Ari Spencer. The real problem was the new boss. A big fat streak of do-gooder there, surely? Educated; privileged; teenage years spent protesting about the climate – as if there were any point complaining about the weather. Making a fuss about human rights and so-called police brutality. If people didn't put their heads across the line, they wouldn't get them broken, would they? And the Angela Warner thing, of course. Jessica had been thirteen: an impressionable age. Sources suggested she had taken it hard. It might have clouded her view of the police, which wasn't what you ideally wanted in a Leader. *She* was the reason there would be a public inquiry after all these years.

So, no: Ari was just doing a job the way he had been born and bred. Then and now. You didn't blame swallows for flying south in winter. But that didn't mean Bob Cole was going to fall on his ceremonial sword to save the slippery fucker's alabaster skin, either. Retirement had its attractions, but he had choices here, and taking the rap for half a dozen deaths could rapidly take the shine off a gold clock. He wasn't an Islander. If the cloud of Cathedral Close could finally be lifted, he might have one big job back on the mainland left in him before he handed in his cuffs.

She might call it closure, or some such do-gooder bullshit, but the Leader would want blood. She was the Child, after all: destined to rule, if you believed all that *Island Story* cobblers. He didn't – it wasn't his island – but there was a fair chance she would. Also, she was Jacob King's daughter. She wouldn't let sentiment get in the way of political advantage. But the beauty of it was, she wouldn't have to: vengeance and self-righteousness could go hand-in-hand. And the blood didn't have to be his. Which was why, that morning, he'd taken the opportunity to drop a word in Jessica's shell-like.

He straightened his shoulders, watching his reflection in the display cabinet's glass doors. He'd changed out of dress uniform;

Commander's tabs didn't ripple quite as pleasingly as gold braid. But they'd do, for now.

No, he wouldn't take it personally. Ari Spencer was just doing his job. For now.

Two blocks away, in his own new office, Ari began to hope that the gentle, indefatigable click . . . tick . . . click . . . tick . . . of Donald's machine might lose its power to irritate, and become instead the sort of white noise that occupies the subconscious, allowing the rational mind to work without distraction.

He had – eventually – taken a bullish line on chairing the inquiry with Jessica. She had as good as agreed. But if Bob Cole wasn't going to play ball, it would make little difference. Even as its chair, he could hardly prevent the commission from interviewing the senior police officer in charge at the time of the alleged brutality they were supposed to be investigating. Especially if that police officer was still in post. In which case he would need to find another way to limit the damage.

Meanwhile, she'd given him other headaches.

Click . . . tick . . . click . . . tick . . .

It was almost better than talking to K while he mumbled and dribbled in the background.

Jessica had said he'd have to drill her a hole somewhere. But what if he didn't? What if drilling a hole somehow came to be seen as worse than not drilling one? Not just politically, but practically? Environmentally?

And then it came to him. The wisdom of crowds.

He was just considering whether to cry *Eureka!* – the entire borehole charade had kicked off with Donald in his bloody bath, after all – when Marion tapped at the door.

"You have a visitor, Chief."

"Marion?"

"Chief?"

"Stop it."

"Stop what, boss?"

"That."

She cocked her head to one side.

"Never mind. Who is it?"

"Lucy Neave. She's in reception."

"Lucy . . .? Really? What's she doing here?"

"Asking to see you, Chief."

"Well, get her up here."

Marion didn't move. "Have you heard about Denis Klamm?"

"I saw him this morning. Wearing K's coat. And what must have been one of his suits."

"He's all over the internet now."

"It did look pretty stupid."

"He's chained himself to the footbridge, boss. I thought you'd want to know."

"Why?"

"Well, Donald would have, boss."

"No, I meant . . . never mind."

"Also, the press office is asking if we're going to comment."

"God, no. Anything else?"

"There's an email from Peter, and another from Sally, that you should probably read before the management team starts in fifteen minutes – and the agenda papers, of course; then you've got a staff induction session at four, a pre-meet for tomorrow's public safety partnership at five, and Scrutiny committee at seven. Just in case you hadn't looked at your diary, Chief."

He hadn't.

"Christ," he said. "Is this how it's going to be?"

"Pretty much, boss. Chief. Congratulations."

Click . . . tick . . . click . . . tick . . .

He looked at his watch. "Fuck it," he said. "Send her in anyway."

He had no idea what Lucy was doing back on the Island,

but he had a job for her. Once he'd sorted out Denis Klamm.

"Also, Marion," he said. "Get me Bob Cole on the blower, please."

❧

Jacob handed Cora back her phone. "So what are you going to do?"

She lifted both hands, exhaled loudly, and let them fall. "If I knew what he was up to, I'd know my next move."

"Why not ask him?"

She looked surprised. "Jacob King, really? You've only been out of office ten minutes."

He thought: and you're not even opposition leader any more.

"But he's your son."

"If he were anybody else's son, it wouldn't matter."

Which was true enough. She wouldn't want to go down there – wouldn't want to fight her way through a scrum of reporters – without knowing what to say when asked if she condoned her son's behaviour.

She was talking to herself again, thinking aloud. "It has to be a protest, though he hasn't said about what. The environment? What does Idiot Son care if the Island disappears under the sea? He hasn't been here in years. Not even to visit."

"A father's death can affect a young man in strange ways."

"You know, I'd almost forgotten K was dead."

Was that sarcasm? With Cora it could be hard to tell. He said, gently, "It's an emotional time."

She laughed. "Right. Denis hasn't spoken to his dad for seven years. And now we're supposed to buy him rending his garments and tearing his flesh in grief?"

"Maybe it's *because* he didn't speak to his father. Perhaps he feels guilty?"

"Oh, don't go getting all psychotherapist on me, Jacob King. It really doesn't suit you."

"He apologized for you. After the funeral."

"He *what?*"

"You had just told me to fuck off."

"Oh, that. You weren't meant to take offence."

He held up his hands, palms out, placating.

Cora said, "No, he's up to something. I just don't know what. Didn't you say he wanted to help? Help how?"

"I don't know." Jacob was enjoying himself now. "I asked if he had any plans, and he said he might stick around and do his bit."

"*Do his bit?* What is he now, a bloody Boy Scout?"

"He said he was going to see the new Leader and offer her his services. Then off he went."

That should give her something to worry about.

"Jessica? He was going to offer Jessica his services?"

"That's what he said."

"Your daughter, Jessica?"

Oh.

"Well, well." Cora pushed her chair back, picked up her empty glass and swirled the dregs around.

He said, "You don't think . . .?"

"Why not? Denis may be an idiot, but he has all his own teeth."

What a shame they didn't all point in the same direction, Jacob didn't say. Such restraint: welcome to the elder statesman.

"And, yes, he may be a bit of a waster now, but he'll soon be rich."

Diplomatically, Jacob said, "Not too soon, I hope."

"You old smoothie. But in fact he's already loaded; he just doesn't know it yet. K's will set up a trust. The bloody lawyers wouldn't let me change it."

The waitress reappeared and asked if she could take their plates. "How was everything?"

Jacob said everything was fine and could they have the bill, please? But Cora said they needed drinks. For a toast. She looked at the menu. Brandy would do, even if it were Spanish.

"Seriously," she began again, when the waitress left.

"Seriously?"

"Well, why not? One of those political alliances. Two great families united. The War of the Roses. That sort of thing."

It was preposterous. Who did she think they were? In which century did she think they lived? Then again, it was only that morning that he'd cast himself as William Cecil to Jessica's Elizabeth.

"You think Jessica and Denis should start a new dynasty?"

"And everyone lives happily ever after."

That wasn't quite how he remembered Tudor history. He said, "Do you not think Jessica might have something to say about who she marries? Or *if* she marries?"

"Oh, she's young . . ."

"She's twenty-three." Young to be Leader, certainly, but old enough to know better than to get involved with Denis Klamm. "She's also smarter than the rest of us put together."

"You're only saying that because you're her dad. And she beat you."

Was he? He didn't think so. He was proud of her. Now that it was over he could even appreciate the way she'd outmanoeuvered him. He would not bear a grudge.

"It's true," he said. "She is."

"Then she can be the brains for both of them."

The waitress returned with two brandies.

"It's just as well I know you're only teasing," Jacob said.

Cora lifted her glass, winking. "The happy couple!"

She was teasing. Surely she was only teasing?

"I tell you what," she said. "We could make it a double wedding."

He left the restaurant a troubled man. Outside it was already getting dark. Street lights and shop windows glowed antiseptically. She had been joking. Of course she had; she'd just buried her husband. Grief affected people in strange ways. He watched her walk away, shoulders rolling, alternately leaning on her stick and lurching forward – less the frailty of old age than the cussedness of a disgruntled bulldog. He shook his head, trying to dislodge her, like water in his ear. He buttoned his coat against the wind, pushed his hands deep into the pockets and turned towards home. Then he stopped abruptly, causing a passer-by to swerve and mutter. Jacob watched him, too, for a moment, before turning again and walking slowly in the opposite direction, downhill.

Home was still the penthouse at the top of Central Block. He had always known that Jessica was safe there, as safe as she could be. Wherever he had to go, however hard he had to work, however long into the night and however early the next day, and the next, and the next again, he'd always had the comfort of knowing she was there, safe: separate and protected. When she ousted him as Leader he had asked pre-emptively if she wanted to swap rooms, to reflect their change in status, hoping she wouldn't say it would be better if he left altogether; to his relief, she'd laughed, but she'd also said that thing about *domestic arrangements*. Perhaps it was just awkwardness. Perhaps. The flat was still home, still safe. Nothing had changed, there. But everything had changed.

He picked up his pace a little, with no particular destination in mind, just heading downhill, away from the Castle. She hadn't asked him to leave, but perhaps he should go anyway? He wouldn't turn into K, hanging around, stinking the place up with his cigars, casting a rheumy, cynical eye on his successor's success. Besides, his job was done. Jessica was an adult, now, not just a politician. She had to build a life of her own. Leaving might be the last best gift he had to give.

TEN

A RI HAD READ the emails but not the meeting papers when Marion returned, looking wary. Before she could say anything, he held up his hand. "Don't tell me. There's a primary school falling into the sea. A homeless man . . . no a homeless woman, a homeless woman and her unborn baby and a puppy have been found starved to death in a delicatessen doorway. Am I close?"

"Nope."

"Go on, then."

"Commander Cole's office says he's too busy to talk to you."

"Is he now?"

"But he was expecting your call, and left a message. He can't play golf this weekend. In fact, he says – and they were very clear he wanted you to hear this – he says he might be giving up golf altogether. Too much work to do, he says."

"Oh, does he? Well that's just perfect."

Ari flopped back in his chair. It wasn't a great surprise, given what he'd heard from Jessica that morning. Like the bishop, Cole must be harbouring mainland ambitions, because even a plod could see there's no way he'd be staying on here. Well, the man wasn't an Islander, Ari thought, and in the end that made a difference. But the only way he'd get promoted off the island would be to come through the inquiry unscathed; and the only way he could do that would be to deflect blame up towards Ari – and Jacob, of course. But Jacob had retired, leaving Ari firmly in the cross hairs. Fair enough. But Bob Cole would need more than a get out of jail card vis-à-vis Cathedral Close: he'd need a halfway decent reference. Which Ari would be happy to provide, if he were in a position to do so; if not, the reference would rather depend on Jessica. But the annoying thing was, none of that was what Ari wanted to talk to him about right now. Well, not directly.

"I didn't know you played golf, sir."

"I don't. And please don't call me sir."

"I thought not. It wasn't in the diary."

"It's a message, Marion."

"Like a code, boss?"

Ari nodded. "Exactly like a code."

"Meaning he's not going quietly?"

Ari looked up sharply. Marion was standing in front of his desk holding a sheaf of papers for him to sign, looking like butter wouldn't melt. He'd only been Chief Exec a few hours. He'd have to get used to working with someone smart, and who had access to all his emails.

"Tell me, Marion: what would Donald have done?"

She thought for a while. "It's hard to imagine Donald *in* this situation."

Which was about as helpful as *I wouldn't start from here*, but he knew what she meant. What struck people most about Donald was that he had appeared to do so little, if anything at all. Not that he was lazy, far from it. He turned up, he read the reports, he chaired the meetings and signed the things he had to sign; only occasionally did he lecture his staff on the Enlightenment principles of human perfectibility. Decisions were made; things got done. But it was always hard to see what role he had actually played in those decisions, or what impact he had on their outcome. And yet, and yet. Donald had been Chief Exec for twenty-three years: he had survived two changes of Leader; and – setting aside, as most people did, the fact that bits of the Island kept falling into the sea and the ever-growing number of people sleeping in the streets – the machinery of the Authority had run ever more smoothly over those years. Costs were down, public satisfaction up. In the end, it took a cancer-riddled prostate gland to prise away his grip on office. So what exactly was it that Donald had done when it looked like he was doing nothing? Ari watched the flywheels spin, the ratchets slowly tick, the springs coil and uncoil. Could it really have been *nothing*?

Marion said, "Lucy's on her way up; management team's in five minutes."

"Send her straight in. And let them know I'll be late."

"Your first meeting, boss?"

"Exactly."

She left the papers on his desk. As the door closed Ari called the bishop on his mobile. He could do without being stalled by anybody's functionaries. In some ways, Bishop Grendel was a trickier proposition than Bob Cole: both were focused on the mainland, and neither would have any qualms about destroying him, if that was what it took. But when it came to the plan Ari had in mind, it wasn't obvious which way the bishop would jump. After all, belief in the Great Simulation was surely heretical? Grendel himself used to say as much, reminding Islanders in rounded episcopal tones that it was to God, not science, that they owed their creation. That had been a while ago, however; his subsequent career showed he could be a more supple theologian. Might he suggest, if necessary, that God's creative powers operated in myriad mysterious ways, including quite possibly through the Simulators themselves? Who was to say that an artificial island, and the threat to its existence, was not, in a very real sense, a test of faith? He would have to take care not to overdo it. The bishop might not need a reference from the powers that be – Ari was hazy on the actual appointment process for arch-bishops, and made a mental note to look into the matter – but he could presumably not afford to frighten the doctrinal horses too much. Ari would have to rely on the bishop's ability to navigate such theological niceties – it was the man's trade, after all. The question was: how to nudge him in the right direction?

"Morning, Binkie," he chirruped, when his call was answered. He'd be buggered if he was going to call the jumped-up mountainous old God-botherer *My Lord*. "Just a courtesy call, really."

"Jessica passed on my message, then?" The bishop's voice was surprisingly light: a tenor, not a bass, in any church choir, and a reedy one at that.

"Indeed, indeed," said Ari. "So I thought I'd let you know right away that it's no problem."

"No problem?"

"Not at all. I mean, thanks and all that, but our thinking has moved on. We *are* re-booting the borehole idea, but we're no longer looking at church sites."

Go on, willed Ari: *ask*.

But all the bishop said was, "No?"

"No."

Go on: you know you want to.

"Then . . .?"

The door of Ari's office opened, Marion in the doorway, Lucy right behind her. They stopped when they saw he was on the phone, but he beckoned them silently in.

"Oh, I really shouldn't say," he said. "We haven't gone public yet. But, as it's you: the sanctity of the confessional, and all that."

"I'm not a Catholic, Mr. Spencer."

Mr. Spencer? The pompous prick. He waved Lucy towards the chair in front of his desk. Marion pointed at her watch. He held up two fingers, knowing he'd be longer, and she left.

"Of course not, Binkie," he said. "But if you can't trust a bishop . . . ?" He paused, but Bishop Grendel did not seem to consider any response necessary. "So, if you promise not to mention it to anyone and, as I say, as a courtesy, really, given how helpful you were to Cllr King - the previous Cllr King, I mean - on the issue, I'll just say that we have a handful of possible sites in mind, but the favourite - I mean, if you were a betting man, which obviously you're not - you'd want to bung the roof repair fund on the Cathedral Close."

He hung up and turned to Lucy.

"There," he said. "Let him stick that in his thurible and smoke it."

Lucy didn't even try not to laugh. "I see responsibility hasn't changed you."

"I should hope not. You, on the other hand, you're . . ."

"Older?"

"Back. How come?"

"Diana tracked me down."

Well, that made a kind of sense. Diana had been Cora's spad – until she'd stabbed her in the back and stolen her job. There was a vacancy. And with Cora on the look out for revenge, Diana would need someone she could trust not to run off to her rival. Lucy fitted the bill – if only because Cora had already sacked her once. But what had persuaded Lucy to accept? Life on the mainland must have had its downsides, beyond poetry.

"So how did she find you?"

Lucy pantomimed offence. "I'm not that obscure. She asked my agent."

"You have an agent?"

It was hard to imagine. Even if she was any good – and he'd have to admit he wouldn't be the best judge – there surely wasn't any money in the poetry game? And twenty percent of diddly-squat was pretty much the square root of fuck all.

"And what does he think of you returning to the sticky maw of Mammon?"

"*She's* all in favour."

"Oh, yeah?"

"She thinks it has epic potential."

"Epic, eh?"

"The sea-borne wanderer returns home after years away, to put her world to rights. She mentioned Virgil."

"The Thunderbird?"

"And Homer. She thinks the Island might need a laureate one day. Well, she did when I described it to her. She hadn't actually heard of the place."

That was more convincing. This agent was obviously in it for the long term. He wondered what the going rate for poet laureates might be. He wondered what Jessica would make of the idea, and realized he had no idea. Which was the nub of his current predicament. There would always be problems, that was just life; but now, for the first time in his career, he couldn't be sure how his Leader would react. If Jacob had ever been confronted by the notion of a poet laureate he would no doubt have refused, pausing only to pour a little scorn upon poets in general and any proposed candidate in particular. Cora would have been equally adamant, but – once she stopped laughing – would have expressed herself with greater force and riper vocabulary. K would have shaken his head silently, allowing the suggestion to die with whatever dignity it could muster. But Jessica? He just didn't know. Her reaction might be equally sound: she was her father's daughter, after all; but she was also the Child. A potential wild card. She had upped and made him Chief Exec, after all, which hadn't been in the plan. Not his plan, anyway. Such uncertainty was a flaw in his confidence, a narrow crack through which trickled a cold fear: could he be getting things all wrong?

"Ari?"

Lucy was watching him like a small dog whose owner has inexplicably suffered a sudden stroke. He recalled the time she brought him word of Cora's hysterical reaction to Donald's Archimedes moment. And, just like that, a previously obscure detail of his plan snapped into place.

"I'm sorry," he said. "Miles away. Comes of being the new Donald."

"Oh, yeah. Congratulations."

"So I've heard."

He expected her to ask why Jessica had done it, which was what he would have wanted to know. Instead she pointed to the contraption that occupied most of his office. "So how does it work?"

Not what he expected, but it was an opening. "It's a perpetual motion machine, Lucy. The clue's in the name."

"But that's . . ."

"Impossible." He paused. It would be important to get the next step right. "And yet . . ."

"You're not telling me Donald succeeded? Even he knew that wasn't going to happen."

"Well, not Donald directly, perhaps. But . . ." *Softly, softly, catchee monkey.* "Tell me, Lucy, do you believe in Simulationism?"

"Of course not."

He nodded slowly, indicating that, naturally, that was the reply he had expected. Then he said, "But would you bet your life on it?"

"Yes. But it's hard to see why I'd have to."

"Is it? Do you remember the borehole project? All the plebiscites?"

It was like playing chess, Ari thought. He was staking out positions across the board, obliging Lucy to respond. His moves might seem random – he hoped they would – but they would slowly come together, tighter and tighter, until she'd suddenly find she had nowhere to turn.

"Of course I remember," she said. "We did little else for years."

"And you remember how bitter and divisive it all was?"

She nodded. How could she forget?

"So why do you suppose Jacob and I put ourselves through all that?"

She must know it was a trick question. But what was the trick?

She said, "Publicly, because Jacob felt he should have a mandate for such a momentous decision, which of course, he never got. Privately, because *you* wanted to keep the rest of us squabbling like hyenas round a dead gazelle."

Maintaining the tone of a patient teacher guiding a student towards a higher truth, a tone he knew was likely to annoy Lucy and so cloud her judgment, he said: "But *why*, Lucy?"

"Because it kept you in power."

"Good. But why was that important?"

"Because you're a sadist who loves dicking around with other people's heads? Because what else have you got?"

Perfect. He changed tack again. "Do you remember Cora's initial reaction?"

Lucy's burst of anger turned predictably inward, to guilt. "I remember telling you she was hysterical," she said.

"You told me she was going mad."

Lucy said nothing.

Time to toss in another distracting bauble. "Whereas," he said slowly, "she might just have been the only sane one there."

"Apart from you?"

He ignored that. "She was laughing because she thought the borehole idea was ridiculous, that Jacob was digging his own political grave. And what does a Leader naturally do when the opposition says their policy is mad?"

Lucy did not respond, so Ari answered his own question. "He doubles down. He *commits.* Because whatever he thinks of the policy itself, it drives a wedge between him and the opposition that voters can see."

"But you pushed the drilling project for years."

"Did I, though?"

"I heard you. Heard Jacob, anyway, reading out words you must have written."

"And yet . . . have we drilled anywhere?"

He sat back, letting that sink in. They had not drilled anywhere: she would infer, however, that had he really put his mind to it, *of course* the project would have been achieved. She would: he was relying on it. These things should not be said aloud, at least not by him.

She said, "You sabotaged it?"

Precisely the sort of thing that shouldn't be said aloud. He appealed to their common experience: "Lucy, Lucy. When you worked for Cora Klamm did you strive to make sure *all* her ideas came to fruition? Did you commit yourself to them equally, without discrimination?" If she had, she wouldn't admit it. No one in their line of work would admit to not being smarter than their boss.

"I was . . . determined to stop him." He paused again. "I was determined," he repeated more quietly, almost whispering, forcing Lucy to lean across the desk, to come closer, "because Cora was right, even if she didn't know why. Because Donald's borehole idea *was* insane. It still is. And do you know why, Lucy?"

Lucy, hanging now on every word, shook her head.

"Because the Simulationists are right."

He sat back.

"But . . ."

"The Island's a boat, Lucy. There are not, so to speak, rocks all the way down, any more than there are turtles. If we drill far enough we won't hit magma, we'll knock a bloody great hole in the hull and the Island will sink. It will go down with all hands. I couldn't let that happen."

"But the Island *is* sinking."

"The sea is rising, Lucy. There's a difference."

"We're not floating, though, are we?"

Which was exactly what he hoped she'd say. "We're not. And why? Because, in their limited wisdom, the Simulators anchored the Island in place. Think about it, Lucy. If they hadn't, we could have drifted off anywhere."

"I don't know."

"The fact is, with the storms we've been having, the Island *has* moved. The cables must be as thick as your thigh, and the anchors the size of a bus, but they've started to drag. We're at least a couple of degrees east of where we used to be."

Lucy looked doubtful. Of course she did: he'd turned her world upside down. But after a while she said, "Who knows?"

Yes, he thought. *Yes.*

"K, and I. And now you."

"K?"

To a lesser man, her yelp might have suggested that he'd lost her. That he'd been reeling her in too quickly, and she had slipped the hook. But Ari knew the hook had merely sunk a little deeper.

"K knew, because he was one of them. He was the lead researcher: that's why he came here. And K told me; and now he's dead."

"Why you? Why not Cora?"

"You've worked for Cora." He didn't say: *would you entrust knowledge this dangerous to someone as barking mad as Cora Klamm?* He didn't have to.

"But she was his wife."

He simply allowed that to curdle. They were both single, but the thought of Cora as a spouse was sufficient. And yet, Ari thought, K had married her. If that had been dedication to research, the man deserved a Nobel Prize.

"I know it's hard to take in, but it's true."

"It sounds like something you'd hear in the pub."

"Sometimes the man or woman in the pub knows more than we like to think."

Or in the cemetery, he thought, waiting.

"So what do we do?"

And there it was. Just like that. He was on his way.

"With Cora's help – with your help, Lucy, though neither of you knew it at the time – I fought Jacob to a standstill. A stalemate. But it couldn't hold. Now Jessica is Leader and determined to do something to save the Island." He skipped over his own role in making sure the standstill hadn't held, in bringing Jessica to power: best not to let Lucy dwell on that. "She wants to drill in the Cathedral Close."

"But that's . . ."

"Just far enough above the current water line to work. It would make sense – if drilling anywhere made sense."

"But it would cause outrage. Just when she's promised an inquiry. The tenth anniversary? The victims' families would be furious."

"There is that," Ari said, as if he hadn't already thought of it. "Which makes this all the more important."

"Makes what important?"

"Our understanding. Jessica won't listen to me on this – I'm too tarred with the old divisions and delays. She'll think I'm using the

115

inquiry just to slow her down the way I did her father. That's what she thinks. You know, it occurs to me now, that might be why she shoved me in here." He gestured at the office around them, at Donald's machine. "Keep me busy, keep me out of the way. But if she goes ahead, to quote your old boss: *We're all going to fucking drown.*"

"Hashtag?"

Ari nodded again. "It's just a shame Cora isn't leading the opposition any more."

"But Diana is."

"Exactly, Lucy."

"You want me to tell her, because you can't?"

"I'm the Chief Executive," he said, pained innocence incarnate: he could get used to this. "It's not my place to go behind the Leader's back."

"You want Diana to tell everyone the Simulators are right? That if we drill a hole we'll sink the Island?"

"Yes. But more than that."

"That's not enough?"

"She mustn't sound like she's just getting in the way. You've heard of Noah, I take it?"

"Noah two-by-two Noah?"

"The mistake Noah made was not thinking about propulsion, or steering. Leastways, the Bible doesn't mention it. The ark drifted, until it ran aground. Surely we can do better than that?"

Lucy was looking doubtful again.

"Diana needs a positive message," he explained. "She has to say the real way to save the Island is to cut the cables, and build a sail."

"A *sail?*"

"A sail, Lucy. Once we're floating, we can choose which way to go. Take control of our destiny for the first time since the Great Simulation itself."

What was in it for Diana? A line of attack that could out-messiah the Child while drawing a line between herself and Cora. Which cut both ways. If Diana could be nudged to push a Simulation line, he could rely on Cora to cleave to the science, hoping to create a rift in their party and a route back to its leadership. It was conceivable K's death might have led Cora to reconsider her priorities, but the odds were vanishingly small. She had lost, and she would want revenge. If Diana supported diving to cut the cables, Cora would demand drilling with equal or greater ferocity – especially if she thought doing so would undermine him. Diana had humiliated her within their party, but Ari's much older treachery had cost her the leadership of the Island. She would not have forgotten that. Which was fair enough. He would never have survived the game if he'd resented the other players' animosity: the important thing was to play upon it, just as one might exploit another's ambition, or idealism. He would work out what made Jessica tick in time; meanwhile, he could see Lucy had bought his proposition. She was sitting straighter, her hands curled into fists. In her eyes gleamed the light of renewed dedication. She had returned; she would save the Island. She would help take back control. And she'd probably write a poem about it.

Sometimes Ari loved his job. His real job.

ELEVEN

IT WAS FULLY, utterly dark – the seaward sky a moonless, starless void – long before Denis sobered up. Being February, and with the wind shifting to the north, it was also very cold. And lonely.

True, there had been crowds of onlookers and reporters, earlier. But, grateful for his timing, the reporters had met their deadlines – pieces filed for the evening editions, reports to camera in the can for the six o'clock news – and left, their day's work done: hot drinks or cold beer awaited, according to taste. The onlookers lasted little longer. Once everybody had discovered what everybody else was there to see; once those within earshot had called out their questions – and received no reply – or hurled their insults, to equally unsatisfactory effect; once the younger and more reckless among them had tested whether it was true that sticks and stones might succeed where mere words had failed, and had been restrained by the responsible adults present; once, that is, there seemed no prospect of further amusement or enlightenment, the crowd had thinned, dispersed and finally disappeared like rabbits beneath the silent passing shadow of a hawk.

He was alone.

And, left alone, Denis's thoughts turned not to the object of his passion, as might have been expected in a romantic hero, but to the variable relationship between the sun, the moon, the earth and the vast body of water covering four-fifths of its surface, and to the consequent semi-diurnal rise and fall of that body of water in relation to a fixed point such as a bridge, to which a man might, for reasons thus far undisclosed to the multitude, have attached himself: in short, to the tides, to which he'd never before given much thought. Or any thought, really. As the afternoon drained into evening and the water lapped inexorably higher, he discovered it was one of those times in the year when the moon, positioned directly behind the earth, not only gives no light, but adds its gravitational pull to that of the sun, raising a spring tide that would eventually wash around his knees. By six o'clock – just as curious Islanders were busy spotting their neighbours on the TV news and wondering what on earth a man like Denis Klamm (child of not one, but *two* previous Leaders) thought he was up to – by six, or six-thirty at the latest, the initial agony had passed and he could no longer feel his toes. By eight o'clock he was numb from the shins down. It would be another six hours and thirteen minutes – a little after two in the morning – before the moon and sun would drag the water back to its lowest level, giving his feet a chance to drip dry and so begin the entire excruciating process all over again. By the time those Islanders blessed with homes and sufficient income tucked into a healthy breakfast, he would be up to his knees in it again. The respite would have been all too brief. Trench foot seemed likely; gangrene and double amputation a distinct possibility. From the waist up, meanwhile, matters were little better. A harsh wind blowing straight from the remnants of the polar ice sought out the slightest chinks in Denis's ill-fitting wardrobe. Having pinioned, outstretched arms increased the size and number of such chinks; it also, after the first hour or two, produced an unanticipated pain in his shoulders, elbows and wrists that could not have been more severe, he felt sure, had his limbs been torn from their sockets by wild horses startled into hoofing it for the hills by the largest, loudest starting gun imaginable.

Sober, he was feeling rather sorry for himself.

TWELVE

IF DENIS WAS sober, his mother was not, although the casual observer would never have been able to tell. Cora absorbed alcohol the way a shark absorbs oxygen: it was simply part of the medium through which she swam; to stop drinking would be to die. Neither was she prone to self-pity, a sentiment she regarded as the curse of mewling adolescents, with no place in the mental life of rational adults.

She had left the restaurant in the highest of spirits, rejecting Jacob's offer to pay the bill. Lunch had been her suggestion, she pointed out; besides, she'd consumed five times what he had. The cost – and she'd even added a generous tip – had been worth it just to see the look on Jacob's face when she made that crack about a double wedding. Priceless. The odd thing was that he'd tried to be a gent about it. Something must have changed in the brief time he'd been out of power. The old Jacob would have been much blunter. Even so, he couldn't quite hide the panic in his eyes. There had been more desperation than gallantry in the way he'd said he'd have that brandy, after all. Not to mention the way he swallowed it and immediately ordered another. It had all been good clean fun, she thought, if not exactly flattering. More to the point, it had the benefit of making a match between Denis and Jessica appear less outlandish by comparison. Because she hadn't been joking about that.

It was nearly six by the time they finally left, pitch dark and freezing cold. He offered to walk her home – something really must have come over him – but she asked if he wasn't scared she might invite him in for coffee, at which point he recalled an engagement that had previously slipped his mind. She told him to give her regards to Jessica. She hoped they would meet again soon. That should keep the old bastard on his toes, she thought, as she stomped away, leaving Jacob looking shell-shocked on the kerb.

She headed back towards the Cathedral and home, spearing litter with her walking stick as she went, just to keep her eye in. She thought with pleasure about Denis, exposed to the weather. A night in the cold would do him a world of good. It might make the little pillock pleased to see his mother for once, not to mention a tad more open to suggestion. Because, although he didn't know it, Denis was now the key piece in a plan taking shape in Cora's mind. If he'd only do as he was told.

There seemed to be more litter today than usual. Cellophane, handwritten notes, leaves and ragged flower petals all swirled around her feet in the blustery wind, pressing against her shins like over-eager puppies. She looked up. Cathedral Close was spared the worst of the north wind by the bulk of the Castle, looming atop the hill. On the southern side of the Close, outside Houghton Tower, an informal memorial to those killed still lingered on, ten years after the event. Someone - not the Authority, which periodically cleared away all such traces of unpleasantness - had continued to bring fresh flowers, and to attach more or less ephemeral signs to the fencing around the developers' cherry trees, the trunks of which had over the decade grown thick and sturdy, as nobbled and creased as an elephant's legs. The tenth anniversary was approaching: that would explain the greater volume of trash. She had better prepare a press release. Or - no. That would be Diana Ford-Marling's job. For now.

Grief was a funny thing. That morning she had dressed all in black, for the benefit of the media - or, more precisely, her image in the media: black would claw back some of the twenty pounds the cameras would add. She wasn't really a mourning person. Ha, ha. K was dead at last, and now buried: he'd had it coming. We all do, but K longer than most. There'd be no flowers on his grave in ten years' time. In ten days, come to that, if it were left to her.

Funny? Hilarious.

Back in the flat she poured herself a gin and tonic - it would clear the palate after that sickly Spanish brandy - and looked for the remote. Why did nothing ever stay where it was put? Inanimate objects had no right to wander the face of the earth the way they did. It would be Denis's fault. He'd have watched TV when she went to bed last night and put it somewhere stupid because he was an idiot. He'd have fallen asleep in front of a shopping channel or some late-night porn and the remote would be stuffed down the back of the sofa. It wasn't. It was on the kitchen counter underneath her coat - what kind of an idiot would have put it there?

She turned on the TV and caught the end of the six o'clock news. "And finally" - there he was, the quirky human story intended to restore the viewers' will to live after the real news has relentlessly banged home just why there is so little point. She was pleased to see them playing up the mystery: there were theories galore as to what he might be up to, but nobody knew for sure. In the vox pops, a woman with a baby strapped to her chest said he was very brave, whatever he was doing, while a man in a cap and a tweed suit said it was a lot of fuss about nothing: "Climate can't change fast enough as far as I'm concerned." A second man with a thick accent said something about love. Another said Denis was a modern day King Cnut proving you can't hold back the tide. "It's all to do with the immigrants, isn't it?" "Well there you have it," the female reporter in a padded coat said, straight to camera. "At the end of the day only Denis Klamm knows what he's doing here. And he isn't saying."

Good lad, thought Cora, for the first time in many years. Just keep it up.

She switched off the TV, picked a battered, well-read copy of *The Idiot* off the shelf and settled down for a quiet evening at home. The book was one of a handful of K's that had survived the move to Houghton Tower. He had read and re-read Dostoyevsky, but when did she ever have the time for Russian novels? Well, now she had more time than she wanted. Prince Myshkin had barely returned to St Petersburg, however, when Cora fell asleep, book on her chest, empty glass in hand.

She was woken minutes later by a noise like an electric eel strapped to a defibrillator. Her mobile was vibrating its way across the polished granite surface of the kitchen counter. With an agility that would have surprised any witness to her earlier stick-assisted widow's gait, she launched herself from her armchair and caught the phone just as it toppled off the counter but before it hit the tiled floor and shattered the way her last one had – really, who made these stupid things? – but not before the call diverted to voicemail.

Diana Ford-Marling, the unbroken screen alerted her. Diana Ford-fucking-Marling. What on earth did *she* want?

The message was brief. Apparently Diana wanted Cora to call her. Urgently. Well, fuck that. What Cora wanted was another drink, and maybe something more to eat. It had been a couple of hours since lunch, and she'd been asleep, however briefly, which always made her hungry. She poured another gin, and stood before the open fridge, weighing her options. Which were basically wine, pesto, jam or a ready-made fish pie that claimed it could not be microwaved. (So why the fuck had she bought it?) By the time she'd managed to set the temperature on the oven she had never used, curiosity got the better of her. And by the time she'd finished her return call, she was delighted that it had. What on earth could Diana have been thinking? *An issue so vital and so urgent they must set aside their differences?* Cora spat gin across the kitchen when she heard that. To think she'd once employed the woman (not to mention lost a party to her). Could Diana Ford-Marling really be that stupid? It was as if she were holding out a gift. All Cora had to do was tug the ribbon and it would all be hers.

A sail? A fucking *sail!*

It was beautiful. It was almost too easy. Sure, she wanted revenge; she wanted her party back; but she'd expected to have to *work* for it, at least. Diana's schoolgirl amateurism might almost take the fun out of destroying her. Almost.

Cora stopped herself. Surely there had to be a catch? Could Diana *really* be that stupid? She went back over the conversation in her mind, replaying everything Diana had said.

Cables? A sail?

Before hanging up they'd agreed that Diana would phone the bishop while Cora phoned Bob Cole.

So: could Diana be that stupid? Cora was forced to conclude that yes, improbable as it seemed, she really could. And if she were wrong? If Diana had laid some trap she hadn't spotted? Well, then, they'd see, wouldn't they? Cora knew a thing or two about making mistakes and clawing her way out again.

She spotted the book on the floor: it must have fallen when she'd scrambled to her feet. She picked it up. Who was the idiot now? Well, Denis, obviously, but Diana was running him a close second. Now they'd both, in a favourite phrase, become *useful idiots*. K had once told her that although it was generally attributed to Lenin, the phrase was in fact the invention of Cold War anti-communists. But she also knew that Lenin *had* attributed to Napoleon (albeit doubtfully) the motto *On s'engage, et puis on voit*. Well, she was about to commit to the fray; and then, she thought, they'd see. Then they'd fucking see, she added, aloud.

Before calling Commander Cole she rang a TV producer, who took some persuading. It would be yesterday's news, he said. Unless Denis actually drowned, where was the story?

"You don't want to know why he's doing it?"

"Not really."

"You don't want to be there when I save the Island?"

"Is that what you're going to do?"

"Trust me," she said, and the producer, who was long enough in the tooth to remember when Cora had actually been Leader, laughed. But he'd be there, she knew, or at least his telegenic reporter and her camera crew would. And once word got out - as she would make sure it did - that TV was on the way, the rest would cluster round like flies on shit. Unsure if this made her or Denis the turd in this analogy, she corrected herself. They'd be there in the morning, waiting for her, like wasps all over a cream tea. She just hoped Denis would keep his mouth shut and not blow it all before she arrived.

On s'engage, she thought, dialling Bob Cole's number, *et puit on* bloody well *voit*. He'd been appointed by Jacob King, and had never served directly under her, but their paths had crossed from time to time. She wondered if his phone would recognize her number, and, if so, whether he would answer it now. He did.

"What-ho, you old poof."

If Bob Cole had recognized her number, he probably wouldn't have answered. And that, he concluded once the call was over, would have been a big mistake. He'd never liked Cora. He suspected that, beneath her crude, no-nonsense persona there beat a truly vicious and self-seeking heart of ice; he suspected that, if the decision had been hers, he would never have got the job, and that her jokey, you-know-I-don't-mean-it-really homophobia would have had a lot to do with it. But if what she had just told him were true (and she'd assured him that she had it straight from the horse's mouth) and if what she had suggested they both might do – and not do – in consequence were to pay off as handsomely as it seemed possible they might, then it would be as well to answer Cora's calls as often as she cared to make them.

In her immaculate kitchen, meanwhile, Cora switched off her phone. She was done for the evening. An insistent pinging from the brand new oven announced that, finally, her second pie of the day was ready. A glass of wine to go with that, perhaps?

THIRTEEN

THIS PART OF the job, though, he could do without. Scrutiny Committee. Started at seven and finished when it finished. There was supposed to be a guillotine at ten – introduced after some ancient councillor died in the chair at two in the morning, ostensibly of a heart attack but more probably of boredom – but the committee could always vote to extend the pain in half hour blocks: a particular form of torture, Ari often thought, like water-boarding, in which false hope and nagging doubt played constantly on the minds of those forced to attend. As a spad, he'd always had a degree of freedom to pick and choose the meetings he attended, and how late he stayed. Now, he'd be there till the bitter end. Still, he wouldn't allow himself to be downcast. His success with Lucy, and the anticipation of reporting to Jessica that the solution to her problems was in hand, had carried him through the afternoon and would not fail him now. There was only one item on tonight's agenda: surely there was a limit to how long even this gaggle of throwbacks could string it out?

First, however, the chair wanted to welcome the new Chief Executive to his post with "Just a few words" – which, as ever, proved more than a few too many. Cllr Ford-Marling responded on behalf of the opposition: she was fulsome in her praise of Ari's qualities. The choice, she conceded, had been unusual, but amply justified by his strategic insight and life-long commitment to the Island. Those councillors who had, over the years, been on the rougher end of Ari's previous manoeuvres looked surprised, then put Diana's enthusiasm down to her own past history as a spad. Ari, however, knew what it meant. It meant Lucy had already spoken to her, that Diana had bought the package. Which only increased his impatience to see Jessica: more than a little gloating would be justified.

The committee proceeded to review a proposal to replace lost housing with shipping containers on what used to be the golf course. Everyone knew it was a stopgap: the golf course would itself be under water in a year or two. The lead member for finance asked if the Authority could afford it. Sally must have got to him. Had there ever been a time when Sally or her predecessors had not muttered darkly about the state of the Authority's budget? And yet, here they still were: not bankrupt. For light relief, he began to check messages and newsfeeds on his tablet while pretending to scroll through the committee papers, until he hit the words: BREAKING: FORMER LEADER BACKS SON'S BRIDGE PROTEST:

Former Leader Cora Klamm will tomorrow (Tuesday) visit the footbridge to which her son Denis has chained himself. While Denis has kept silent – prompting widespread speculation about his motives – his mother is expected to say that he has "put his life on the line to save the Island," and that "as a mother" she could not be more proud.

"Mr. Spencer? Is that correct?"

Back in the committee room, the chair was pressing for a view.

In a blistering attack on her successor Jacob King – and a direct challenge to new Leader, Jessica King – Cora Klamm will claim: "for far too long, the Authority has shuffled deckchairs while our Island sinks." She is expected to say that time is running out and

"Yes, of course," Ari said.

"Are you sure?"

He nodded.

"It's just," said one of the other councillors, "it's a bit of a change of direction."

Oh, shit. What had he just endorsed? He'd spotted nothing new in the reports he'd flicked through, but he'd better make sure. Reluctantly, he said, "Perhaps Peter could just run us through it one more time?"

Even then, he didn't really listen, not after the first few words.

It looked as though Cora was getting her retaliation in before Diana even got off the starting block.

Did that matter? Maybe not. It could work just as well this way round – as long as Cora hadn't gone Simulationist herself. He scanned the rest of the short article. Not for the first time, he blessed the debased journalistic ethics that made competitive editors happy – desperate, even – to print politicians' press releases about what might happen, rather than waiting to report what did. *The Authority must stop talking and start acting before her son drowned*, he read. But nowhere did Cora say what should actually be done. Which was no great surprise: she would save that for tomorrow. For now, all she wanted was to ratchet up the temperature, which was fine by Ari. He wondered if she might also be positioning Denis, saviour of the Island, as a potential future leader. With ample parental guidance, of course, although even that seemed a little too selfless for Cora.

The chair was looking at him again. "Is that a no?"

"No."

"No? Or no, it's not a no?"

Ari had no idea, either. "I think perhaps we should come back to this," he said at last, "when we have a proper risk assessment and a comms strategy, don't you, Chair?"

Peter certainly didn't, that much was obvious, but he was hardly going to disagree publicly when Ari was already implying that he hadn't done his job. Which was unfair, Ari reflected, but such was life. He'd find another way to make it up to Peter. In the meantime, at least it brought the meeting to an early close.

❧

Back on the seventh floor, Marion was still at her desk.

"How come you're still here?"

"The Leader called, boss. She wants to speak to you."

His heart sank. Keen as he was to speak to Jessica – and confident of his success when he got the chance – he didn't want to start off on the wrong foot. With so many plates spinning, he had to weave between them with care. Upsetting Jessica unnecessarily would not help.

"Why didn't she call my mobile? Why didn't you?"

Marion looked as if she'd just noticed he was wearing spats and clown shoes. "Because she said not to disturb you, boss. But to ask you, and I quote, to pop up as soon as you get back."

"When was this?"

"An hour ago." Marion looked up at the clock on the wall. "Hour-and-a-half."

That wasn't great. He said nothing for a while.

Marion said, "But she . . ."

"I know. It's not your fault. Another time, though? Text me."

It really wasn't Marion's fault. They were all going to have to get used to Jessica. She was not her father, after all.

He took the lift. It was only one floor, but he needed to breathe, slowly. Calmly. Jules – also, unbelievably, still at his desk: didn't these people have homes to go to? – ostentatiously checked his watch as Ari entered.

"Ha bloody ha."

Jules waved him straight through into the Leader's office.

She was standing by the window again, and did not move towards the sofas when he entered. "Good meeting?"

"Fine thanks. Nothing special. The prefab project's on hold."

There, he thought: get that in before it looks like I've got anything to hide. But Jessica had other things on her mind.

"I had another call from the bishop this afternoon."

That was quick, Ari thought. "That's a coincidence," he said. "So did I."

"He says *you* rang *him*."

"Technically, yes, but . . ."

"Ari, what's going on?"

He looked past her for a moment, out of the window. In the vast blackness beyond their own reflections he could just make out the lights of a large boat near the horizon. He wondered where it had come from, where it was going.

He said, "I told him . . ." – this was it, the moment of truth, or something like it – "I hinted that we're going to drill in the Cathedral Close."

"I know. He made that very clear. What I want to know is: *why?*"

"Because I knew it would wind him up."

"And?"

"And I anticipated he might call Diana. Or she might call him."

The look on Jessica's face suggested this did not explain very much, which was fair enough: this way she'd enjoy it all the more when he got to the point.

"Because I'd already got Lucy to warm her up to the idea you were keen to get on and drill, and that we had to find a way to stop you."

"To stop *me?*"

He nodded. He was walking a tightrope. Which was part of the fun.

"And, even supposing it had been my idea," Jessica said, with exaggerated patience, "and even supposing that were your job, why would you want to stop me?"

"Because drilling anywhere would sink the Island and drown us all. Cathedral Close was just the icing on the cake. To annoy the bishop."

"*Why*, Ari?"

"Because we want him siding with Diana."

Jessica snorted. Was he pushing his luck a bit too far? She spoke slowly, as if to a young child. Or an idiot. "Why would it sink the Island, Ari?"

"Because it would puncture the hull the Simulators built, and we wouldn't be able to bail out fast enough."

"The Simulators?"

"Who else?"

"And she *believed* you?"

"I think so. Not that it really matters. What matters is that it gives her a line of attack. She'll say we need to stop drilling and

130

start diving down to cut the anchor cables. So we can float on the rising seas – and be free."

Jessica thought about that for a moment: thought, Ari sensed, like a politician at last. She said, "So we can say she's spouting hysterical nonsense?"

"No."

"No?"

"So that Cora Klamm – who is already working out how to capitalize on the fact that her half-wit son has chained himself to the footbridge, and is more than ever determined to get her revenge on Diana now that K is dead – so that Cora puts two and two together, declares herself all for solving the climate emergency before it drowns the sainted Denis, swears Diana is spouting hysterical nonsense, as you put it, and demands we begin drilling immediately. Binkie Grendel chucks his lot in with Diana, because – he says – drilling in the Cathedral Close before the inquiry even takes place would desecrate the memory of the dead; but campaigning with the opposition lets us rule him out of chairing the inquiry. So we revert to Plan A: I chair it. I land whatever blame there is to be landed fairly and squarely on Bob Cole, who fucks off to play golf whether he likes it or not. You, meanwhile, the new Leader untainted with historical political baggage, you rise above it all, serenely weighing the arguments and listening to the people's views. Your shit smells of roses, and everybody's happy."

It was perfect. K would have been proud. He had a fleeting mental image of Donald's machine ticking slowly away, a floor below, ticking not quite silently, but relentlessly on. It would fail one day, as no doubt would he, but for now it was as close to perfection as any human artefact could be.

Jessica said, "Happy?"

"Well, you're happy. They're all fighting like rats in a sack. Again. It's perfect."

She said, her voice still even, giving nothing away: "Okay."

Okay? Was that all? It was more than okay. But Jessica continued:

"Perhaps we could have a referendum?"

A bit retrograde, but maybe. It had worked well enough before.

"Dive or Drill?" she said.

There was something in that. It had a ring to it. Being around the Castle all these years, something must have rubbed off on her.

She said, "We could ask people to vote on Simulationism – once and for all – a vote on whether the Island is real or not."

Now *that*, he thought, was genius.

He said so.

But Jessica hadn't finished. "And in the meantime," she said, "the Island will continue to crumble away, there'll be more and more people sleeping in fewer and fewer doorways, and the man really responsible for Angela Warner and half a dozen others getting their heads staved in still won't be held accountable."

Well, yes, Ari thought. That was rather the point. Part of it. She really wasn't her father's daughter, after all.

"You win some, you lose some?" he said hopefully, knowing it was too late.

"Try again, Ari. You've got twenty-four hours."

FOURTEEN

IT WAS A much-chastened Denis, then, with only the faintest
recollection of what he was doing or why, who – as the last vestiges
of alcoholic courage drained like the turning tide from his veins
and the Island's remaining pubs called time – heard with relief the
approach of footsteps and a soft, familiar voice close behind him
say:

"You want chips? Islanders eat many chips, I think."

Yes, he wanted chips. And brandy. He pictured a shaggy St
Bernard bearing a barrel the size of an actual barrel. But more than
anything, he wanted not to be alone. Even if it meant spending more
time with the man who'd stolen his credit card.

"I get chips," Pavel said. "Also card. This afternoon, I forget.
Sorry for misunderstanding."

A hand appeared from behind and reached across Denis's chest,
slipping his credit card into the breast pocket of his father's jacket.
Another hand appeared over the opposite shoulder, holding a greasy
potato chip in front of his mouth. This hand was slimmer, the nails
painted a shade of dayglo orange so bright it hurt his eyes.

"I bring Eva, also."

"Pleased to meet you, Eva," said Denis, over his shoulder, feeling
he had never spoken a truer word. "I'm Denis."

"We know," she said. "Denis Klamm. We saw the news." She
fed him another chip, and then a third. "So, Denis. What are you
doing here?"

"I tell her," Pavel said, "is for love."

Eva ate a chip herself, then fed another to Denis. "Pavel is a
romantic. Which can be nice, I suppose, in a poet. But not everyone

thinks that way. Some people think you're insane." Another chip. "Why didn't you tell the reporters what you're up to?"

The water lapped around his ankles; the pain in his shins and calves was growing as the circulation returned to numb flesh; the agony in his shoulders and elbows, meanwhile, continued unabated. All the same, Denis found his condition eased a little by warm food and company. Why hadn't he spoken to the reporters? In all honesty, he could barely remember. There had been a napkin involved. A boat. An SOS. It seemed ridiculous. His own best friend, had Denis possessed such a thing, would never have cited self-awareness as his strongest suit. Yet now he glimpsed from afar, as if through fog, a painful recollection of embarrassment. It had been a novel sensation. The more the drink wore off, the closer the gloom of an incipient hangover approached, the more ridiculous his position had seemed. It wasn't that he no longer wanted to attract Jessica's attention – he wanted it more than ever, now, or all this *pain* would have been for nothing – it was just that, having ensured maximum publicity for anything he might say, anything he did say publicly would sound ridiculous; which would not help. He really hadn't thought this through, had he? Watching the crowd gather and the reporters arrive, however, he had rationalized his own timidity: silence would be mysterious. Intriguing. People would go home and discuss what he was up to. That would ratchet up their curiosity and maximize the impact of his gesture, whatever it might be. He'd worry about that later, when he had a bit of peace and quiet. By the time quiet arrived, however, the pain had set in too, and he'd been unable to think about anything at all.

He said, "What are they saying on TV?"

"Is love," said Pavel. "That's why you choose here. The bridge with all locks."

"One woman said that," said Eva. "A guy with a beard said it was a crisis of masculinity. A posh woman with a voice like a dental hygienist's drill thought it was a grief thing, about your father: an atavistic attempt to reconnect with the chthonic rituals of the past.

Something like that. But mostly they're saying it's a climate protest or you're nuts. Could be both, of course. Or more. All of the above. Sorry about your father, by the way."

"Thanks."

"I always liked the old guy."

From Eva's voice, he didn't think she could be old enough to remember K in office. He said, "I didn't."

He had bemoaned his father – and his mother – to plenty of young women before. He'd told them, hesitantly and in a low voice, working gradually up via clipped bitterness to a barely restrained fury, just how hard it had been growing up the son of politicians who had a million things to think about – including booze and Dostoyevsky – before they ever thought of him. He'd never bothered to ask himself if it were true. It was just a way to get young women into bed. This was different. Something about Eva – about Pavel and Eva – seemed to make it easier to tell the truth. Perhaps it was that he couldn't see them, chained here facing out to the uninterrupted blackness of the sea. Or maybe it was the overwhelming pain. Whatever.

He said, "It was – is – love."

Pavel hooted and clapped his hands. "I tell you so!"

"Who's the lucky lady?" said Eva. "Assuming it's a lady?"

"Jessica," he said, aloud, for the first time. It was that simple.

"Jessica King?"

"Yes." A politician, he thought. With a million things to think about.

Eva whistled.

"Ridiculous, isn't it?" Denis said.

"Is beautiful!" Pavel whooped. "Is Romeo and Juliet."

"Steady on," said Eva. "She's not fourteen."

"Klamms and Kings: Montagues and Capulets!"

"More like Olivia and Malvolio."

Denis hadn't paid much attention to Shakespeare at school, but suspected this wasn't a compliment. Normally, it would have bothered him – both the insult and the not knowing – but in his present penitential mood he felt it was probably fair comment, whatever the comment was.

"I wanted to get her attention."

"Well," said Eva, passing him the last chip in the bag, "you've done that. She'll have been briefed already. So what's your next move?"

Which, of course, was where Denis's plan crumbled. Now he had Jessica's attention what could he do that wouldn't make her despise him?

"He proposes!" said Pavel. "When cameras come back. He ask: marry me? On TV."

"He can't do that."

"Why not?"

"She's right, Pavel. I can't do that."

"Is romantic!"

"It's abusive," said Eva. "There's nothing attractive about a man you don't know declaring undying love in public. He'd look like a stalker."

"I declared love for you."

"Yes, and what did I do?"

"You slapped me in face."

"Punched, Pavel. I *punched* you in the face."

"But then you love me."

"Like a brother, Pavel. Remember?"

To Denis she said, "You see what I have to put up with?"

He didn't, not really. The nature of their relationship was not at all obvious. But it also wasn't his problem.

"So what do I do?" he said. It wasn't a question he'd asked anyone – certainly not a woman – in years. Not honestly. Not because he wanted to know what they thought.

She said, "You have to make it not all about you."

"I've chained myself to a bridge. How can it not be about me?"

"As I understand it, Pavel chained you to the bridge because you couldn't do it yourself."

"Well, yes. But it's still me here getting hypothermia."

"But for something bigger than yourself."

"Is love," Pavel said.

"Not love, Pavel. It's . . . well, it's obvious, isn't it?"

Not to Pavel, it wasn't. And not to Denis, either, for whom the concept of something larger than himself was still proving rather difficult to grasp.

"Most people who don't think you're mad think you're protesting about climate change," Eva continued. "So let's run with that."

"What do I care about the climate?"

"Honestly? You can't tell me it wasn't in your mind when you picked this gesture? Exposing yourself to the rising waters?"

A napkin. A heart. Arseholes.

"There was a lot on my mind at the time. But it was mostly alcohol."

"And Jessica," said Pavel.

"And Jessica."

"But mostly alcohol," said Eva. "Well, sunshine, you're in the front line of the climate crisis now. Stay here long enough and it'll drown you."

Denis thought about that. It made sense. He'd never thought much about the environment before yesterday, when the harbour wasn't there. But it could work – as a gesture that wasn't just about himself. Better than lovesick pining: pining with a purpose. He liked that. He'd never taken the sea level stuff on the news seriously because he wasn't the one going to drown. Well now he was. It could be about him after all.

"I could be a figurehead," he said.

"Or prophet," Pavel said, "Like in Bible."

"The Island's Greta Whatshername."

"You're about the right height," said Eva.

Denis ignored the jibe, warming to his theme. "A lone voice in the wilderness. A one-man crusade. The wanderer returns to save the land of his birth."

"Like Prodigal Son."

"But without the fatted calf. Mum didn't exactly lay on a feast."

Eva suggested Cora might have been more concerned about her husband.

"Why? He's dead."

Eva sighed. "You might want to work on that line a bit, you know? In case you ever get to talk to Jessica."

"Right," said Denis, remembering a similar thought he'd had that morning. "Because her mother's dead, isn't she? And I could – what's the word? – empathize?" He sounded as if he were reading a menu in a foreign language for a dish he wasn't sure that he should try.

"Something like that," Eva said.

"Excellent. Are there any more chips?"

"Sorry. All gone."

"Pity. Still, soldier on. Bit of grief. Empathy. Bingo. But for the moment, I get it: concentrate on the lone voice stuff. One-man crusade, and all that. Save the Island. Save Our Souls."

"Right. Except you're not just one man."

"I'm not?"

"There're two men here. And one woman."

"We can't all be in love with Jessica."

"But we can help."

"I fetch chains," said Pavel.

Denis heard Pavel's knees crack as he stood up, followed by clanging footsteps as he walked off the iron bridge.

To Eva he said, "Why would you do this?"

"I told you, Pavel is a romantic."

"And you?"

"I'm Pavel's sister. Sort of. As far as Immigration is concerned. He's a good man, but a certain amount of lunacy goes with the territory."

Pavel clanked back onto the bridge, dragging heavy chains. Eva climbed over the rail and sat, perched on the iron ledge, a few feet to Denis' left, allowing him a glimpse of her for the first time in the orange glow of the riverbank streetlights. She was about his age, maybe a little younger, although it was hard to tell in the dim light, and not made any easier by the huge padded parka she wore with the hood pulled up, from which a wisp of blonde hair played across her face. Her legs dangling out beneath the coat suggested that she must be slim, and tall. But what did it matter? His heart was taken: and so was hers. She was here to help him. He wondered about that punch, about just what sort of sister she was to Pavel. No matter. He was not *interested*, he told himself, just . . . interested: it was only natural, wasn't it? Of course it was.

Pavel leaned over and looped two chains around Eva and fastened them to the bridge with heavy locks. "Don't do the arms!" Denis implored. But Pavel proceeded to zip-tie her wrists to the fretwork. "It's just,' Denis added a sheepishly, "it bloody hurts after a while." She smiled at him and said, "We're in this together."

"But how's Pavel going to . . ."

"I prepare," said Pavel. He moved to Denis' right and held out his arms, measuring the space he would occupy. He threaded two heavy chains and two zip-ties through the ironwork at appropriate points.

A thought struck Denis. "Before you do," he said, "any chance you could get more chips?"

"Is closed," said Pavel. He climbed over the rail, locked the chains around his chest, slotted his hands through the plastic loops and, with remarkable insouciance, grasped the ends between the thumb and third finger of each hand, and pulled them tight.

He said, "To love!"

"To love," Denis muttered, sotto voce.

"Well," said Eva. "Here we are."

⚜

Denis managed perhaps an hour's sleep, while the tide was at its lowest. The first touch of cold water on his just-thawed toes, however, woke him to the certain knowledge that the sea would continue to rise again for several hours. Only the narcotic hallucinatory joy of hypothermia could distract him from the pain to come, or from the agony that, after just long enough to imagine rest might have given some respite, was already tearing through his shoulders and elbows as if each nerve were being individually stretched, plucked, thrashed, twisted, bent and strangled, like Jimi Hendrix torturing his guitar. One of the objects of his undergraduate lust had been into heavy Sixties rock and human rights abuse: in her pursuit he had endured interminable drum solos during detailed descriptions of "enhanced interrogation techniques" in Long Kesh and Abu Ghraib. Another had preferred the baroque, and had one Easter exposed him to four hours of Johann Sebastian Bach. Only now, however, did he understand the true import of a term like "stress position", let alone the Passion of the Christ.

"Fuck!" he bellowed, shaking his head from side to side. "Fuck, fuck, FUCK!"

In the darkness, from his left, Eva said, "Are you all right?"

From his right, he heard: "Is good. I read swearing cancels pain."

"Then how come you're not screaming?"

"This?" Pavel shrugged. "This easy. In my country we say: piece of piss."

"Really?"

"No. I translate. You get picture."

Denis did, and yet he didn't. He understood Pavel's words, but not how they could be true.

"Is easy. We breathe."

"Well, I breathe, too. And right now, I have to say, it fucking hurts."

It was true. With every inhalation, the cold air burned; much worse, the weight of the chains across his chest had turned the simple rise and fall of his rib cage into the sort of endurance sport where they shoot laggards for their own relief.

"We breathe in," said Eva, softly. "And out."

"Is there any other? Fucking? Way?"

"In," said Eva softly, ". . . and out. In . . . and out."

"In," said Pavel, ". . . and out."

And in, thought Denis involuntarily, and out. And in . . . and out . . . and in time they wore down his resistance, his breathing fell into their rhythm, and their rhythm slowed, and slowed, and his slowed with it.

"And listen," Pavel whispered.

"And listen," Eva whispered.

"I'm listening," Denis said. "I hear the waves."

"Listen," said Eva, "for your heart."

If the bastard poets were to be believed, it was his fucking heart that got him into this mess. His breathing sped up and became erratic, and they had to start again.

"And listen," Eva said, when the time came, "for your heart."

And Denis did: and he heard his heart, he heard the systole and the diastole, distinct, he heard blood pushing through his veins, and pausing, and pushing on. And on, and on, and he felt nothing, he felt empty, he felt ethereal, he felt vast, he stretched effortlessly across the sea from shore to shore, horizon to horizon and he was everywhere and nowhere and nothing hurt, and nothing, and "Fuck me!" he said, "It works!" and had to start again. But that was fine, Eva said, they had all night, and that was how they spent it, the three of them, and when the water rose around their legs they felt no pain, and when it began to ebb away they felt no loss, and when the light began at last to creep across the eastern sky, they felt nothing at all.

FIFTEEN

OVERNIGHT, THE DEPRESSION that for days – since the election at least – had squatted mulishly across the northern seas with the Island at its navel, finally span lazily off towards the east, like a drunkard ambling out of the beer tent at a country show in search of a bush to piss behind, before falling apart somewhere over Siberia. In its place, a band of high pressure scrubbed away the accumulated grime of the previous week, allowing the sun, when at last it staggered blear-eyed over the horizon, to paint the cloudless sky the colour of a rare unblemished blackbird's egg. It wouldn't last long at this time of year – neither the daylight nor the fine weather – but it would be perfect while it lasted, Cora thought, gazing complacently out across the Cathedral Close where, she imagined, Diana Ford-Marling would later that morning assemble her pathetic gang of Simulationist nutters. She hoped the turnout wouldn't be too small.

Cora was up and dressed and even washed behind the ears much earlier than usual. Never a heavy sleeper – far from it – she had found since packing K off to St Julian's that taking a cup of tea back to bed, scouring the news websites, bombarding the world with scabrous tweets, and harrying her underlings by text and email, was pretty much the ideal way to spend a morning. She tried to imagine leadership before the internet, before smart phones, and couldn't: it was before her time, a concept she really could not comprehend.

This morning, however, was different. There was work to be done: arrangements to check, arms to twist, promises to redeem, radio interviews to exploit, dog whistles to be blown. All of which she could have achieved from bed – she had in the past – but which today she felt the urge to seize fully prepared, caparisoned from head to toe in shining silver armour. When Henry V (was it?) or Richard III or – no, Marc Antony, that was it – when Marc Antony cried havoc and let slip the dogs of war he didn't phone it in from under the duvet, did he? Maybe Antony wasn't the comparison she wanted – she couldn't actually remember what kind of an end he came to, even if he did get to shag Elizabeth Taylor in the movie, who as it happened some people said she, Cora, resembled, but whether that was before or after the whole business on the steps of the Capitol she wasn't quite clear, and anyway wasn't the point, which was that there's a tide in the affairs of men, and probably women – definitely women – which taken at the flood leads on to fortune. And this was it, all her political instincts screamed: this was the flood that might drown half the Island, but which would lift her, Cora Klamm, back to the pinnacle of power. And that had to be worth a decent suit and a bit of slap, now, didn't it?

She left the flat in buoyant, optimistic mood. She was not alone. She had decided to walk – without her stick – down to the shore. As she crossed Houghton Square and followed Riverside ever lower, ever closer, she could feel the electricity of a sense of common purpose among those around her: they were all heading in the same direction, all for the same reason – unaware, even those who recognized her, that they did so at her instigation. Never had she felt more Napoleonic, the fate of whole peoples, whole nations bending to her will. The whole Island, anyway. What was left of it. An image of the emperor staring out to sea from St Helena rose unbidden to mind: she crushed it. This was no moment for doubt. She was *engaging*, wasn't she? Well, then. They'd fucking well see, wouldn't they?

What she herself saw at the footbridge, however, gave her pause. There was Denis, all right, with his back to her, to the whole Island, perched on the outside of the bridge, draped in K's outsize overcoat, arms outstretched, heavy chains looped across his back. You had to hand it to the little pillock. He might be an idiot, but he wasn't doing things by halves. That wasn't the problem. The problem was that he was not alone. To his left was a blonde woman in a coat that looked like she was wearing the Michelin man; to his right a small, dark-haired man in a thin bomber jacket, who must have been as cold as fucking charity. Not that Cora cared if the little bugger froze to death, so long as it didn't interfere with her plans. Who were these interlopers? What were they doing here? More to the point, what difference did it make? The crowd was growing again, bigger than ever. And would get bigger still as word spread. As the TV cameras and reporters arrived. That was what mattered. A couple of hangers-on merely showed what pulling power Denis's stupid gesture had for stupid people. So long as all three of them kept their mouths shut, there would be no problem.

⚜

Lucy Neave was up and about early, too, although in her case it was less a matter of vaulting ambition than direct instruction from Diana Ford-Marling, who apparently never slept at all. Lucy had spent most of the night re-casting a sonnet sequence – concerning Island treasures lost to the encroaching sea – as a series of villanelles, for reasons that Diana's abrasive voice had driven completely from her mind. It had seemed a good idea at the time.

So had staying here, in the flat her father had died in, and which she – far away on the mainland – had never cleared out. One day she'd get it steam-cleaned and on the market. Right now, though, breakfast seemed like the best idea, that and warm clothes. Get your precious poetic backside down to the footbridge, darling, Diana had said; check what's going on; report back to me. I simply must know what Cora Klamm's up to; I *must* know if it's working, she'd said. Don't let her see you, she'd said. We're all on the same side here, but, you know. Just don't let her know. Wheels within wheels. Then she'd hung up. Which was all very well, Lucy thought, but how long was she supposed to hang around down there? It might

144

have stopped raining, Earth may well not have had anything to show more fair, but Lucy wasn't fooled: the beauty of the morning would be all the chillier for a sky that happened to be bright and glittering in the smokeless air. Porridge it was then. Wordsworth would doubtless have agreed. A couple of years past its sell-by date, but what was the worst that could happen to an oat flake? She pulled on jeans and a tee shirt, a flannel shirt, a jumper and a jacket over that; plus a greatcoat she found in her father's wardrobe, the sort of thing a Russian general might have worn while setting Moscow alight and hunkering down to starve out the Napoleonic horde. All topped off by a woolly hat with ear flaps and a bobble that said Prince Myshkin more than General Kutuzov.

Lucy's was a sensitive soul, and felt the cold.

⁂

Diana Ford-Marling, meanwhile, having long since downed a breakfast of kidneys, raw kale and iron filings, now flossed her teeth with razor wire and painted her lips the exact colour she imagined Jessica King's blood would look like wiped off a stiletto. She had deployed her spies and advance guards, detailed minions to chase the printers, the coach hire company and the conductor of the Island's second-best brass band, while she herself tracked down and terrorized the very radio producers whose calls she was not to know Cora Klamm had already taken. The bishop was on board, bless him; Cora seemed to have taken the bait, and would have squared Bob Cole. Nothing would go wrong. There would be plenty of people, plenty of banners, plenty of noise. The airwaves and the internet would be awash with the message: #DiveDon'tDrill.

It would have to be carefully calibrated, though. Cora might be playing it straight: she might really think they were in this fight together. It was even possible she believed in the danger of drilling, in boats and sails. Possible: but unlikely. Chances were, she'd be down at the footbridge declaring her son a martyr and demanding Cathedral

Close be dug up by lunchtime. But that was okay, too. It would be as well to know – that's why she'd sent Lucy Neave down to keep an eye on things – but whichever way Cora jumped, Diana would come out on top. If Cora supported diving, well that was Diana's campaign and it would cement her leadership of the opposition; if she supported drilling to oppose Diana, well, controversy and conflict were valuable parts of the process. You couldn't build loyalty without an enemy. And, while the ultimate enemy, of course, was little miss Jessica, the Chosen-bloody-Child, a first round skirmish with Cora Klamm would not only settle scores, cauterizing recent wounds before they had the chance to grow old, it would bind her own troops to her, seasoning them for the greater battle to come.

Diana couldn't believe her luck. Not luck, she corrected herself. Breeding. There had been Ffordes and Marlyngs at Agincourt. At Malplaquet a Ford-Marling, having lost a leg and a favourite horse to a stray cannon ball, soldiered on to trounce the Spanish. She had been in the job less than a week, and today was going to be glorious.

In his episcopal apartment overlooking the cathedral – now over-looked in turn by Houghton Tower – Binkie Grendel counted aloud each time his flail struck lacerated flesh. He struck lightly, though. The flail was itself a holy relic – having ironically once belonged to that great scourge of relics, Martin Luther himself – and must be treated with care. The practice would be frowned upon by some congregants, he knew, but for the bishop pain, however slight, however fleeting, drew Man closer to the passion of the Christ. Thus did he reconcile mortification of the flesh with the great tradition of his church: moderation in all things, even passion. Especially passion.

Commander Cole held rather different views of passion, and had no time for pain, except in the context of its legitimate use in the restraint of uncooperative wrong 'uns. Or do-gooders: he wasn't fussy. But Commander Cole was asleep; or rather, half asleep, enjoying that blissful state in which it is possible to recognize that one is dreaming, and to extend the dream: his reverie that morning was undoubtedly passionate, and certainly immoderate.

Down at the waterfront, Denis and his new friends breathed in . . . and out. And in . . . and out, oblivious to the crowd that began to gather again, having seen that there were three of them, now, to wonder aloud if this were the start of something bigger, if more and more people, perhaps, would take to chaining themselves up until there was no space left on the bridge. And even when the reporters, dragged back to a story they frankly thought they'd finished yesterday, began to ask the same questions but more pointedly and more persistently, when they called out Denis! Denis! – not knowing the names of the other two and who the hell were they? Some new extremist group? – when they tried to provoke a reaction, even then, when one of the reporters called out "Denis, what does your mother think?", they said nothing, he said nothing, Denis, but continued to breathe in . . . and out, to hear the blood rush from ventricle to ventricle within his heart, and to say nothing, not a word, until he thought he heard the other reporters pick up the question, Cora they shouted, Cora Klamm!, and then he heard, two inches from his left ear, the once-familiar hiss so close he felt the spittle on his cheek, which broke the spell, and when his mother said "That's perfect, Denis, just keep schtum," he said, "Shit. Mum," and when she said: "Hush, darling," it sounded like a threat, and he said "What . . ." and when through rigid, barely parted lips she said "Just shut the fuck up," the pain came roaring back to fill his world.

Inside the Castle, on the third floor of Block 2, Ari stared his own reflection in the eye. His face was always pale. Now stubble rimed his cheeks and chin. Incipient pouches beneath his eyes smudged grey; the eyes themselves were buried deep within his skull. He had slept little, which was not unusual. Over the course of the long insomniac night, however – at his desk, pacing the floor, slumped in an armchair with his dressing gown adrift and cold air chilling his legs – he had achieved precisely nothing, which was more than unusual: it was unprecedented. For all that the skies had cleared and the day had dawned bright and fair, he no more knew this morning what he would say to Jessica than he had last night.

He pictured her, on the eighth floor of Central Block, in the kitchen of the penthouse, grinding coffee beans and chopping an under-ripe banana into her muesli bowl. Jacob, meanwhile, still occupying the larger of the bedrooms, would be sleeping the sleep of the just, gurgling, farting, dreaming of nothing. And a floor below, in his empty office, Donald's legacy would tick on unregarded, approaching, however slowly, its inexorable end.

Ari turned away from the mirror. Among the myriad Simulationist sects, he knew, two principal schools of thought prevailed. One held that the original Simulators had lost interest decades ago, moving on, perhaps to bigger, more ambitious projects; the Islanders were cast adrift upon a rickety craft that, without maintenance, was always already falling apart. The very crumbling of the ground beneath their feet, they said, showed the incontrovertible truth of their argument. Believers of the second school, however, held that the Simulators were very much still present in their lives, although they disagreed amongst themselves about the extent and nature of the active intervention it was reasonable to expect. Were the Simulators mere observers of an experiment they had created? Or were they routinely engaged in directing the life of the Island? Was there anything the Islanders themselves could do to influence the Simulators? Praise? Entreaty? Sacrifice? Or, perhaps: good work? Was there any reward for contributing to the future success of the Island? Or sanction for not doing so? But they all believed, more or less consciously, that the Island's recent disintegration was punishment for the Islanders' collective failure to maintain their precious home. Donald would have been horrified to hear himself compared to any breed of Simulationist, Ari knew; but it was clear that in the nothing he had done that was actually not nothing, he had demonstrated his own form of active stewardship, constantly maintaining and improving the way the Island worked. Such was the price of humanity: ultimately, failure was inevitable.

Which was all very well, Ari thought, but no help at all right now. Twelve of his twenty-four hours had already passed.

"Morning, boss," said Marion, when he arrived on the seventh floor. "Bad night was it?"

Was it that obvious? And was "boss" better or worse than "Chief"? Probably.

"Have you seen the news?"

"Denis Klamm's chained to a bridge, I know."

"There's three of them now."

"One Denis was more than enough."

"Ha, ha. Boss."

"Have they said why?"

"Apparently not."

Ari let out a heavy sigh. It was not yet eight o'clock, and already things were taking on a life of their own.

"Get me Bob Cole on the phone, please. And don't take any bollocks from his PA."

"As if I would."

He went through to his own office, listening out for the faint tick of Donald's machine before he even realized what he was doing. It must be like having a pet, he thought; or a child. Standing outside its door, listening for breath. Knowing it would die eventually, but – with luck and a fair wind – not before oneself.

Marion buzzed. Commander Cole was not available.

"You mean he's still in bed?"

"Couldn't say, boss. They say he'll call when he gets in."

"Am I the only one who does a proper day's work around here? Apart from you, Marion. Obviously."

He filled time reading reports for the day's meetings. Talk about perpetual bloody motion. In the past, he'd always been able to dip in and out. Now he had to actually read most of this stuff he discovered just how much of it there was. He was relieved to be rescued from a turgid and interminable screed about digital transformation of the Parks Service – one area, he'd thought, that might have been immune to the deathly touch of techno-babble – by Marion's announcement that Commander Cole was on the line.

He picked up his phone. This was where the real work was done.

"Morning, Bob. Thanks for calling back."

"You got my message then?"

Ari played innocent. "Message?"

"About . . . golf?"

"Oh, yes. But that's not why I called."

"No?"

"It's Denis Klamm, and his two chums."

Bob said nothing.

"Forgive me if I've missed it, Bob, but you don't seem to be doing anything about it."

"We're not."

"Could I ask why?"

"Because they're not breaking any laws."

Since when had that been the issue?

"Obstructing the highway?"

"It's a footbridge, Ari. And they're on the outside. They're not obstructing anyone."

"Criminal damage?"

Bob sighed. He was obviously enjoying himself. "Half the Island's clamped padlocks to that bridge. You want me to arrest them all?"

"It's a thought."

"There's at least half a dozen that say 'Jessica'."

Which might just be coincidence, Ari thought. But might not. He pictured three people, arms outstretched, dangling over the water.

"Blasphemy?"

"You'd have to ask the bishop about that."

"Come on, Bob. I'm sure you could think of something."

"I dare say I could, but . . ."

"You're not going to?"

"Let's just say, Ari: taking your advice on operational policing matters hasn't always worked out too well, has it?"

He could hear Bob's grunt of satisfaction down the line as he landed that. So they were going to have to talk about golf after all, were they?

Apparently not: the Commander had hung up.

Ari wasn't used to people hanging up on him. But at least it told him one thing: Bob Cole was serious about not cooperating. Well, they would see about that. He'd only wanted Denis arrested to help wind up his mother – on whose combative instincts his plan relied – and to neutralize the other two while he found out who they were, and whether they mattered. It was not the end of the world, however. Leaving them in place could add a certain piquancy to the diving versus drilling debate that even now, he thought, would be kicking off for real. Because anywhere they drilled would have to be uphill from the current waterfront, or they'd never have time to do the work. Not that he was thinking of drilling just anywhere. Or anywhere at all, or . . . the plan was still a plan. Still genius. If only he could find a way to make Jessica see that. If only she would open her eyes, and start thinking like a politician. If only, if only.

If only.

Ari mouthed the words in time with Donald's machine.

Perpetuum mobile.

SIXTEEN

TODAY WOULD BE glorious, Diana repeated, threading her way through the crowd gathering in Cathedral Close. Few of them recognized her, but that was only to be expected. She'd been just four days in the job. But by the end of today, there wouldn't be an Islander who didn't know her face. A shaft of low winter sunlight sliced between Houghton Tower and a department store, glittering on the cellophane-wrapped flowers stacked around the leafless cherry trees like diamonds in a gutter. It was perfect.

She had deliberately not arrived too early. It was important to show a little faith in her newly assembled team; also, to hold herself back. It would not do for a future leader to be seen fussing about petty administrative details. She would not be the kind of politician who helped stack chairs and lay out leaflets. She had people for that now. Little people. And, look! Those little people had done her proud.

On reaching the cathedral side of the close, she found a stage already erected, complete with a twenty-foot high *#DiveDon'tDrill* backdrop and a sound system that looked as if it could rattle the Castle walls, all set behind parallel rows of interlocking metal fences. They were the type of barriers the police used to block roads and control crowds; and yet, she couldn't help noticing, there were no police. Lined up to the left of the stage, the brass band honked their instruments at will and drained spittle from the valves. The band leader tapped his baton against the music stand to little effect until the bass drum slammed hard twice – *ba-bom!* – a giant's heartbeat that brought the players and most of the people in the Close to sudden attention. The leader tapped again and a solo trombone launched into the opening plaintive wail of 'A Change is Gonna

Come' before the rest of the band kicked in behind. An unexpected choice, Diana thought: some might even say offensive. Would Sam Cooke have been a Simulationist? She shook her head, sweeping aside petty distractions. Who cared? It was perfect. A change *was* gonna – going to – come. She felt the weight of ancestry propelling her to be that change. Klamms and Kings had been in charge for far too long.

Making her way backstage she was challenged by a steward in a hi-vis tabard. Really? It was one thing for the crowd not to recognize her – yet – but her own staff? *Don't you know who I am?* Knowing grace to be a better look than petulance, however, she showed the man her Castle security pass.

He peered at it dubiously. "This isn't the Castle."

"No. But I am, as it says – just there – Diana Ford-Marling."

"And?"

This was stretching a point; but she would not succumb. She closed her eyes and hummed a few notes with the band. A change was going to come. *Noblesse oblige.* Today would be a glorious day.

Her patience was rewarded by the arrival of a puppyish young member of the press team who looked horrified to see what was going on. She scowled at the steward, who remained unimpressed but pulled back a section of the fence to let Diana through.

"I'm so sorry, Councillor," said the puppy.

"That's quite all right. Better safe than sorry. Is the bishop here?"

"Not yet."

Diana turned back to the steward. "I know you're just doing your job, young man. And I thank you. But when you see an older gentleman in a purple shirt and a white collar, do be a good fellow and let him in, won't you?"

After a brief pause, the band launched into 'We Shall Not be Moved'. Which wasn't entirely appropriate, either, Diana thought, given what she had in mind for the Island. But they weren't to know.

She ascended the stage and, from the back for now, surveyed with satisfaction the result of all her efforts. The crowd was building nicely; by the time the coaches scooping up supporters from the outlying villages arrived, she could reasonably claim to have filled the Close. She had not yet heard from Lucy, but whichever way Cora jumped her support could hardly rival this. Diana, after all, had the resources of the official opposition at her disposal. Her morning media round had gone well. To all speculation about a possible split within the opposition, she had responded with well-rehearsed self-righteousness. On this question, she had explained, honestly held differences of opinion were inevitable; the salvation of the Island was *so* much more important than party politics: as Leader of the Opposition, she would not criticize members of her own party for making their position known. But it was her responsibility, as an Islander and as *Leader* of the Opposition (she said it slowly, lingering extravagantly on the first word), to face the truth, and to challenge the Authority urgently to do what must be done. To all the questions about why she had not previously endorsed the Great Simulation, she had simply replied, "I think you'll find I have," leaving flustered interviewers and their off-air producers scrambling for examples – or better still counter-examples – and finding none. She accepted that she had not been so forthcoming with her views in the past, but that was simply because matters of faith were personal and best left out of politics wherever possible; where, however, such matters impinged directly on a question fundamental to the Island's safety – indeed, to its very existence – it was her duty, as *Leader* of the Opposition – just as it was the duty of Bishop Grendel – to make plain the truth. There: she had reinforced her position as a responsible, principled stateswoman, and had flashed her trump card: God was on her side.

Right about now, she thought, watching the coaches disgorge their passengers, God – or at least His principal representative here on the Island – should indeed be literally at her side, warming up the crowd for the main event. Where was the old fool? She retraced her steps and found him, held up at the barrier by the same steward who had earlier obstructed her. Now there was an oik who never wanted to work on the Island again. Some people you just couldn't save.

⁂

Lucy waddled seawards with all the grace her multiple layers of heavy woollen clothes allowed: like a penguin, she thought, that – after balancing an egg upon its feet throughout the winter storms – pummels its atrophied muscles and stumbles off across the ice in search of water and a decent meal. Like the penguin, she was not alone, but found herself among a growing band of pedestrians with a common, unacknowledged purpose, all heading resolutely downhill, a trickle growing steadily into a stream, merging with other tributaries, a sense of unexpressed excitement, at first barely detectable, but which swelled irresistibly until it burst out in shouts and cheers and undeniable fellow feeling the moment they caught sight of the sea, of the footbridge, and of the backs of the three brave martyrs pinioned against it. Even Lucy – here merely to observe, a spy amongst the crowd – could not help getting swept up in the moment. Here were people finally doing something to save their homeland. Not just talking, not manoeuvring for advantage, but coming together to demand – demand! – action. To insist that the drilling – delayed so long that most of them had forgotten it was ever a possibility, and resisted by many of them when it was – must now start at once.

There would be a poem in this feeling: there had to be. The people, rising like lions after slumber. Not *that* poem, obviously, which was already taken. But *a* poem, no doubt about it.

No doubt, that is, until – after she had been standing as close to the bridge as she could reach for almost an hour while the crowd continued to expand, like prose poetry, to fill the space available; then to compress, like a haiku in a bottle, pushing in upon her from all sides – Cora Klamm returned, and Lucy's residual political instincts tugged the scales from her eyes. This crowd was no spontaneous expression of popular will; and she had a job to do.

For her part, following her early morning call to arms, Cora had judged it best to withdraw from view, to allow the power of publicity to work its magic. A second breakfast seemed called for, and a spot of research. The two peasants flanking Denis might be wholly insignificant, but it never hurt to know who you were dealing with. Also, she would collect her stick, which had played so well at the funeral.

Now, a couple of hours later, Lucy watched her make a more dramatic entrance, disembarking from a large black Range Rover accompanied by two large men in black suits with curly wires behind their ears, connected – had the crowd but known it – to nothing. A flurry of excited recognition rippled towards the bridge. Cheers were followed by unnatural silence as people pushed each other back to make way, like the Red Sea parting before Moses, Lucy thought, had Moses been four foot two, thirteen stone and leaned heavily on a stick. She was shaky on the details: if the Bible ever mentioned Moses' height, it would have been in cubits, which wouldn't really help. She pictured a tall man, though, with a long beard, robes and a staff, not a stick. Or was that Gandalf? She couldn't be sure. In any case, Cora and her entourage repelled the crowd before them, which instantly reformed behind, a bubble of clear space passing through the dense press of bodies, like a magnet dragged across a field of iron filings. Did that work, Lucy wondered, as a simile? Was that how magnets worked? If it and the filings were both negatively charged? She could see the image in her head, the sheet of paper, the grey filings like shaved whiskers in a basin, but, again, was uncertain of the details. Perhaps best to leave it out? As the bubble approached, then passed, she plunged in and surfed the wave of Cora's progress, right up to the footbridge, where she would hear every word of Cora's address to the crowd; hear, too, Cora's asides to Denis and his companions.

"Hello again, darling," Cora half whispered, while facing the chanting Islanders, beaming and waving. Denis growled, but his mother ignored him.

"Good morning, Eva; good morning, Pavel."

"How do you know us?"

Still beaming, still waving, conducting the alternating chants of "Drill now! Drill now!" and "Cora! Cora!" she murmured: "There are ways of finding these things out, Pavel. You and your . . . sister are quite famous, in your own way."

The threat wrapped in her gentle tone was unmistakable. She'd put air quotes around "sister". Some asylum seekers were more welcome here than others. Pavel swallowed, but persisted. "You take Denis to his love?"

"Oh, no. I think it would be so much better if we brought the fair Jessica down here, don't you? To witness Denis's heroism at first hand. As I have."

At the sound of his own name, Denis, like the invalid at Bethesda ordered to shoulder his mattress and hop it, miraculously revived. "That's okay," he said breezily. "We've made our point. No need to overdo things, after all."

Cora ignored him. She gave her full attention to the crowd, motioning downwards with both hands to silence the chants.

"Fellow Islanders!" she began, before telling them how proud she was of her son and his friends. They were, she said – to massive cheers – willing to lay down their lives to save their Island home. Eva and Pavel remained impassive; Denis alone looked unconvinced. Cora called upon the Authority to act immediately. She would make no bones about it: drilling must start at once, and it must start in the Cathedral Close. The Close, she said, was the perfect spot, the nearest practical option to the current shoreline: drilling there would minimize the loss of land, lives and livelihoods. This was news to her audience, if not to Lucy, but they were in no mood to quibble. If that's what Cora said, she must have her reasons. She went on to announce the plan for the day: they would shortly march upon the Castle, to make their demands loudly and clearly in the very heart of power. They would call upon Jessica King, the new Leader, to return with them to the footbridge, to look Denis,

Eva and Pavel in the eye, and to promise them that drilling would start by the end of the week. And if Jessica King wasn't willing to come with them, not willing to make this pledge? Well, then, she said, more quietly - waiting for the expectant silence she knew would fall, holding the moment as long as she could, then drawling - *pianissimo* - Well, then. If she will not do her duty, we must show her that *we* are the people - *crescendo* - that she is here to serve *us*, not the other way around - *Forte* - To show her she has no choice in this -*Fortissimo* - To *drag* her here, if need be! - *Diminuendo*, now - Because we, the people - *Sforzando* - will not be denied! To the Castle! To the Castle!!

At this, amid cheering and thunderous applause, not all of it unpremeditated, Cora Klamm strode from the bridge, stick aloft, back into the crowd, which in its enthusiasm to touch, congratulate and pledge loyalty to their newly-reborn prophet, showed at first less willingness to part before her than they had when she arrived. With the assistance of the two large men in suits, however, along with others in bright yellow vests and carrying placards, order was imposed. Cora was re-positioned not in the midst of a shapeless mass of bodies, but at the head of an organized battalion of marchers, across the front of which unfurled a banner: *Drill Now - or Drown Later!* The battalion took on greater definition and discipline as, slowly at first, but with gathering momentum, it made its way from the footbridge uphill through the city, stepping over the sleeping bodies of the homeless on its way.

Down at the waterfront, Lucy, rising a little - a very little - like a lion after slumber, shrugged off the chains of Cora's rhetoric and pulled out her phone to text Diana Ford-Marling: Crowd huge. Demand: drill now, Cathedral Close. CK leading march on Castle. Capture JK? She hesitated. Had Cora really threatened to apprehend the Leader by force? It seemed implausible. That wouldn't be campaigning, or even politics: it would be treason. Surely it was just rhetoric? She deleted Capture JK? and typed Mass support, adulation, tempers high instead. She hit send. Diana would not be pleased to hear how successful her rival had been, but that was what Lucy was here for. If Diana didn't want the truth, she shouldn't have sent a poet.

She turned to leave. Somewhere in the crowd, she'd lost her bobble hat, but under the Russian greatcoat, her jacket, her jumper, her shirt and tee shirt, she was sweating like a pig. She could feel it, gathering in her armpits, trickling into that hollow beneath her breasts – just at the bottom of her sternum, just above her belly: was there a name for that? – trickling into the crevices of her hips and groin, the backs of her knees.

By the time the now ex-steward made his way home, after threatening strikes and employment tribunals to no effect, the bishop was at the microphone addressing a crowd of perhaps a thousand people. (Diana would say twice that; the police, had they been present, might have put it at three hundred.) Having made the case for a Christianity that must on occasion rise above the injunction to render unto Caesar that which was Caesar's, and to challenge, as our Saviour had in reality Himself challenged, the powers that be, he had moved on, to the evident indifference of the crowd, to tackle all those doubting Thomasses who questioned whether a two-thousand-year-old religion should really endorse a claim that the Island had existed for less than half a century. Even as he spoke, the bishop said, some cynical journalist was *no doubt* preparing a cheap sarcastic column in support of which a dozen armchair pundits would *no doubt* fire off their far less witty twitterings. *No doubt*, the bishop boomed, a little too close to the microphone, they would press 'send' and consider their work accomplished. They would not recognize in themselves the priest and the Levite who passed by on the other side. He paused. But at least the priest and the Levite did not congratulate themselves in print, he joked, for leaving their neighbour, the poor man, robbed and bleeding on the side of the road. In the crowd, no one laughed. "Today, that poor man is our Island, and we are all its neighbours: we must all be Good Samaritans. And do our current-day sceptics not believe," he said, getting back into his stride, "that the God who made the stars and the ocean, who made the bounteous earth and every living creature, that such a God could not also create men and women capable (with His guidance) of simulating a small island? Of simulating the very Island on which we now all stand? And is it not our duty in the eyes of God, who sees everything and knows everything, is it not the duty of every one of us to protect and nurture to the best of our ability His vicarious creation?" This time the crowd, despite for the most part having little idea what "vicarious" meant, or even much belief in God, nonetheless recognized a rhetorical crescendo when they heard one, and responded accordingly.

Diana observed all this, continuing her mental self-appraisal. Her media round had gone better than well; it had been a triumph. How did she square her ancient lineage with a belief in the recent Simulation of the Island? Her focus was upon the future, she had replied, not the past. But – unlike some second-generation migrants (unlike, she implied, but did not say, their current Leader) – she was proud of her Motherland. Even a supposedly tricky question about how diving would help the Island's growing number of homeless people had been easily turned to her advantage: homelessness was of course a very serious issue; the spectacle of people sleeping in doorways in the twenty-first century was appalling, and the Authority must do everything it could to prevent it. "But, in the end, as I am sure your listeners will understand, Nick, if the Island sinks – if Jessica King sinks the Island – we will *all* be homeless. Or worse."

The bishop meanwhile signalled he was moving on – dropping both the volume and the tone of his voice, albeit the effect was rather undermined by a wail of feedback – to the reason for holding this demonstration here, this morning, in Cathedral Close. "As the flowers and the ribbons and the pictures of loved ones pinned to trees and fences all around us show, it is now almost ten years to the day since seven brave men and women were mown down like grass for doing nothing more than we are all doing here today. That is, nothing more – but also nothing less – than demanding that our earthly leaders respect the sanctity, the God-given holiness of the ground on which we stand, the Island on which we live and the sea in which that Island could – and one day will – float free."

There was, of course, no reason to suppose that the original protestors in Cathedral Close had favoured unshackling the Island. Indeed, Diana thought it highly unlikely: in those unenlightened times, all things Simulationist had been despised and ridiculed by the *bien pensant* Castle elite and their lickspittle cheerleaders in the media. No matter.

"And for that," the bishop continued, "the vengeance of the Authority, like that of a wounded beast, was swift and it was mighty. The police," he said, "on the orders of the Sodomite Commander Cole, cruelly beat to death those seven brave witnesses to the truth."

Diana, who never prayed, prayed now that the word *sodomite* might be lost in the wind or in the bishop's struggles with the PA, or at least taken by the crowd in a technical, Biblical sense as a resident of Sodom. The Commander was from the mainland, after all.

It was at this point that her mobile buzzed; she read Lucy's text. So be it, she thought, the blood of her ancestors stirring in her veins: bring it on.

"No," the bishop was booming, "we will not simply forget. We will not pass by. We are here today because the bitterness of their death is most decidedly *not* past." There was a huge answering roar from the crowd. The allusion may have been lost on them, but the sentiment was not. "We are here because the Authority, having failed for so long to deliver the inquiry the families and friends of the brave victims have so long demanded, now has the effrontery to propose this site – the very ground on which we stand, this sacred spot on which our fearless predecessors fell – to propose *this* site, I say, as the very epicentre of their callous, suicidal – *Godless* – project to destroy the Island altogether!" A third roar of approval crashed over the little stage, followed by chants of "Dive, don't drill! Dive, don't drill! Dive! Don't! Drill!"

It was time to take back control. This was Diana's demonstration, after all; God was just the support act. Conducting the chants with both hands, she leaned into the microphone – "Dive! Don't! Drill!" – gently edging the bishop out of the way. Finally, she calmed the crowd and thanked the Right Reverend Binkie Grendel, making clear that he had had his say, before launching into her own peroration on the bright future that awaited the Island once it was set free of the all-too-literal chains that bound it. When they could steer their own path in the world, unfettered by the blindness, inertia and bigotry that had blighted their lives and now threatened their very existence. Today was just the first step, she said. They would not rest – *she* would not rest! – until Jessica King was forced to promise that there would be no drilling, and gave the order to start diving. "Until then," she bellowed in a voice that would have carried a thousand Boxing Day hunts, "until then, we will occupy this sacred ground, as my good friend the bishop has said. Until then, we have a message for the police, for Jessica King and" – pausing for effect – "for Cora Klamm who, even as I speak, has rounded up a pathetic rabble of unbelievers to distract us from our cause. And that message – my message: *our* message – is: we are here, we're here to stay!" It wasn't quite enough, she realized. Working herself to a fever pitch she cried – in an inadvertent gift for the journalists and the armchair pundits the bishop had so excoriated – "We're! Going! Nowhere!!"

At this, the Island's second-best brass band launched once more into 'We Shall Not Be Moved', to be joined by enthusiastic singing from many of the older members of the crowd, above which those on the seaward fringes of the throng could just make out the distant grumbling call-and-response of Cora's approaching marchers.

SEVENTEEN

LATER, ARI WOULD remember little of what he'd done with the rest of that morning. He must have attended a meeting or two, had a chat with Sally about Peter – or Peter about Sally: one or the other – must have read some stuff, and signed some stuff, cleared it or not cleared it, because that's what he did now, wasn't it? This was now his life. Somewhere along the way he must have taken a moment to check the newsfeeds, because he remembered seeing Cora Klamm demand drilling start as soon as possible. She'd urged all Islanders, whatever their political allegiance, to join her in celebrating the stand her son had taken at the footbridge, to take up his fight for common sense and all their futures; following the rally, she'd said, they would march up to the Castle. Diana Ford-Marling, meanwhile, had occupied Cathedral Close, declaring publicly that the Great Simulation was real, while denying she'd ever said anything else. Any attempt to save the Island not based on this simple fact was doomed to fail. It was time, she was quoted as saying, that the bureaucrats in the Castle stopped sneering at ordinary Islanders, and recognized the Island had been simulated for everyone who lived on it, not just those who had usurped its rule for far too long; time for every Islander of good faith to fight to save their birthright.

It was perfect, Ari reflected bitterly. It was more than perfect. Everything was turning out exactly as he had engineered. By the end of the day Jessica would be in a position to declare a final referendum, a chance to settle the question once and for all. Which would, of course, settle nothing, but during which she would retain a principled neutrality while Cora and Diana tore each other apart.

Except she wouldn't.

And why not?

Because Jessica King was too blinded by youth or idealism or *Our Island Bloody Story* or whatever it was to see the political advantages it could bring. Or if she saw them, too innocent properly to appreciate their value. Because Jessica King, despite having grown up at the heart of power, had somehow failed to understand how power worked. Because, for all the adoration Jacob heaped upon her, she was simply not her father's daughter.

Because she believed.

But also because he, Ari, had failed to see or properly to appreciate that fact. He had failed. Which was not like him, and which he found he did not like.

He left the office, telling Marion to clear his diary for the day. She said, what with the demos going on, the Public Safety Steering Group would most likely get cancelled anyway. Senior police and civic leaders would have better things to do than sit around not listening to each other. He wondered how much of Donald had actually been Marion.

He took the lift to the ground floor. After a word or two about the receptionist's daughter Emily, and the clutch trouble Leonard the security guard was having on the car that he'd been daft enough to buy off a bloke in a pub, he made it to the revolving doors. None of this came naturally. But he'd witnessed K in his prime, moving among people like a fish through water, a flick of the fin here, a flick there, effortlessly. He had experienced the subtle power bestowed by such easy familiarity with the mundane details of other people's lives, and had trained himself, working diligently, as if at a foreign language he would need in order to survive behind enemy lines, until his command of the idiom was perfect. Nobody could tell the difference. No one saw the tiny cracks that opened in his soul whenever he talked about children or sport, about ailments, traffic or last night's television.

He left the Central Block and headed for the perimeter. Outside, the sun was shining and the wind had dropped, but it was, if anything, colder than it had been yesterday. Overhead, pigeons and gulls resumed their spiralling tactical battle for airspace, the gulls all brute force while the pigeons scattered and re-grouped, scattered and re-grouped again, theirs a war of attrition. On the roof of the guard's hut by the main gate, a huge black rook – a putty-white patch around its beak glowing savagely in the winter sunlight – stared silently as he passed. He swapped a couple of words with Jim – former soldier; three children (two at university); a diabetic wife and a prosthetic leg – who had manned the red-and-white traffic barrier for as long as Ari could remember.

Finally, he was out. It didn't happen often. Apart from his occasional visits to St Julian's and civic events like yesterday's funeral, he rarely left the Castle. What would be the point? Everything that mattered was inside.

He pulled his coat tighter and began the slow switchback towards the cliffs, then down into the city. Denis couldn't have chosen better weather to demonstrate his commitment to whatever he was faking a commitment to. If he was seeking attention, he'd certainly got that – at least until his mother pitched up, muscling her way into the limelight. It was always possible, as Cora had proclaimed, that Denis was laying his life on the line to save the Island: possible, Ari thought, but unlikely. He'd been happy enough to get away to the mainland; happy enough not to come back. So what had changed?

There was an obvious answer to that: K was dead. Denis's father was dead.

And there it was: grief. Bereavement. The way people react when other people die.

Ari told himself it wasn't a topic he knew much about. When his mother died, he'd been too busy scavenging a living to stop and wonder how he felt. What good would that do anyone? If he'd cried at night, at first, it had been because he was hungry, and cold; and anyway, it hadn't lasted long. He found some blankets, a sandwich toaster and an electric heater, rigged up curtains for his requisitioned meeting room; he was fine. As for his father: who knew? He might still be alive; more likely he was dead. Somewhere in the Authority's files there'd be a record – a note of the date, the cause, the disposal of the remains – but it wouldn't be filed under S for Spencer.

Ari shivered. It was cold: he should go back. He could still see Central Block from here, most of the lights on most of the floors already burning at midday. Or he could go home, get something to eat, talk to himself – which was pretty much all talking to K had been for the last few years anyway. He should stop making excuses. Go home: get on with the job.

Instead, he headed downhill, into the city, towards the sea. He passed a café where the proprietor stood in the doorway, smoking a thin dark cigar that looked almost black against his nearly clean white tunic. He nodded noncommittally as Ari passed; Ari nodded back, but neither of them spoke.

He crossed Houghton Square. So-called. On the next block, men and women wearing several layers of shabby, mismatched clothes arranged their scant possessions with the ritual attention to detail of museum curators; others settled down to sleep already, in the middle of the day, because – honestly – what else was there to do?

K, you old bastard. Okay, you *were* old: that didn't mean you had to die.

Except, of course, it did.

Ari stopped outside a shop selling handmade leather shoes; then began to walk again. All this – this introspection – was not like him. A functionary thought about problems, not himself. He made things happen – or not happen. *He* did. Not Cora or Jacob or Jessica. Not Daniel-bloody-Houghton, for all his money and his luxury flats: him. Ari Spencer. For more than twenty years, that had been his task: changing what needed to be changed – Leaders, mostly – so nothing really changed at all. There would be no end to it.

The future would grind on. The Castle would endure, however high the sea might rise. The *Island Story* was a lie, not because it wasn't true, but because it wasn't really a story. Stories end. They build to a climax: everything gets worse, until finally it gets better.

His life would not get worse, or better; it would peter out, like K's. So what? It was enough. Until then, he'd keep spinning yarn after yarn, rigging tightropes to cross from one rock to the next, never escaping the rapids. So what had changed?

He stopped again. Something – somebody – was blocking his path.

"Ari?"

The storyline he'd spun Jessica had been one of his best.

"Ari, are you alright?"

A devious Machiavellian thriller. But it hadn't worked. She hadn't let it work.

"Ari?"

Jacob was clicking his fingers in Ari's face.

"I'm fine."

"Fine? You need a drink."

"It's not even noon, Jacob."

"I'm retired."

"But I'm not."

"You should try it."

He turned Ari around and led him back past the café, where the proprietor was stubbing out his half-smoked cigar against the wall, then on a few yards more to an iron staircase that led down to a basement bar Ari hadn't even known existed. It was dark inside, scarred wood and tarnished brass. It could have been any time of day, or night. Jacob ordered whisky and whatever his young friend wanted; Ari said he'd have a whisky, too. Jacob said there really must be something wrong.

He led them over to a quiet booth. The seats leaked stuffing.

"Keep your head down," Jacob said. "That's what I'm doing." He'd been down to see what was going on, he said. Couldn't get near the footbridge for Cora's minions, but Denis was still pinned out on the bridge, a funny little guy on one side, rather attractive woman on the other.

"What does he want?"

"Who knows? He says he wants to do his bit. I tell you what, though – you'll enjoy this. Yesterday, after the funeral, I had dinner with Cora. She reckons it's his way of declaring undying love for my daughter."

"What? Wait. You sat down with Cora?"

Jacob laughed. "You think that's more surprising than her idiot son fancying Jessica?"

He did, actually.

Jacob held up their empty glasses. "Another?" He went back to the bar without waiting for an answer.

There *was* something wrong, Ari thought. But it wasn't K; it was Jessica. Jessica was Leader. That's what had changed. What *he* had changed. Could he discuss that with her father? The man they'd ousted? Why not? he thought – or perhaps the whisky thought. He'd talked to K about Cora, hadn't he? About Jacob, and Jessica?

But Jacob wasn't K.

Which only meant he was not yet dead.

In the end, over a couple more drinks, he told Jacob his story, the one Jessica had spiked. Jacob nodded encouragement, kept him talking, before finally delivering his verdict: "I'm not surprised. I mean, there's nothing wrong with the script, *per se*. It's beautiful. If it had been me, I would have bitten your arm off, you know that?"

Ari nodded.

"But Jessica's not me."

Ari shook his head sadly.

"So what's plan B?"

Ari shrugged, playing along. "There is no plan B."

"That's not like you."

"I've got twenty-four hours . . ." – he looked at his watch – "I've got six and a half hours to come up with one."

"So what's the problem?"

"I can't give her what she wants."

"Come off it, Ari. That's what you do."

"No."

"Yes. Of course it is. You did it for Cora. You did it for me. What's so different about Jessica?"

"You wanted to keep going. She wants a solution."

The words came easily, without premeditation. But that was the nub of it, Ari realized. Jessica still believed in endings. She thought she was the Child – of course she did. *Our Island Story* was real and she wanted resolution. Redemption. The triumph of good over evil, the discomfiture of the malefactors. Jacob said not to go away, he'd get them both another drink.

When he came back, Ari said: "What if Cora's right? What if, instead of a political thriller, we make it a rom-com after all?" He paused, but only for effect. "Denis falls madly in love with Jessica; she thinks he's a waster, but after some hilarious ups and downs, discovers there's more to him than meets the eye. But he's a Klamm; she's a King: their love is forbidden, until . . . united in their opposition, their parents – that's you and Cora –"

"I know who my daughter is."

"– their parents learn they have more in common than just hating each other. They, too, fall in love. There's a double wedding –"

"Funnily enough, that's what Cora said."

"She did? There you go. Wait. *Cora* said that?"

But Jacob had picked up the baton. "What about Diana?"

"Oh, I don't know. Yes, I do. We expose her somehow. She gets her comeuppance. A nasty end."

"How?"

"Details, details. To be confirmed. Did Cora really say that?"

Jacob ignored him again. "So what happens to you?"

"Oh, I get to marry Bob Cole. The bishop does all the marrying. Something for everyone and everybody's happy."

Jacob sat back, his hands behind his head. "There you go then. Problem solved."

"Except it isn't, is it? My round."

Ari stood and walked towards the bar. The floor rolled slightly, like the deck of a ship, he imagined, never having been to sea. For an

Islander that seemed suddenly ridiculous, although it was much more common than most people – most mainlanders – might suppose. The bar was crowded now; he would have to wait. No, the problem wasn't solved at all. The story couldn't end with weddings, any more than it would with a referendum. Because it couldn't end at all. The real problem was that Jessica wanted salvation – for the Island, not for a handful of its politicians. Which meant tedious, interminable efforts to mitigate global warming and house the homeless – which wasn't a story at all, was it? Nobody really wanted to think about the endless, boring stuff, much less do it. Or vote for it. *That* was what was wrong. Jessica wanted answers: solutions, salvation, Armageddon: The End. But there were no answers: nothing was ever resolved, no one ever saved. A political problem, by definition, was one that *couldn't* be solved. Everything else was just engineering and management. History didn't end; politics didn't end. K might be dead but the young would see as much and live just as long; and it would be just as dull. Which was why, for the first time in his career, he couldn't deliver what his Leader wanted.

The barman was asking what he wanted.

You can't save a life, K used to say, only defer a death.

He ordered a whisky for Jacob, water for himself.

Our Island Story would be a disaster if it were ever allowed to come true. Luckily there was no chance of that.

The floor stopped shifting under his feet. The tension in his neck and shoulders – so habitual he hadn't noticed it was even there until it wasn't – drained away. He hadn't solved anything. He never would. But at least he knew what he would say to Jessica. It wasn't perfect, but it would have to do.

Back at the booth, he said: "So Cora proposed? What *did* you say?"

EIGHTEEN

C ORA HAD SENT scouts ahead. Now word filtered back
that Diana's demo wasn't at all the depthless fiasco some of
Cora's own lieutenants had predicted. Well, so be it. Cora smiled, a
disconcerting sight for those around her. The Close was on a direct
path between their current position and the Castle; confrontation
with Diana was just as much the point as challenging Jessica King.
The scouts assured her that what their own march lacked in reli-
gious imprimatur and musical volume, it more than made up in
sheer weight of numbers. Boots on the ground were what counted
here. And for every pair of boots – or trainers, or court shoes, or
chunky vegan sandals – that Diana had contrived to muster, Cora
could count on three. She couldn't have been happier. Diana might
have a bishop but, as Napoleon knew, God Himself could reliably
be counted on the side of the big battalions.

Onward. They would brush aside Diana and her pet clergyman
as the Emperor had crushed his enemies at Austerlitz! More than
that, she would take control of the Cathedral Close, not only to
demand drilling, but to begin the work herself. At her command,
they would rip up the cobbles and the paving stones: *Sous les pavés,
la plage!* Or, if not the beach, exactly, then the borehole (the French
for which escaped her). Then she would lead her loyal band onwards
and upwards, ever upwards, to storm the Citadel itself!

It wasn't Napoleon, Cora reflected later – or at any rate he was
certainly not the first – who said no plan survives first contact with
the enemy. But it was definitely a boxer who said everybody has a
plan till they get punched in the fucking mouth.

The trouble with a static demonstration, Diana mused – as opposed to a march, where forward motion at least kept everyone heading in the same direction – was that one could not prevent these people milling about, bumping into old friends, peeling off to the café on the corner of the Close for drinks and light refreshments; meanwhile opportunistic retailers of snack foods, newspapers and party paraphernalia had descended like wasps on jam, lending the whole affair an atmosphere more redolent of a summer fete, despite the February temperatures, than of serious political protest. The band didn't help. Well, it did help, of course – it made a lot of noise and attracted people to the Close, which was all to the good – but, after several rousing renditions of 'We Shall Not Be Moved', 'Jerusalem' and 'Things Can Only Get Better', some of the crowd, and no doubt some of the band, chaffing at their status as the Island's second best, had become restless. In response, the band leader – a diminutive pedantic man, whose mouth, even at rest, retained the pinched embouchure of the confirmed cornetist he had been before taking up the conductor's baton – seized his moment in the sun, offering to take requests, thereby adding to the festival atmosphere at the expense, Diana could not help thinking, of the more serious message of the Island's Simulation and salvation. Some of her supporters began to treat the occasion as an opportunity for large-scale open-air karaoke. In the Venn diagram of their talent, their musical tastes and the band's repertoire, however, the area of intersection was small, although even Diana had to admit that the young woman who had belted out 'I Will Survive' certainly possessed a fine pair of lungs. And the message was at least tangentially relevant. They would survive. By diving not drilling, Diana bellowed as loudly as she could, having involuntarily ceded the microphone to the singers: they would not drown. They might lie down, but only to protect the Close, to save the Island: not to die. They would survive. More than survive. Under her leadership they would . . . By the time this burst of inspiration overtook her, however, the band leader's hubris – "You hum it, we'll play it" – had shattered on the rocks of 'Lady in Red': even Diana's piercing, aristocratic tone was drowned out by the good-natured boos and catcalls of a crowd showing every sign of enjoying itself.

Which was not at all the point, she thought.

The intervals between numbers became longer but less frequent as the bandleader demonstrated his familiarity with the concept of the *segue*, even if his players sometimes struggled with the practicalities of unrehearsed changes of key and tempo. In those moments of relative peace and quiet, however, Diana began to make out more and more clearly the distant heavy tread of marchers and the tightly rhythmic call of "What do we want?" being met with "Drilling!"

"When do we want it?"

"Now!"

She knew – the bloodline of Ford-Marlings from Crecy to Waterloo whispering in her ear – that if her supporters really were to remain like trees planted by the waterside, she would have to get some order into their ranks, now, before it was too late.

❧

One corner from Cathedral Close, Cora Klamm paused, and held her walking stick aloft, signalling for silence. Gradually the marchers behind her slowed, bunched up, ran out of road and finally came to a gentle patient halt. An eerie quiet rippled back through the column, followed closely by the unmistakable sounds of '(It's Fun to Stay at the) Y.M.C.A.' being belted out a block away by a slightly ragged brass band and several hundred discordant but undeniably energetic voices.

"Ours is not to reason why," Cora said, dismissing any notion that the Charge of the Light Brigade might not be the most appropriate military manoeuvre to emulate. She had rather more than six

hundred at her command. She and her troops would march right through the Valley of Death. *Ours is but to do or die.* Well, that was on the nose, at least. Without the borehole, weren't they all going to fucking hashtag fucking die?

She climbed the stone steps outside a bank so that she could be seen above the crowd despite her diminutive stature. "Sisters!" she bellowed into a megaphone, "Brothers! Islanders! We approach a moment of truth! Our route to the Castle, to the legitimate and peaceful expression of our just cause, lies through Cathedral Close." Most of the marchers seemed to be listening, although a few were wrangling children or, at the back, starting up half-hearted chants. "We chose this route because the Close is the best possible site to drill the borehole our Island needs. What do we want?" she shouted, and the better part of three thousand voices roared right back:

"Drilling!!"

"Where do we want it?"

"Cathedral Close!!"

"When do we want it?"

"NOW!!!"

Cora basked in the wave of noise. If only all of politics could be like this. In the real world the answer would have been: "As soon as public consultation and a preliminary geological site investigation reasonably allowed." But where was the fun in that?

She lowered her voice as far as she realistically could while addressing a crowd in the open air, over a booming Village People tribute somewhere in the neighbourhood. "But now we hear the Close has been occupied by Diana Ford-Marling . . . and her deplorable alliance of God-botherers and Simulationists."

The mention of Diana's name was greeted with satisfying boos and catcalls, many of them, Cora noticed, from party members who had probably voted the bloody entitled upstart into leadership in the first place. So far, so good: politics was a fickle affair. Her characterization of Diana's supporters, however, produced a more muted response. There must be God-botherers in her own ranks, she supposed: statistically, it was inevitable; tactically, it was a subject best avoided. Simulationism, on the other hand, she would have to confront head-on.

"Now I know," she said, "that many of you – perhaps in the past; perhaps even today – have found yourself wondering about the Great Simulation. I know I have." There was heckling she couldn't quite make out, followed by some laughter. She was treading a tightrope here: getting to the other side without falling would make eventual victory all the sweeter. "It's fun to ask yourself: "What if it were true?" Fun to argue back and forth over a couple of pints on a Friday night. Or a cup of coffee on a Tuesday morning," she added, hastily. The common touch was all very well, but there was no mileage in offending the abstainers. "And it *is* fun: harmless fun. But there comes a time when we have to ask ourselves serious questions. When idle speculation becomes a real threat to our very survival, we need to face the danger resolutely. We must ignore the cynics who try to stop us taking anything seriously. Because this *is* serious. Survival is serious. We must ignore the voices – even, especially, our own, internal voices – that say: *"You never know"*. Because we *do* know. *Science* knows."

She was aware of vibrations in the tightrope, ripples of unease amongst the crowd: nobody here had signed up for a lecture. Get to the point, she scolded herself.

"Which means we cannot allow Diana Ford-Marling . . ." – more grateful boos from an audience keen on villains – "and her Simulationist friends to set their faces against Science, against progress, against *survival* by occupying the very site we need to save the Island!" Cheers, applause and shouting told Cora she had recovered the energy of the march: now she just had to let it loose.

"When we enter Cathedral Close, we do so with our heads held high, with dignity, and with discipline. They may try to stop us" – more shouting, and some laughter – "the police will try to keep us apart." (They'd better bloody not: not after what she'd promised Commander Bent Cop Cole.) "But we will fight. We'll fight like hell. And make no mistake," she cried, her voice firm and resonant: "we *will* take back the Close!"

She shook her stick in the air like a spear, more Boudicca than Napoleon.

"Onward!" she cried, descending the steps to begin the march anew. "Onward and upward!!"

And so, as the tuba player in the Close made a creditable attempt at the baseline from 'One Love', Cora and her shock troops turned the corner and marched slap bang into what appeared to be a jamboree.

There was dancing in the Valley of Death. And the police were nowhere to be seen.

⚜

For her part, Diana tried and tried to get some order in the ranks, but to no avail. Having lost control of the stage, she addressed them from the Cathedral steps, but was once more drowned out by the band. She mingled with the crowd on the south side of the Close, warning that Cora Klamm and her mob of God-less anti-Simulationist drillers would be upon them at any moment, urging them to link arms, to sit down and peacefully resist. "They shall not pass!" she bellowed, clutching her paste pearls (this was no place for real jewellery) as they bounced to the rhythm of her screams, "They shall not pass!" – only to be told that those were not the words to 'Agadoo'. In desperation, she called Bob Cole's private number, but was diverted straight to voicemail.

The mood changed, however, when Cora Klamm and her column of marchers hove into sight. All the festive party-people and the karaoke give-it-a-goers turned, if not as one, then at least with the ragged coordination of a 'Top of the Pops' studio audience. By the time Cora's march entered the Close, everyone within had realized the threat. Some tried to slip away, recalling urgent appointments or their employers' attitudes to those arrested on previous demonstrations – where *were* the police, anyway? – but many more surged forward, curious or determined, blocking off any possible retreat for those in the front line.

"The blast of war blows in our ears! Imitate the actions of the tiger!" shrieked Diana, as 'One Love' groaned to a discordant halt.

In the brief, electric silence that followed, the low February sun caught the inch-thick glass walls of Houghton Tower, projecting a rainbow into the no-man's land between the opposing lines of demonstrators. A seagull – oblivious to the surrounding tension, much less the miracle of physics that painted its white feathers blue, indigo and violet – landed, cocked its head to one side then the other, squawked and took off again, apparently unimpressed. Something in the seabird's nonchalance seemed to trigger every ounce of stalled violence in the human hearts of those who witnessed it. From immediately behind Cora a former fellow-councillor and member of the Planning Committee – bearded, and with halitosis bad enough to shrivel a cactus – bellowed "CHARRRRRRGE!!!!" and she found herself swept irresistibly into the very epicentre of the action. *On s'engage,* she just had time to think, *et puis . . .* she watched the megaphone in her hand – *her* hand! – descend with some force onto the skull of a primary school teacher-turned-Diving fanatic. Those around Diana, meanwhile, having ignored her attempts to stiffen their spines, now found themselves throwing punches, lashing out with their boots, or cowering behind their companions as instinct, temperament or long-forgotten parental choices dictated. Further back, someone never to be identified in any subsequent inquiry used a placard pole to prise loose a damaged cobblestone that the Authority, or the Church, should have fixed years ago, but which, owing to a dispute about their relative responsibilities, neither had. Once one stone was loose, those around it soon came free; once the first protestor picked one up, his neighbours quickly followed suit. Afterwards, nobody would ever know whether it was a Christian or a Simulationist Diver who hurled the first stone, just as no one would know – or admit to knowing – which of Cora's Drillers first picked up the stone that landed at his feet and hurled it back. What is beyond doubt is that when, during the general *mêlée* that followed, the bishop was spotted scuttling through the wicket gate within the Cathedral's vast Gothic doorway, a small band of Drillers peeled away from the main fight to lob their missiles after him. Seeing those projectiles bounce harmlessly off the ancient oak, they took to hurling rocks at the irreplaceable stained glass instead. And when horrified Divers condemned this act of wanton cultural vandalism, the Drillers responded by asking why, since they believed the whole thing had been knocked up in the 1980s, the Divers gave a shit? Blows followed; heads were cracked; but, on this occasion, no one died.

The motive behind the attack on Houghton Tower was less clear. Some suggested it was in retaliation for the desecration of the Cathedral; others that it was a response to the sight of the flats' occupants pouring drinks and ironically cheering on the rioters from their balconies high above the fray; others still that it reflected the long-held grievance of elements within both Drillers and Divers at the razing of a much-loved boozer in favour of inexplicably-priced investment opportunities for the already rich, and at the stench of corruption surrounding the Authority's decision to approve the scheme. Perhaps it was some combination of all three – and of other, more random and more personal prejudices, which, obscure as they may well have been to the perpetrators themselves, no inquiry, however thorough, could ever hope to uncover. What is certain, however – it's there on CCTV for anyone to see – is that both Diana Ford-Marling and Cora Klamm (the latter perhaps more energetically, given her personal interest in the outcome) sought to intervene, to protect valuable private property from their people, or each other's people. Neither succeeded. A heavy iron fence post, with its hand-written memorial to those who died ten years earlier still attached, was ripped from its attendant cherry tree and hurled, javelin-fashion, at the plate glass lobby. With a soft grunt, the glass splintered, shooting out a spider's web six feet high and six across, but did not break. At a second blow, however – this time the post was not thrown but swung low, sweet chariot, like a battering ram – a hundred thousand shards of glass (no two, like snowflakes, entirely identical) collapsed into a glittering jewel pile, like granulated sugar spilled from a punctured packet in a supermarket aisle. Within moments the protestors – Divers? Drillers? No one could be sure – were inside; within minutes, those thousands more outside, had they paused in their fighting, their fleeing, their aimless milling or their energetic Facebook posting, could have seen the glow of flames, dulled by heavy, tinted glass, that licked through the second floor and up into the third. By the time they spotted the streams of thick black smoke trickling from the building's ventilation system and – such was the density of immolated toxic materials within them – sinking towards the ground before gathering the strength to rise and merge into great dark thunderclouds of disaster that overhung the Close, it was already far too late. It was perhaps a miracle that although many were badly affected by the smoke, no one – that is, not a single resident or protestor – died. Not a miracle, Houghton Developments would subsequently claim in their marketing material, but design: it was precisely the high-end safety engineering possible in buildings of this quality – and price – that had ensured that no one died. No one, that is, except Mrs. Emily Harper (née Foot) who, having some years earlier lost her husband to an industrial accident and subsequently lost her home after ill-health forced her own employers – reluctantly, they said: but what else could they do? – to let her go, had latterly been sleeping – illegally, and apparently without the knowledge of the building's uniformed security staff – in a basement cubbyhole, where she had survived on the scraps that slithered down the refuse chutes from residents' kitchens into the vast collective bins those residents never saw, where she did no one but herself any harm, and where her charred remains would lie unsuspected amid the rubble, soaked by the hoses that firefighters played for two days upon the glowing embers, frozen by the late winter ice that followed, undiscovered, other than by the rats that gnawed her thawing flesh in Spring, until the site was cleared for redevelopment, by which time there would be nothing left to identify her corpse but half a lifetime's dental decay and ill-set fractures that traced the history of the violence she had endured throughout her life.

NINETEEN

OWN AT THE waterfront, the caravan had moved on. It was quiet again: quiet, and cold. The march had left; the cameras and the press had left. Denis, Eva and Pavel faced the sea alone, unobserved – except, that is, by Lucy, who had not yet left, but stood huddled in an empty alleyway allowing her sweat to cool, watching Pavel, Eva and Denis as they, in turn, watched the tide recede.

"How long?" said Denis.

To his right, Pavel replied, "How long what?"

"How long do we have to keep this up?"

"It's your romantic gesture, lover boy," said Eva, from his left. "You tell us."

He was hungry. He was freezing and he was wet and he felt so tired he could die if only the pain in his shoulders and his hips, his wrists and his legs, would let him. But it wouldn't; counting his breaths no longer seemed to help because the gnawing in his stomach would keep getting in the way.

Last night's chips were long gone. Denis would now happily have eaten the ones he'd dropped, if they hadn't been scavenged by seagulls before they even hit the water.

Pavel said, "You want chips?"

Yes, he wanted chips. He was starving. But he also wanted clinical-grade painkillers and a bed to lie in and perhaps a massage and maybe then, perhaps, after a day or two, he'd want Eva. Jessica. He meant Jessica. Not that it made any difference. He was chained to a bridge: he wasn't getting anything he wanted, was he?

"Chips? Yes?"

"Fuck off, Pavel."

"No chips?"

"Stop tormenting me about fucking chips!"

"Only, now no one is here, I go to chip shop."

"What? How?"

With a sort of rippling shrug Pavel slipped free his right hand, then his left; he raised his arms above his head and pulled himself upwards, leaving his heavy, crisscrossed chains dangling like the abandoned chrysalis of a giant butterfly.

"Chips?"

"But . . . how . . .?"

Eva laughed. "You don't think we'd be dumb enough to wrap ourselves in chains we couldn't escape, did you?"

Denis, who had assumed they'd been precisely that dumb, said: "You mean? We can just walk out of here?"

"We can," said Pavel. "You can't."

"Why not?"

"You tense muscles?"

"What?"

"Like Houdini. Tense muscles. Relax afterwards, slip off chains?"

Denis shook his head.

"Of course you didn't," said Eva. "Besides, you can't just walk out on love."

"Watch me," Denis said.

"No, no. We'll all stay. But there's no need to starve, is there?" And, although it was hard to say, because he could only see one side of her face out of the corner of one eye, it looked to Denis very much as if she winked at him.

"He's going to get food, come back and climb into his chains again?"

"Of course."

"Pavel," Denis called over his shoulder, "you're insane. You're a braver man than I, but you must be fucking mental."

"We are hungry," Pavel said simply. "I fetch food."

A doubt struck Denis. "Wait. If you go to the shop, they'll recognize you. They'll know we're cheating."

Pavel shook his head, though Denis couldn't see it. He said, "I am taxi driver. No one recognize taxi driver."

Denis examined his own conscience. It didn't take long. "You're like the invisible man?"

"Is true. Is my superpower."

"Then take my wallet," Denis said. "Get chips. Get fish, get sausages in batter, get pickled eggs and anything else they've got. Get the fucking lot."

The morphine and the massage could wait. If only the card would work again. Miracles had already happened. Eva was still there.

Jessica.

Eva.

Jessica.

It was quieter than ever. Even the seagulls seemed to be giving it a rest. The waves slapped rhythmically at the shore, then ground their teeth as they pulled back.

Eva4J4eva.

He was conscious of not knowing what to say.

He said, "I'm starving."

Eva laughed. "You're just hungry."

"I hope Pavel buys everything in the shop."

"No use spoiling the shit for a ha'p'orth of lard?"

Denis was surprised. It was the sort of thing his mother might have said. Though she'd probably have squeezed in a couple more expletives. "Do they say that in your country?"

"What country?"

"Your country. Where you and Pavel come from."

Eva affected outrage. "Denis, I'm an Islander. I was born here."

"But Pavel is your brother. You said so."

Dropping her voice an octave, in Pavel's accent, she said: "Perhaps I lie. Perhaps I Pavel's wife."

He gave up. She was impossible. He had no idea where he stood.

Dangled. He let his head slump, chin to collar bone.

"The Authority," said Eva, speaking normally again – if that *was* her normal voice: how would he know? – "thinks he is my brother. And the Authority is always right."

He closed his eyes. He tried to picture Jessica King – it was a vision of Jessica that had brought him here in the first place, after all – but all he could see was Eva. Even wrapped in a ridiculous coat that was to all intents and purposes a duvet, she was so very, very beautiful. And she teased him cruelly. Which was, if she only knew it, the perfect combination to reduce his immature heart to abject devotion. She probably knew it. All men were probably the same to her, all equally pathetic. Or perhaps she was just teasing.

He began to breathe again, and to count his breaths.

"You really don't remember, do you?"

Lazily, he said, "Remember what?"

"We were at school together."

"You and Pavel?"

"You and me, Denis. You and me."

Really? He was about to say he was pretty sure he'd have remembered that when Pavel returned, hauling two large bags of deep-fried food. He helped them eat, fed them chips and sausages and chicken and fish until even Denis had to admit that he could take no more. Then he cleared up the greasy paper, folding it roughly into one of the plastic bags before tying its handles and dropping the whole lot into a commercial waste bin he found in the mouth of an alley where a red-faced young woman in a huge overcoat pretended not to watch.

He returned to the bridge, stepped over the rail and slipped back into his chains. "Is better?"

"Much better," Denis said.

He contemplated the waves for a while, found himself breathing again in time to their ebb and flow, to the rhythm of the universe. How was it, he thought, that mere food could so ease physical pain and induce such mental stupefaction? Because everything *was* better, much better, of course it was. Except he was still here, they were still here, still hadn't answered his question: how long?

Eva said, "I was two years below you."

She must mean primary: he'd been to an all boys' school after that.

"The same class as Jessica King. Before she dropped out."

"Would she remember you?"

Eva paused. "We'll have to wait and see, won't we?"

"About that . . .?"

"No," said Pavel, firmly. Denis hadn't even been aware that he was listening.

"No," Pavel said again. "Your mother says bring Jessica here. Meet you. You cannot stand up lady."

"Well, if you put it like that . . . let's go."

"No."

"What are you now, my gaolers?"

He turned as best he could towards Eva, but Eva was not listening: she was staring straight out to sea.

He turned back: he stared, too. Low bright sunshine danced across a muscular swell; the waves, unhindered by the harbour defences they had swallowed long ago, rose and fell to the heartbeat of distant storms. Across the glittering horizon, silhouetted ships that would eventually pass the Island by seemed motionless. Closer to shore, something black, and round, appeared and disappeared with the roll of the ocean. A buoy? A rock? A seal?

It waved, desperately.

Denis opened his mouth, but Eva had already slipped out of her chains, dumped her padded coat and kicked off her shoes. She dived straight off the bridge and struck out towards the struggling figure at a fast crawl. Stupidly, as if he were her mother – although not his own – Denis found himself wishing she wouldn't swim so soon after eating. He watched her reach the flailing body, only to be dragged under by his – her? – panic at being grabbed and held. He watched Eva overpower the desperate castaway and return to shore at a slow backstroke. By now, Pavel had freed himself and was bellowing encouragement from the water line, leaving Denis alone pinned out against the bridge.

As Eva approached, Pavel waded in waist-deep to help her drag the limp figure of what was now obviously a woman up onto dry land. Between them – Eva with her arms looped under the woman's shoulders, Pavel lifting her feet – they carried her to the road, beyond Denis's peripheral vision, and laid her out on the crumbling tarmac. He heard her cough up seawater, heard her heavy, effortful gasps as she struggled to regain control; heard, too, Eva's softly-murmured reassurance, Pavel's fussy staccato questions and offers of assistance.

After a few minutes, Eva sent Pavel over to tell Denis what was going on.

"This woman half-drowned. We take her home, dry clothes, food. Maybe hospital."

"Fine," said Denis. "Just get me out of this lot and I'll give you a hand."

"You must wait here. For Jessica King."

Wait? Alone? No way. He had seen Eva dive into the sea, save a life, and emerge sodden but undaunted. He no longer cared what Jessica did or did not do, what she thought or did not think, of him. Which would of course be: nothing. But he couldn't say that. Not to Pavel. Not after all his help. Pavel was a romantic, after all.

He said, "She won't listen to my mother. Why would she?"

"You will wait to see. Perhaps things happen today that change situation."

"Pavel, please. She's not coming."

But Pavel was already on his way back to Eva and the rescued woman.

"*Please.* I'll do anything. I'll pay you. I have money."

He didn't have money, but he had the prospect of money, which was surely just as good? This was no time for pedantry, after all. But Pavel took no notice. Between them, he and Eva helped the rescued woman stand and walk across the road to Pavel's taxi. With the engine already running, however, Eva hurried back to the bridge, her waterlogged clothes dripping as she knelt behind him.

"Help me," he said.

"I'm sorry, Denis. Pavel really wants you to wait for Jessica. He'll be upset if you don't."

"Fuck Jessica."

"I promise not to tell him you said that."

"Fuck Pavel, too. Get me out."

"I can't do that."

"You can."

"Pavel says you have to stay. Be patient."

"She's not coming. Unless my mother actually kidnaps her, there's no way."

"I know."

"So let me go. I've had enough."

Eva sighed, resigned. "Right now, I need Pavel; I need his taxi. When I know the baby is all right, I will come back."

Baby?

"The mother will be okay. She hasn't been in the sea long. But she is, as Pavel puts it, with child."

"She's pregnant?"

"Very pregnant. I'd say at least eight months."

Jesus, Denis thought. A refugee, a castaway, with a child. With child. Child. Whatever. Which must mean . . .

If Jessica heard that, she might just come down here after all. Or at least send spies.

In her alleyway behind the waste bin on the far side of the bridge, Lucy Neave had come to the same conclusion. From the moment they laid the woman out on the road, the protuberance of her belly, even under heavy, sodden clothes, made it obvious that childbirth was imminent. She should text Diana, she thought. Or, she could head directly to the Castle, giving Cathedral Close as wide a berth as possible. She was an employee, after all, just as she'd told Ari years ago when she thought Cora must be losing her mind. Even if it got her sacked again, Lucy's first duty was to the Authority. Besides, she'd give a lot to be in the room when Jessica King heard the news, let alone to be the bearer of that news herself. If nothing else, there'd be a stanza or two in it. Epic, indeed.

Lucy slipped out of the alleyway unseen, and headed uphill, inland, missing the moment when Eva said, "Goodbye, Denis," and kissed him on the cheek. Standing up, she added: "I'll come back. I promise."

A moment later, Denis heard the taxi pull away; apart from the seagulls, he was alone. And Pavel still had his wallet.

TWENTY

CLIMBING BACK UP the metal staircase from the bar, Ari was surprised to find it still light outside and checked his watch. Two-thirty. Of course it was still light.

He hadn't drunk much, really. More than he was used to, maybe. Definitely. The fresh cold air would sort him out.

Half an hour later, back at the Castle gate, Jim saw him coming and moved to raise the traffic barrier. "I thought it might be easier, sir, the way you're walking."

Shit. Was it really that obvious?

On the seventh floor Marion said, "I'll put the kettle on, guv."

He winced. It must be. Even so: *guv?*

"Are you all right, guv?"

"Tell me, Marion," he said, leaning against her desk, "what did you call Donald, when he was Chief Exec?"

"Donald, guv."

Was that a question or a statement? She was good at this game, he thought; his next move would need to close her options down.

"You called him Donald?"

"Yes, guv."

"Not Chief? Or boss? Or guv?"

She shook her head.

"Donald?"

"Yes, guv."

"Then why won't you do the same for me?"

"Because your name's not Donald?"

"Ha bloody ha." He'd walked right into that. No: she'd walked him into it. Talking to Marion helped after all. The desperate and rather feeble move he was planning for his meeting with Jessica seemed somehow less desperate, less feeble.

"Tell me, Marion," he said again, "do you enjoy your work?"

"Love it, guv."

"Good," he said, "that'll make it all the sweeter when I sack you."

"Ha bloody ha," said Marion. "I've cleared your diary for the day. The Public Safety thing definitely isn't happening" – which was just as well, Ari realized, because it would have started an hour ago – "but I've put you in with Jessica at four. Not quite the full twenty-four hours, but I thought you'd want to get it over with."

She was right, of course. Four o'clock was perfect – just long enough to review his approach, not too long to stew. But how did she even know he needed to see Jessica – and that he'd want to get it over with? But of course she knew. It was what she did.

"So you're not going to sack me, are you?"

Of course he wasn't.

"I'll make the coffee. Boss."

In his own office, at his own desk, he checked his emails – those Marion hadn't already dealt with. He read, replied, deleted or filed them one by one, but his mind wasn't really on the task. At the other end of the room, Donald's contraption continued to disturb the universe, but only just. Its soft ticking seemed softer than ever, more the tentative suggestion of a sound than the thing itself. Ari pressed his tongue gently against the roof of his mouth; then ever so gently pulled it away. The click it made was satisfyingly slight, inaudible, he was sure, outside his own skull. He tried to match the machine's tempo, but kept rushing the beat. He forced himself to slow down. But no matter how hard he tried, the machine was always slower.

He glanced at the top right corner of his screen: 15:20. Forty minutes left to fill. Marion brought a pot of strong coffee, placed it on the desk, and left without a word. He poured a cup, sipped twice and began running through, again, the conversation he would have with Jessica, anticipating her responses, preparing his replies. He knew how it would go. That is, he could foresee three or four ways in which the conversation might proceed, and would be prepared for each.

How certain could he be, though? If it had been Jacob – or Cora, Diana or K, each of whom, in their own way, played by the rules of the game – he'd have known where he stood. But Jessica? Jessica was the Child. She just wasn't a politician.

He sighed aloud, finished his coffee, refilled the cup and forced himself to read another email.

Perhaps he was exaggerating? With Jessica it could be hard to tell. Which was precisely the point.

During the night he had dredged deep and come up with nothing. If there had been a way to save the Island, he would have offered it long ago, but that wasn't the point. What he needed was a way to save Jessica from herself.

In the bar with Jacob, it had come to him. Not much, but better than nothing. Desperate, maybe, and more than a little feeble. With Cora, say, or Jacob, it would have been ridiculous. But wasn't that the point? Jessica wasn't any other Leader. But she was still, when you got right down to it, her father's daughter, wasn't she?

Wasn't she?

That had to count for something.

Ari shifted uncomfortably in his chair. Which wasn't his chair at all. It was Donald's chair at Donald's desk in Donald's office where Donald's bastard contraption with its endless clicking and shuffling now sounded louder than ever. And it was Jessica who'd put him there.

❧

Half an hour later, Ari took the stairs, not the lift, up to the eighth floor. A slow heavy tread felt right, ascending the scaffold. Jules greeted him like a cheery hangman.

"Hello, Ari. Rough night, was it?"

Still that obvious? He'd hoped a couple of coffees might have restored some semblance of animation – or at least sobriety – to his demeanour. He made a show of rubbing his eyes with the heels of both hands, opening his mouth in a parody yawn that somehow became real. Too much? He could hardly hope to imply he'd spent the night in wild debauchery. Jules would know as well as Marion – maybe better – what was happening here.

"It's the afternoon already, Jules," he said. "How are you?"

"I'm fine, thank you for asking. Though I *did* have rather a rough night, as it happens."

Ari pretended not to know that he was being teased. "I'm sorry to hear that."

"Oh, don't be. All of my own making."

While Jules swooned as if remembering details of the very debauchery Ari could not pretend to, Ari pretended not to notice. Life worked so much better when everyone followed the rules.

"I'll see if she's ready for you."

Jules rose, pushing himself up with his elbows out and just his fingertips on the padded arms of his office chair, reminding Ari of a large ungainly bird, a heron perhaps, settling its wings. He crossed to the inner office door, opened it slowly but without knocking, and slipped inside. Ari was still a few minutes early; Jessica would keep him waiting until they were a few minutes late – those were the rules, after all. But before he could complete the thought, the door swung wide and Jules gestured broadly, beckoning him inside.

"Coffee?" he asked, as Ari passed.

"Not for me, thanks," Ari said. "I'm fine."

He wasn't. But more coffee wouldn't help. Besides, the delay while Jules made a pot and brought it in would necessitate a round of inconsequential small talk he could do without. Now that he was here he might as well get on with it.

Jessica, however, seemed, if not relaxed, at least willing to approach the matter gently. She said hello, she asked him how he was, she pointed him towards the sofas and sat opposite him – although without any break or tension in her voice that might acknowledge the threat implied; she observed that Denis Klamm seemed to have acquired a couple of companions. Which, if not wholly unrelated to the topic at hand, wasn't exactly going for the jugular. The relative warmth of her words raised the mists of alcohol in his mind once more: he would be all right.

"Just so, Leader."

"Do we know anything about them?"

"Not much. Brother and sister, apparently. He's a taxi driver."

"And the woman?"

"No one seems to know anything about her."

Jessica left a silence Ari didn't enjoy, then said: "I was at school with her."

"Really?"

"When I was at school."

Which would have been a dozen years ago, he thought. They'd have been eleven.

"She didn't have a brother then."

"Are you sure?"

"It's a small island," Jessica said.

And getting smaller, he might have added, but decided this was not the time. Instead, he said, "Do you suppose she remembers you?"

Jessica didn't answer for a moment, and when she did Ari thought there was more regret than arrogance in her words: "I'm sure she does."

He took the silence that followed as his cue, finally, to come to the point. Just as he had rehearsed, he said: "I'm sorry, Leader. I have nothing new to offer."

"Nothing?"

"Nothing. But I'd like you to understand my thinking a little better."

"You mean it's my fault I can't see why you're right?"

"Not at all, Leader. It's just that there are some things, some important considerations, you may not be aware of."

This was it, Ari thought. Delicate ground. She would say she was aware the Island was disappearing into the sea, or something of the sort, and he would say: well, yes, but there was nothing they could do about that, really, and it was the Cathedral Close inquiry he wanted to talk about. At which she would get angry or sarcastic about his climate fatalism, and argue that if she, as Leader, did nothing about the fact that they were all going to drown, who would? Or she would ask him to enlighten her, icily inviting him to tiptoe further into the minefield. One of the two. Ari steeled himself, waiting to see which route she'd choose. Either would lead, in a few more steps, to where he needed her to be.

But she chose neither.

"Ari," she said, "you're going to say you're only trying to protect me, aren't you?"

Ari, who had been going to say exactly that, although not just yet, bit his tongue.

"You're going to say a real inquiry wouldn't just expose you – that none of this is about you, really – but would expose my father. Because it was never you, was it, who insisted the police use maximum force? You would never take it upon yourself to say such a thing – would you? – unless your Leader had expressly told you to?"

Which was a breeze strong and cold enough to blow away the last of the whisky-mist. Galloping to catch up, Ari said, "I argued with him."

"Of course you did. No doubt you told him it was unwise. No doubt you told him it was unnecessary."

"Exactly, yes."

"But did you tell him it was wrong?"

"Of course. We didn't need . . ."

"Not a tactical error, Ari. A crime. A moral outrage. A sin, if you will?"

A *sin*? Of course he hadn't.

"And you did it anyway, didn't you?"

"I made my point. I was overruled. Your father overruled me."

Jessica did not respond.

"It happened. Sometimes. We disagreed and we moved on. It's the way things work."

She had to understand that, surely?

Apparently she did – or felt no need to argue – because she nodded again. "And then you were going to appeal to a daughter's love for her father, weren't you? You were going to say I couldn't really want to expose my father – *my own father* – as the man truly responsible for battering seven people to death. Weren't you?"

"Yes."

"For battering Angela to death?"

"Yes."

"And when I pointed out you were talking to a daughter who – with your help – had already challenged and defeated her own father to become Leader, what were you going to say to that?"

What could he say? He couldn't say any of it now. All the same, he said: "I was going to say that Jacob always knew that you'd take over sooner or later, in fact it was what he always wanted."

"Of course you were. And then you'd have said that was a world away from destroying his reputation and exposing him to the risk of prosecution, and surely I wouldn't want that, would I? And what would I say then?"

"No, of course not."

"Really?"

"It was possible," he said, feeling as if he'd stepped into a lift and found only empty shaft. It wasn't that he and Jessica had different views and disagreed: that would have been part of the game, of the way things worked. It was that he'd known all along his moves were feeble, but still hadn't expected her to outplay him.

She said, "You were wrong, I'm afraid, Ari."

He knew that now.

She said, "I send not peace, but a sword."

"A sword?"

"Yes."

Which was all very well, but what did it *mean*? The image of Bob Cole in yesterday's dress uniform flashed across his mind. To be fair, he recognized the allusion. His eclectic, pre-loved library included a King James Version he'd once discovered inexplicably concealed in a Block 4 toilet cistern: *not peace, but a sword* were the words of the Christ Himself. *A man's foes shall be they of his own household*, Christ said; *he that loveth father or mother more than me is not worthy of me*. At fourteen, fifteen, having neither father nor mother, he had read those words, and re-read them. But apparently hadn't understood them, because he still didn't know what Jessica King meant, now. What she would do, as Leader, now that she was Leader. Now that he had made her Leader.

Had he perhaps for the first time not done the right thing, after all?

TWENTY-ONE

THE ARRIVAL OF the fire brigade – but still no police – hardened the mood in Cathedral Close. Idiots on both sides turned from throwing rocks at each other to hurling them at fire-fighters instead.

Until this point, Cora had been undecided. Should she march on to the Castle now, or linger awhile to savour final victory in the Close? Trouncing Diana's motley crew of Simulators was putting the fun, as well as the mental, back in fundamentalism, no doubt about it. But her place was at the head of her people, taking the real battle to the Leader: Diana was just collateral damage. Besides, now that the grown-ups were here, hanging around the scene of a riot might not be too good a look for a once and future Leader. Especially if somebody died. So: what would Napoleon have done? There was no real choice. She'd round up the idiots on her own side and point them back at those on Diana's. She'd tear the rest of her troops away from lighting bin fires and looting artisan bakers' shops, recover the "Drill Now/Drown Later" banner, detail a small but trusted contingent to occupy the centre of the Close, and, with as much semblance of order as she could muster, set off uphill with the rest.

Diana, meanwhile, defeated and in fear for her life as much as her career, disavowing the pride of countless generations, abandoned the field at the first sound of sirens to seek sanctuary in – where better? – the Cathedral, only to find the doors resolutely barred against her.

Inside, Bishop Grendel had not yet stopped trembling. For reasons perhaps more obvious in the thirteenth century than our own, the wicket gate within the Cathedral's main West doors opened about nine inches above the worn stone threshold, leaving that much solid oak to be stepped over; at the same time, it extended no higher than the average mediaeval peasant. Taken together, these constraints required a twenty-first century man of even modest proportions to duck his head severely just as he raised his legs to high step like a prancing pony through the gate. Strait is the gate, and all that, but there was strait and there was eye of the needle. The bishop was a tall man, and a fat one: he found negotiating the wicket a tricky prospect at the best of times and preferred, when the main doors were not fully open, to enter and leave via the North transept. On this occasion, however, as the cobblestones flew around his ears, haste had prevailed over better judgment: he approached the gate at a run and – almost as if it had been pre-ordained – tripped, sending his considerable bulk hurtling into the nave, where it came to rest, with a dull and sickening crump, skull-first against the ancient font. Blood trickled, then poured, down his forehead, a flood only partly dammed by the thick, unruly eyebrows he had always believed gave him the look of an Old Testament prophet, and which he had accordingly never trimmed. Ordering the dean urgently to lock and bar the gate, and to admit no one, he rose unsteadily to his feet and staggered the length of the aisle, leaning for support on every second pew. Finally, he reached the sacristy, which offered not only one more lockable door between himself and the Babylonian horde, whose taunts and cries he could still hear above the sound of splintering glass, but also the wherewithal to prepare himself for the trial to come.

For it seemed to the bishop, as the blood continued to flow and the pain to rise, that the hour was indeed at hand.

Outside, a terrified Diana turned from the gate to find herself surrounded by a ring of protestors, and wished her face had not become so recognizable after all. In desperation, she pointed across the Close, shouted, "She went that way!" and was surprised to find that, if the posse did not thunder off as one towards the smouldering ruins of Houghton Tower they did at least pause, confused, just long enough for her to kick off her heels and run flat out around the back of the Cathedral.

Inside, behind locked doors, the bishop removed the plain black cassock he had worn to address the people, stripped off his purple episcopal blouse and matching underwear, and stood, arms splayed, large and naked in the presence of his Lord.

Before his eyes the words appeared, as if written in the air:

For he hath judged the great whore, which did corrupt the earth with her fornication, and hath avenged the blood of his servants at her hand.

Slowly, deliberately, he sponged and cleansed the still-slick blood from his face. Enrobing himself, however, he made no attempt to avoid staining the dazzling vestments of white silk and gold thread that were normally reserved for conducting the Eucharist on the most holy Sunday of our risen Lord. If he were to meet this day his martyrdom, he would do so fittingly attired.

And he was clothed with a vesture dipped in blood: and his name is called The Word of God.

Yet still he trembled.

And bled.

And still the roar of the unrighteous could be heard from without, while the righteous voice spoke clearly from within.

And he hath on his vesture and on his thigh a name written, KING OF KINGS, AND LORD OF LORDS.

His *thigh?*

What, like a tattoo? Or was he supposed to have been doodling with a biro during evensong?

No matter.

The bishop's unruly thoughts were interrupted by a knocking at the sacristy door. "My Lord," the dean called from the other side.

"I'm busy."

"My Lord, will you open the door?"

"I told you: I'm busy."

"There is a woman at the North transept seeking shelter. Should I admit her, my Lord?"

"A woman?"

"It is Diana Ford-Marling."

Had he not already judged the great whore?

"You said not to let anyone in? But they're throwing rocks at her?"

"And the remnant were slain with the sword of him that sat upon the horse."

"My Lord?"

"Which sword proceeded out of his mouth."

"That's a no, is it?"

"Tell me," said the Bishop, standing, unlocking the sacristy door and addressing himself directly to the dean for the first time, "have you ever seen that woman set foot inside the house of God?"

The dean, startled by the bishop's appearance in full bloodstained regalia, racked his brains, but could not recall having done so. He didn't wish to be uncharitable, but Diana Ford-Marling had not even attended K's funeral with all the other Godless politicians. "No, my Lord."

The bishop removed his mitre to step through the door, then replaced it, drew himself up to his full, extraordinary height, and intoned:

"It is done."

"What . . .?"

"He that overcometh shall inherit all things . . . But the fearful, and unbelieving, and the abominable, and murderers, and whoremongers, and sorcerers, and idolaters, and all liars, shall have their part in the lake which burneth with fire and brimstone."

"My Lord?"

KING OF KINGS, AND LORD OF LORDS.

He was no longer trembling. But he was bleeding, and not just from the head: from both hands, both feet and – could the Dean but see it – from between the ribs on his right side where the spear had entered.

"And the city had no need of the sun, neither of the moon, to shine in it: for the glory of God did lighten it, and the Lamb is the light thereof."

That should just about do it.

LORD OF LORDS.

His thigh, though?

Outside, Diana's expensively-manicured fingernails gouged scratches in the ancient woodwork of the northern door before catching and tearing on its ironwork as she was dragged away, feet-first, by the mob that Cora left behind, while Cora herself, flanked by the two large men in dark suits and those stewards in high-vis tabards still nominally under her control, continued her ascent - less Napoleon than Alaric surfing a wave of excitable Visigoths towards the gates of Rome.

"To the Castle!"

TWENTY-TWO

A RI WAS STILL wondering – and Jessica still declining to elaborate – what exactly she might have meant, when the phones on her desk and in his pocket both began to bleep and hiccup with unusual intensity. He wouldn't allow himself to check what was going on before Jessica did, and she showed no sign of moving, or even speaking.

Jules knocked and immediately entered, breaking the impasse. "We've had Comms on the phone, Leader. They want to know what line we're taking on the riot."

So that was it, thought Ari. Not exactly in the script, but hardly surprising. Or unwelcome. It would buy him some time, at least. And it would keep Bob Cole busy.

Jessica turned back to him. "Ari?"

He did not answer immediately. He would make a show of considering the options. He asked Jules what they knew so far.

"Pitched battle between Cora's mob and Diana Ford-Marling's – both sides lobbing rocks at each other. The bishop came out for Diana, and is now holed up in the Cathedral. The Houghton flats are on fire. Some of Cora's lot are advancing on the Castle as we speak."

"Any casualties?"

"There must be, but no one knows."

"The fog of war, eh?"

There was a silence. Jules obviously saw no point in answering what had not really been a question, and Jessica was awaiting Ari's advice. He left it as long as he dared before saying, as he'd always been going to:

"We say this behaviour is wholly unacceptable in a democracy.

Perpetrators of violence must be met with the full rigour of the law, but for now that is a matter for the police."

Jessica nodded, but Jules said: "That's just the problem. Apparently, there *are* no police."

Really, Ari thought, that *was* a surprise.

"Ari?" said Jessica. "Is this your doing? Have you been having a 'quiet word' with Bob Cole again?"

"Me, Leader?"

For once he did not have to affect innocence. "It's not my place to interfere with operational policing decisions." He enjoyed the phrase, but immediately regretted it. He was innocent - of this - but hinting that he might not be was none too clever in the current circumstances. The look on Jessica's face suggested she neither believed him nor appreciated the joke. He said, "I've learned my lesson." Which was probably no better.

In the queasy silence that followed, Jules said: "Leader? The line?"

Jessica didn't take her eyes off Ari as she replied. "What he said. Full rigour of the law. But chuck in something threatening about how there will come a time for a full inquiry. Answers will be found. Justice delayed is no justice at all. Something like that. Threatening, remember. I'll have Commander Cole's head on a spike."

"Thank you, Leader. One other thing: Lucy Neave is outside. She says she needs to see you urgently."

"Lucy? Diana's spad?"

"Yes, Leader."

"What does she want?"

"She wouldn't say. Just that it's urgent."

"Well, well. What do you think, Ari? Should we let the opposition in?"

Ari pondered, because it seemed appropriate, then said, "I would think so. Lucy is generally sound . . ."

"For a spad?"

"For a poet, Leader."

It had been a while since Lucy had been here, in the Leader's office, and she was surprised to see how little had changed. The same exploded street map on the wall, the same low leather sofas. Jessica King had only been in office a few days, but even so. Somehow, Lucy had expected more from the woman who'd always believed she was the Child.

Ari was there, too, which was no surprise at all. It was only yesterday he'd fed her all that guff about the Great Simulation. Cables and what not. Had she believed him? She had. Sort of. But she'd done a lot of standing around in the cold with not a lot to do since then, during which she'd come to the conclusion that she had allowed herself to believe him, for a while, because . . . it would have been right. Aesthetically. It would have made a better story; poetic justice wasn't really about poetry, after all. Well, even Ari couldn't have foreseen the next twist in the older story she was about to deliver.

Jessica asked her what was so urgent. "Is it to do with the riot?"

"No, Leader."

"Then what?"

Lucy took a deep breath. She'd left her father's greatcoat in Jules's outer office, but she was still wearing far too many layers to be comfortable indoors. She breathed again, trying to steady her heart rate. On the way up from the waterfront, she'd rehearsed what she would say, exactly how she'd say it. She'd stick to the facts, of course. But that didn't mean she couldn't choose her words with care, hone them, polish them up to shape the way they'd land and fall. Though perhaps not make them rhyme. Best not try her luck.

Another breath. When she opened her mouth, the words flowed out faster than she'd hoped. She tried not to gabble.

When she'd finished, Jessica turned back to Ari. "You know what this means, don't you?"

Of course he does, thought Lucy. He wouldn't be Ari if he

didn't. Probably he'd known all along. The question was: had Jessica?

Ari said nothing for a while. Lucy guessed he'd be weighing the options: would Jessica want him to say out loud what they all knew now? He'd stall, she thought. He'd say something like "Of course, Leader" and lob the conversational ball back into Jessica's court. Let her decide how to react. Test the water. Ari would definitely stall.

"It means," he said, "that you can't be the Child."

Lucy flinched. She couldn't help it. But she did bite back a joke about the Second Coming.

Jessica nodded. She brushed imaginary fluff off her skirt, and said, "I'm not the Child?"

"No."

"And I suppose I never was. And my father?"

"Is definitely your father," Ari said.

"That's not what I meant."

"I know, Leader."

"I need to talk to him, don't I?"

To Lucy, Jessica looked suddenly younger: younger and more relaxed. It was not what she'd expected.

Jessica said, "You know, Ari, ever since you came and told me it was time, I've asked myself: what would Angela say? And you know what? *Our Island Story?* The Child? She'd have said it was all bollocks, wouldn't she?"

"I can just hear her saying it, Leader."

Jessica shrugged. "And yet, here we are."

Lucy couldn't tell whether she meant *here she was, Leader anyway,* or: here we are, *the real Child has arrived:* that, for all their rational scepticism, the Island Story was turning out to be true after all.

Ari said, "Just so, Leader."

Which might mean that he agreed with her. The new child really was the Child; or that she was Leader, anyway. Or just that he had no idea what Jessica meant, either, and was playing safe. Lucy couldn't tell any more.

"I should call my father."

Ari stood, and Lucy followed suit, struggling out of the low seat in her heavy clothes, but Jessica, with her mobile to one ear, waved them back. They sat again and waited while the call diverted and Jessica hung up.

"He never picks up messages. Lucy, would you please go and find him for me? Tell him we need to talk."

Ari said, "It might be better if I did that, Leader? Lucy should track down the pregnant woman, and bring her up to the Castle."

"All right. I'll get on with disembowelling Commander Cole and inserting a spine into whoever his number two might be."

"Not peace but a sword?"

"Indeed."

"Try not to enjoy it too much, Leader."

He rose again, but Jessica said. "Did he know?"

"Your father?"

"Yes."

That he was a fraud? Lucy wondered: how could he *not* know? But Ari said, "A man's foes shall be they of his own household, Leader?" It made no sense to Lucy, but Jessica seemed to understand. She shook her head. "I don't think so, Ari. But I'm not sure I can forgive him."

"You don't have to."

"No?"

"Being chosen is the opposite of freedom, Leader."

Lucy wasn't at all sure she agreed. There was freedom, too, in not having to choose. But no one was asking her.

"Then perhaps it's just as well I wasn't," Jessica said. "You know, Angela would have ridiculed the whole idea. But she'd also have said you have to do what you can to leave the world a little better than you find it."

Which was surely just the sort of sentimental garbage that would turn Ari's stomach?

He said, "Just so, Leader."

Something must have changed while Lucy was away. Or nothing

had changed. She no longer knew which.

But she wouldn't be the Island's laureate, she knew that much. What would be the point?

TWENTY-THREE

Ari waited for the lift, wrestling with what Jessica had said. Should we make the world a little better? Why? God wasn't watching. Nobody was watching but us; and we were only showing off. Besides, the world would be fine. It was people he wasn't so sure about. You had to ask if they were worth the effort. No doubt Donald would have agreed with Angela: a tweak here, a tweak there would bring us ever closer to paradise. But Donald was dead, too. So what did that prove? The panel of lights above the door tracked the lift's movements up and down, and up – tantalizingly close – and down, never quite reaching the eighth floor. Jules stuck his head out into the corridor. "They've heard," he said.

Had word of the new Child spread that fast?

"About the riots. Everybody's going out to watch. Or coming in to hide."

Walking down eight flights Ari found the place abuzz with unaccustomed energy. It was the energy, though, of the anthill that has been carelessly poked with a stick. For a while they would all charge mindlessly about, excitedly bumping into each other, comparing notes, amplifying rumours, and *doing things*: doing *something*, anything, but none of it to any purpose. Gradually, eventually, the energy would begin to dissipate, the muscles and minds begin to tire, and the soldier ants would start to redirect their movement: supply lines would be re-established, order would prevail and the great task of reconstruction would begin. Again. It was the way these things worked: after each disaster came the tedious, soul-destroying triumph of putting things back the way they were before. It's what he'd always done.

He should stay and play his part. He was the Chief Executive, after all. Instead, amused by the thought, he was abandoning his post, like a ship's captain slipping away in a private lifeboat while the crew panicked and women and children fought on deck. For the second time that day, he was leaving the Castle.

Outside, the weak February light had faded. The sun, having not quite set, squatted gloomily behind a bank of cloud on the silver-grey horizon. That it had been seen at all at this time of year was a minor miracle: tomorrow it would doubtless rain again.

The barbarians were already at the gate, but Jim was single-handedly barring the way to Cora and her pitchfork-wielding mob. Something about a red-and-white-striped traffic barrier they could easily have walked around, or under, or simply have snapped off and used for ammunition, seemed to have mesmerized the rioters. Innate respect for the authority of the Authority? Or had they just run out of steam already? It was hardly impressive, either way. He told Jim to lift the barrier.

"Are you sure, sir?"

"Let them do their worst."

"Only, it didn't end too well for the Romans, did it?"

Maybe; maybe not.

"The thing about the fall of Rome, Jim, is that it didn't really matter. All the power shifted to Byzantium and the Empire lasted another thousand years. If the Dark Ages were ever dark, it was only in damp, insignificant islands in the northern seas that no one cared about."

"Like us, sir?"

"Oh, no. This Island wasn't around until the 1980s. Hadn't you heard?"

Jim chuckled – Ari was the Chief Exec, after all, and you had to, didn't you? – and lifted the barrier. The crowd, taken by surprise, milled tentatively into the car park. Ari nodded to Cora, who leaned heavily on her stick and made no effort to detain him. The fighting and the march up the hill seemed to have taken it out of her as much as any one. She'd be all right, though; she'd rally her troops and lead the assault on the Central Block. A few windows would be broken. And for what? To support a drilling project she must know wouldn't work? To keep Cora herself in place for another thousand years? Good luck with that.

He edged his way through the advancing column, then headed off downhill. All the way back to the Cathedral a trail of destruction belied the exhausted passivity of the marchers at the gate, as if Hansel and Gretel had been violent insurrectionists unsure of their way home. Every hundred yards or so he found an incinerated litter bin, melted and charred, or a huddle of cars like dead cockroaches, upended and burned out, black smoke still drifting up between the buildings, blotting out the sky. Plate glass had exercised its usual fascination. Some of the windows destroyed were predictable enough – the bank, the jewellery shop, the bookies – others, like the charity store with nothing much to loot, less so. In the Close itself, a few hastily erected barriers and half a dozen fire engines, their lights spinning lazily, restricted casual access for sightseers like him. Firefighters clustered in small bands, all urgency dispelled, their helmet visors raised, their breathing apparatus shucked off, like knights whose part in the tourney was now over; a handful of their colleagues played hoses back and forth across the charred bones of Houghton Tower. Opposite, the great bulk of the Cathedral stood, as it had for a thousand years – or less than half a century, perhaps – a squat, brute testament to humanity's unquenchable capacity to belittle itself, in the face of which a few broken windows would make little impact. It had survived the bombing that destroyed its roof; this afternoon's damage was no more than a scratch. Between the Tower and the Cathedral lay a desolate space of uprooted trees, the rubble of dislodged cobbles and the jetsam of placards, banner poles, broken glass, dead flowers and food wrappers left behind by those whose gratification could not be delayed, not even for a riot. Amid all the detritus, Ari spotted bouquets and handwritten memorials for those who had died ten years before. In the distance, the sound of multiple sirens – interweaving, overlapping, creating a soundtrack all their own – suggested the police were finally gearing up to restore order now that disorder had begun to play itself out. He wondered how many more heads would be broken, if any more would die. There was no need for a real display of force. But when had that ever stopped an Acting Police Commander with a point to prove?

He righted an upturned iron bench. It wasn't where it belonged, having been torn up and thrown onto a makeshift barricade, but it was tolerably intact. It would do. He sat, and waited. His mission was to locate Jacob King; but if he waited here long enough, he knew, Jacob would find him.

In the event, it took less than an hour, during which, for the first time Ari could remember – for the first time, certainly, since he had insinuated himself into Cora's staff, since the days of K himself and since his mother died – he did precisely nothing. Neither preparing for the conversation to come, nor reviewing those just past, turning them this way and that like a jeweller looking for flaws. He *did* nothing; *planned* nothing; *thought* nothing: he had not known it was possible.

When Jacob finally appeared, he was trudging uphill from the south, from the shore, and not – as Ari had done – from the direction of the Castle. Would he have seen the extent of the damage?

He stood in front of the bench, looking down at Ari. "Alone, and palely loitering?"

Ari raised his face, white in the gathering gloom. "I could say the same for you," he said. "If I knew what it meant."

"Keats. As if you didn't know."

"You must have mistaken me for Lucy Neave."

Jacob sat on the bench. Together they faced the ruins and the ashes.

After a while, Jacob said: "I've been back down to see Denis."

"And?"

"A bit bedraggled, but he'll survive. He tells me there's been a new arrival."

"I know," Ari said. "More to the point, Jessica knows."

They sat in silence for a while. Three vans of riot police pulled into the Close in a swirl of sirens, and stopped, apparently unsure in the absence of any rioters, what to do next.

Jacob said, "Does she know I . . ."

That you lied to your own daughter all her life? That your entire career – and hers – was founded on that lie? Probably, Ari thought. She'd always been a clever child, after all. "She knows she's not the Child. We didn't discuss you."

"You didn't?"

"She wants to talk. I offered to come and round you up."

Jacob muttered, "Bravely, my diligence! Thou shalt be free."

"Keats?"

"Shakespeare."

After a while, Jacob said, "I had wondered if we might both leave. Go away somewhere, together."

"It's a beautiful thought, Jacob. But I'm too old to leave now."

"Not you, you oaf."

"Sweet," Ari said. "Father and daughter. Like rats from a sinking ship."

"She's still young. What else can she do?"

"She'll do what she can. Leave the world a little better than she found it."

Jacob looked startled. "What on earth does that mean?"

"Buggered if I know, Jacob. But it's what she said." He paused before adding, "She said it's what Angela would have wanted."

"Angela?"

"It's what she said."

The two men fell silent again.

It meant the Island would keep sinking, Ari thought. It meant the homeless – those who hadn't been trampled to death or set alight in the riots – wouldn't find homes; not all of them, anyway.

But at least it meant an inquiry could safely be allowed to proceed. Justice would be done. Lessons would be learned. One out of three pledges would have to do.

"Come on. I've got to deliver you back to the Castle."

They made their way slowly uphill, back past the trail of intermittent violence, Ari pointing out his favourite examples on the way. At the Castle gate, Jim was still at his post, the red-and-white barrier gone. Not the rioters, Jim told them: the police. "Those bloody vans just didn't stop. Must've been a dozen of them."

Inside the compound, as Ari had predicted, the plate glass windows were mostly smashed. There were perhaps a hundred demonstrators left, kettled against Block 5 by twice that number of police. Beneath the broken stub of the walkway protruding from the fifth floor of the Central Block, a ring of police stretched out a huge tarpaulin. Looking up, Ari saw a figure in ceremonial dress dangling gently in the breeze. Jacob said, "Is that . . .?" and Ari said it was. Two more figures were edging their way gingerly out along the bridge towards their former Commander. He'd chucked his lot in with Cora, Ari guessed, and Cora, last spotted being led away in handcuffs, had lost. Not as badly, perhaps, as Diana, but badly enough. Plus she'd be homeless now herself, given the state of Houghton Tower. For now, Jessica's only opposition was a half-drowned woman and her unborn child. It would be enough, in time.

Without a word, they entered Central Block, scuffing their way through the carpet of broken glass and heading for the lift. Ari pressed the button for Floor 8; then, as it began to ascend, pressed 7. When the doors opened he said, "This is my stop." They shook hands; then Ari stepped out and allowed the doors to close behind him.

Marion rose from her desk as he entered.

"Ari? Are you all right?"

Ari: finally.

He said, "I'm fine. Any messages?"

Of course there were. The phone had barely stopped ringing. She'd tried to reach him on the mobile but . . .

"I'd turned it off."

"Yes, boss," Marion said. She didn't say: *In the middle of a riot.*

He thanked her, and promised he'd sign the stack of papers she handed him. He carried them through to his own office and shut the door. He dropped the papers on the desk and sat down. The room was silent. From outside, muffled by seven flights and double glazing, he could just make out the shouts of the police and the clatter of the clean up that was already getting into gear; from inside: nothing.

He stood and walked over to Donald's machine.

Nothing.

He poked a tentative finger between the spokes of a large flywheel; nothing happened. The machine had stopped.

What was it Jacob said?

Thou shalt be free?

He began to read, and sign.

TWENTY-FOUR

DOWN AT THE waterfront, Denis waits for Pavel and Eva
– but mostly for Eva – to return, to set him free, while all
around, the sea rises; and rises.

ALSO BY GUY WARE

The Fat of Fed Beasts
978-1-78463-024-9

Reconciliation
978-1-78463-104-8

The Faculty of Indifference
978-1-78463-176-5

The Peckham Experiment
978-1-78463-263-2

RECENT FICTION FROM SALT

SEAN ASHTON
The Way to Work 978-1-78463-292-2)

KERRY HADLEY-PRYCE
God's Country (978-1-78463-265-6)

LIVI MICHAEL
Reservoir (978-1-78463-290-8)

CHRIS PARKER
Nameless Lake (978-1-78463-258-8)

TREVOR MARK THOMAS
Dry Cleaning (978-1-78463-282-3)

ALICE THOMPSON
Chimera (978-1-78463-254-0)

TONY WILLIAMS
Cole the Magnificent (978-1-78463-278-6)

NEW FICTION FROM SALT

NEW SHORT STORIES FROM SALT

CHRISTOPHER BURNS
Mrs Pulaska and Other Stories (978-1-78463-315-8)

CLARE FISHER
The Moon is Trending (978-1-78463-287-8)

DAVID FRANKEL
Forgetting is How We Survive (978-1-78463-301-1)

DAVID GAFFNEY
Concrete Fields (978-1-78463-303-5)

JONATHAN TAYLOR
Scablands and Other Stories (978-1-78463-294-6)

WILL WILES
The Anechoic Chamber (978-1-78463-328-8)